Coming Back To You

Also by Donya Lynne

All the King's Men Series
Rise of the Fallen
Heart of the Warrior
Micah's Calling
Rebel Obsession
Return of the Assassin
All the King's Men - Prequel

Strong Karma Trilogy
Good Karma

Coming Back To You

Donya Lynne

Dedication

To those in search of true love.

Acknowledgements

No book can be completed without the assistance of a team. I want to thank all my beta readers, critique partners, and pizza-chomping brainstormers and juiceboxers. You know who you are. Notably, thank you to Liz, Sue, Leann, Sandy, Laura, Jill, and Tia. Without your feedback and support, this book would not be what it is today.

To my readers, you're the reason I do what I do. Thank you for loving Mark and Karma as much as I do.

Prologue

They say you never forget your first true love...that one special person who touched your heart before anyone else, and who, with just a thought, can still set hummingbirds to flight inside your stomach. He will always be there, even though he's gone. He will always hold a special part of your soul. A part he ripped from your body — because it belongs to him now — and left an empty hole that rejects any attempt to fill it with a memory. A place that aches so acutely and with such intensity that you feel as though you will never be able to breathe deeply enough again.

I don't know who "they" are or how they came to know such truths, but I know they're right.

Part I

Letting Go

Chapter 1

December 1

"Take off your shirt and get comfortable, mate."

Mark loosened his tie, unbuttoned his starched white business shirt, and placed both over the back of a nearby chair. A moment later, his undershirt joined them.

The tattoo parlor was cold. It almost felt like they had on the air conditioning instead of the heat.

With a shiver, he settled into the black leather recliner that reminded him of the chairs in a dentist's office and waited as Razor, his artist, prepped his station.

"Is your heat not working?" Mark rubbed his palm up and down his arm.

Razor glanced over his shoulder. "No, mate. We keep it cooler in the shop."

"How come?" He didn't remember it being this cold last time he was here. But that had been in October, when it was warmer.

"Helps keep people from passin' out." Razor set out a couple bottles of ink. "Y'see, people's bodies heat up coz of the pain. If the place is too warm, folks'll be blinkin' on us right and left."

Mark nodded once, understanding that when Razor said blinking that he meant fainting. "I see." He wouldn't pass out. The pain his first time around with Razor hadn't been too bad. Today should be a piece of cake. But other people might not have the same tolerance for pain he did.

He stared at Razor's slender back as he prepared his equipment. Other than the mass of tattoos covering his arms and neck, making him a walking billboard for his trade, the guy didn't fit Mark's image of what a tattoo artist should look like. He had imagined a biker type with long hair, leather boots with chains, and a rough disposition. Razor was slim, dressed in designer denim trousers, Doc Martens, and a heather red graphic tee. He kept his greying hair short and tidy. He could have been a banker.

Razor pulled on blue latex gloves, sat on what looked like an ergonomic stool, and swiveled to face Mark. "You ready to finish this sweet piece, mate?" He inspected his previous handiwork on Mark's left pectoral.

"Yes." Mark had gotten the tattoo in October but wanted to make a few enhancements.

Razor pressed his fingertips against Mark's chest and pulled on the skin. "This healed up nice." He tilted his head slightly to one side. "So, you want the glyphs and the surrounding circle to be darker, right?"

"Yes, almost black. And I want some shading around the glyphs. Something with texture that makes the tattoo look more like it's been stamped on my chest."

"Easy enough, ay? Let's make some magic then, shall we?" Razor, a native Australian transplanted in Chicago, had a reputation for being one of the city's top tattoo artists, which was why Mark had picked him in the first place. For something as precious as this tattoo, Mark wanted the best.

"How long do you think this will take?" Mark glanced toward a nervous blonde in the chair on the other side of the room. She winced and had a death grip on the arms of her chair as another artist hunched over her ankle, a buzzing tattoo gun in his hand.

Razor prepped his gun. "Not long. Maybe thirty minutes. Forty-five if I really get into it."

A pained squeak drew Mark's attention back to the blonde. Her artist was a spiky-haired twentysomething with trails of ink up and down his arms and round plugs that looked like small, black wine corks in both earlobes. He glanced up at the girl. "You doing okay?"

The girl nodded briskly as she exhaled and sucked in several small breaths. "Yeah. Yeah, I'm fine."

Razor chuckled, pulling back Mark's attention.

"Got a cherry over there." Razor bobbed his head toward the girl and the other artist. He spoke quietly and rolled closer. "First tattoo, and she gets it on her ankle. Ain't that somethin'?"

"Why? What's wrong with getting your first tattoo on your ankle?" Mark knew next to nothing about Razor's profession except a good tattoo artist raked in top dollar.

Razor poised his gun over Mark's tattoo. "The foot and the ankle are the most painful parts o' the body to tattoo, mate." His mouth curled in amusement as he glanced toward the girl again. "But that's what she insisted she wanted. Wouldn't let us talk her out of it." He turned on the gun, and Mark sucked in his breath as the needle penetrated his skin at blurring speed.

Mark forced himself to relax and take steady breaths. A few minutes later, he turned to check on the girl. She didn't look good. Sweaty and pale.

"We're almost done," her artist said.

"Okay." The girl winced and clenched her teeth.

Why would she put herself through that much pain for the sake of a little ink?

Mark turned toward Razor. "Why did she insist on her ankle if it hurts so much?"

Razor shrugged. "Personal choice." His voice took on a more somber lilt. "She lost her mum to cancer and wanted a tattoo to remember her by. Said it had to be the ankle coz she and her mum shared a birthmark there. So, the tattoo we drew up incorporated it."

Mark glanced back at the girl who couldn't have been more than twenty-two years old. That was too young to lose a parent. "That's awful."

"I know. We hear a lot o' sad stories in this business. Sure, some people want a tattoo coz it's cool or coz they want to look tough." Razor's Aussie accent stroked each syllable. "But more often than not, a tattoo holds special meaning. Each person's ink tells a story. A tattoo is a piece of custom art that stamps that person's story on their body forever. Or maybe it just holds a memory." Razor's gaze flicked to Mark's before turning back to his needlework. "Everyone has a different reason for why they put something this permanent on their skin, mate."

Mark picked up on the unspoken question. He had never told Razor the reason behind his tattoo, but he could tell Razor knew he had one.

Razor's silent nudge caused Mark's thoughts to snap to Karma.

Karma Mason.

The woman he'd spent the summer with.

The woman he'd fallen in love with.

His reason. His story. It was her name tattooed on his chest in Asian glyphs. He'd stamped her name on his body like a brand declaring ownership. Because, in her way, she owned him. He willingly admitted that even if he didn't fully understand how she'd found her way inside his guarded heart.

Since leaving her in Indianapolis in September and driving back to Chicago in a conflicted mess, he'd gone back and forth in his mind countless times about whether he should call her, return to Indianapolis for her, or leave well enough alone. He loved her. Of that much he was certain. But was that enough? For him, maybe. For her, though, he didn't think so.

Karma deserved a man who would not just love her but marry her. And if Mark had learned nothing else from his past, he'd learned marriage wasn't in his cards. No matter how much he loved her, he couldn't get past the roadblock in his brain that gave him a case of the shakes every time he thought about standing at the front of a church waiting for her to come down the aisle.

Then again, he couldn't imagine a future without her, either. To think he would never see her again rattled his cage as badly as thinking about marrying her. Where did that leave him? A hammer on one side, an axe on the other?

A year ago, he'd been self-assured. Maybe not exactly happy, but definitely content. Definitely with a sense of direction. Now he felt like he didn't have *any* direction. As if he were a stalled car. No forward movement. No movement at all.

"So, what's your story, mate? If you don't mind my askin'."

Mark came out of his reverie and cleared his throat. "Maybe I don't have a story."

Razor lifted his head and met Mark's gaze with a dubious smirk. "Everyone has a story, especially when they don't wear their tattoo where people can see it." He returned his attention to his needlework. "And especially when they tattoo the word *karma* directly over their heart, even if the word is written in Asian glyphs." His deep, tobacco-hardened voice sounded suspicious, almost accusatory.

For a long moment, Mark said nothing. Was Razor someone he wanted to discuss his relationship — or lack thereof — with? In a way, it felt good to think he had someone he could talk to about her, but in another, he just wanted to keep her to himself.

He rested his head back on the plastic-covered cushion and gazed up at the industrial, art deco ceiling. "It's not a word. It's a name. Karma's a name."

"Aaaahhh, a name. Now we're gettin' somewhere." Razor's tattoo gun whirred as he circled it around and around on Mark's chest before pulling it back and wiping his towel over the freshly inked area.

"Yes, Karma's very special." Mark drew his gaze

down to his tattoo. The skin was red and swollen, but he could already tell the shading was going to be what kids these days called "sick."

"She your wife?"

Mark flinched. "No."

"Girlfriend?"

Mark bowed his head. "No."

Razor sat up, a concerned frown on his face. "She's not...you know...gone?" He appeared uncomfortable, as if he feared he'd stirred bad memories.

It took Mark a moment to realize what Razor was getting at. "You mean dead?"

Razor's expression dissolved into one of apology. "I'm sorry if—"

"No, she's not dead." Mark smiled sadly, because while Karma wasn't dead, there were times he felt like she was. Times when he was sad enough to consider drowning himself in scotch. Times when he wanted to ignore the voices in his head, which told him he wasn't what she needed and reminded him of the promise he'd made to let the universe decide when—or even if—to bring her back into his life. Times when he just wanted to go to her.

"Then I don't get it," Razor said in his brusque accent. "If she's not dead and so special, and she's not your gal, what's the story?"

"I let her go." Mark gave a derisive chuff and shook his head at how crazy the words sounded. He'd let the one woman he loved go. Why? Because that's what he'd said he would do. And why had he said that? Because he had sworn years ago never to lose his heart again. He would never again risk putting himself through what Carol had done to him when she'd left him at the altar. Mark had never recovered from that humiliation and heartbreak.

Razor returned to his work. "You love this little lady, don't you?"

He'd already opened up. No stopping now. "Yes."

"Then why'd you let her go?"

"Because I can't be what she needs me to be."

"And what does she need you to be, mate? Other than yourself."

"Someone who isn't afraid to commit."

"Oooohhh, I see. You're one of those fellas. Afraid of gettin' involved past a certain point. Is that the way of it?"

"I used to be like that. Now I'm not so sure. I've never felt like this before." Mark had never loved Carol the way he loved Karma. To the point that he ached for her. Karma's absence actually caused physical pain. Much like Razor's tattoo gun whirring over his skin, only deeper and not so sharp.

"You sound like you're not sure you made the right decision by leaving her."

Mark blew out a harsh breath. "You could say that, but I made my decision and now have to live with the consequences and wait."

"Wait for what?" Razor skimmed his towel over the tattoo to wipe away the blood and ink.

"For a sign that we're meant to be together." That didn't sound as ridiculous in his head as it did out loud.

Razor made a throaty noise. "Ah, yes. A sign. I believe in signs."

"You do?" Maybe he didn't sound so ridiculous after all, if a tough guy like Razor agreed with him.

"Absolutely. Life will give you what you need when you need it. If you just sit back, let life happen, and stay open to the signs, all will fall into place."

Razor was beginning to sound like a mystic, but his words resonated with something deep inside Mark, fortifying his resolve to not give up hope that he and Karma would be together someday. But he'd always been such a control freak. Sitting back and letting fate choose his future clawed his nerves.

"It's hard for me to let go. To let something else control my destiny."

Razor shook his head but kept his eyes on his work. "You letting life unfold naturally isn't the same as life controlling your destiny, mate. Your destiny is already set. Your course is charted. You just need to look for the signs along the way that keep you on course." He paused and made a dismissive noise as he sat up. "Hell, even that's not true. Because it's when you're looking for signs that you miss 'em. When you're not looking for signs, you see 'em without even realizing it." He bent over Mark's chest again, and the tattoo gun buzzed back to life, followed immediately by the sting of the needle. "You just need to let go and not force it. If your Karma is meant to come back around, she'll find her way to you and you to her without you even having to lift a finger. Believe in that, mate. Believe in that and have faith that if it's meant to be, it *will* be."

Renewed energy flowed through Mark's veins. Razor was right. Mark just needed to have faith in the agreement he'd made with the universe on his way back to Chicago last September. Unable to reconcile his heart's desire to go back to Karma and his head's demand to let her go, he'd relinquished control so that fate could decide his future. In the months since, his resolve had waned. But now, with Razor's sage advice rolling through his mind, he found new hope.

Hours later, lying awake in bed, staring up at the dark ceiling with a bandage over his tattoo, Mark was still thinking about Razor's words.

Let go. Have faith. Don't force it.

His advice sounded so simple. Mark knew better than to think it would be that easy, but he had to at least try.

Returning to the way things had been before he met Karma would be easier than letting go altogether. Except he couldn't go back. He wasn't the same man he'd been before Karma. She'd changed him. She'd gotten inside. He could never be that man again.

But for her sake, he wanted to be. Karma didn't need a commitment-phobic suitor who could love her but never marry her...who could never give himself completely.

But if that were true, why had he enhanced his tattoo? He'd made it darker, more like a brand. If he really didn't think he had a place in her life, he could have opted to have it removed. Instead, he'd imprinted her more heavily on his body. Why? Because despite thinking she deserved better than he could give, Mark was not just in love with her. He was unbelievably, universally lost in his love for her. She *did* own him.

Not just his heart, but his body and soul, too.

Let go. Have faith. Don't force it.

Razor wanted him to be patient. But patient for what? What could patience give him that could fix his dilemma? He wanted her back, but he feared being with her. How would that work?

Sighing, he ran a hand over his face. He didn't know how it would work. All he knew was that he couldn't stop thinking about her.

Maybe Razor was right. Maybe he just needed to let go. Maybe if he showed a little patience and refocused his faith in the powers that controlled fate, the dilemma would resolve itself.

But damn it, he wanted her back. Even if he wasn't right for her.

Chapter 2

Christmas Day

Karma buried her face in her hands, tears pouring from her eyes even as Macaulay Culkin slapped aftershave on his cheeks and screamed.

How did anyone cry while watching *Home Alone*?

She should be laughing. She loved this movie. It was the quintessential holiday tradition. Karma watched it every year at least three times between Thanksgiving and Christmas. But this year she didn't have much to smile about, and young Culkin may as well have been Scrooge for all the good he did.

This was a time of year meant for snuggling under blankets and making love in front of fireplaces. A time to cuddle on the couch with that special someone and stare at the lighted Christmas tree. A time for playful snowball fights that led to heated sex after stripping out of cold, wet clothes.

Funny how she'd never thought about those things in the past. Until this year, holiday season was for sweaters, football, and snow. But now, the romantic side of winter was all she could think about.

And it was because of *him*. Mark Strong. The sexiest,

most incredible man she had ever met.

She saw his face in her mind. Heard his voice. Felt his touch. Their relationship had been over for three months, but he still gripped her mind. Still held her heart.

Wasn't it time she moved on? That was what her friends and her dad wanted. Especially her dad. He was fed up with watching Karma suffer, as he had made perfectly clear on Thanksgiving.

"You need to get over that *boy*, Karma," he had said as she snuggled with her cat, Spookie, on her parents' couch.

Before she could protest, he'd held up his palm and cut her off. "I told you it would end this way. That he would only hurt you. But you didn't listen to me." He scowled and shook his head. "And now look at you. I hardly recognize you. You've been a ghost for weeks."

The muscles along Karma's jaw and the back of her neck tensed, as did her shoulders. She was as much angry as she was sad. Angry at herself, her dad, even Mark. "You can't blame Mark for this, Dad. He did nothing wrong." *Except leave me behind when he returned to Chicago.*

But Mark had made it clear before she got involved with him last spring that he wasn't looking for anything long term and that he would leave when his job at Solar ended. At the time, that hadn't mattered. She'd just wanted to spend time with him, even if he would leave and their relationship had to remain a secret.

Except her dad had found out about him, anyway. And once he learned Mark was the consultant working at her company, he accused Mark of taking advantage of his position so he could use her. For the rest of the summer, her dad hadn't wasted any opportunity to criticize Mark.

Seeing her so miserable had to be bittersweet vindication for her dad.

The kicker was, she felt bad for hurting him. Before Mark, her dad had been her entire world. The yardstick she measured all men by. Now, Mark was her yardstick. In a way, he had replaced her dad, and that riddled her with guilt, which fueled both her anger and her sadness even more. Because, really, wasn't she the only one here who had any right to be angry and sad? The only one who'd truly lost something—some*one*—special?

In the end, her dad got what he wanted, which was for her to see a therapist who could help her return to the land of the emotionally balanced. Karma simply couldn't stomach the way he'd looked at her with such pity...as if she were fragile. As if she were a *victim*. She didn't want to be a victim, least of all Mark's.

So, the Monday after Thanksgiving, Karma had contacted a therapist named Jan Krakowski and set up an appointment.

Which brought her to the reason for her cry fest this evening.

She wiped tears off her cheeks then rested her fingers back on the keyboard of her laptop. Her new blog waited for her to create a name and fill its pages with every rambling thought about Mark that tiptoed—or whirled like the Tasmanian Devil—through her mind.

But there was something about rehashing her relationship with Mark in written form that brought everything back to the surface so that it stung harder. Talking about Mark in sessions every week was bad enough, but to write about him was like pulling out a magnifying glass. Like observing snowflakes under magnification, where you could see the intricate facets and shards of each frozen crystal and not just a tiny white puff. Writing made the memories more vivid. Details already forgotten would resurface once she began pouring her soul through her fingertips.

Even before writing a single word, the memories tore at her heart, which was why, despite Macaulay Culkin's best comical efforts, tears streaked her face.

After Mark left, a gauzy film had gently shrouded the four months she'd spent with him, taking away some of the vividness of her memories. But with the creation of her blog, the film dissipated like fog in the sun and she recalled the once-blurry details with painful acuity. And with each remembered nuance, another needle pinpricked her heart.

Why was she torturing herself? Why was she unwrapping the recent past and stabbing herself in the heart with it?

Because Dr. Jan had asked her to.

At the end of last week's session, Jan had said that writing about how she felt would help her process her emotions and provide clarity. So far, the only emotion Karma had processed was intense sorrow, and the only clarity she felt was that she still loved him. But then, she hadn't gotten much further with her blog than choosing a template and a mochaccino color scheme.

Maybe once she finally began writing, the magic of blogging her pain away would take hold.

Still, she feared writing down her memories would not only cement them in her mind, but also rip off the Band-Aid from her wounded heart, which was sure to obliterate any progress she and Jan had made toward healing it. But if this was what Jan wanted her to do, she would do it. After all, Jan was the professional.

But before she could spill her memories of Mark, she needed a blog name. Something meaningful yet obscure enough that no one she knew could tie the blog to her if they stumbled across it.

She thought about it for a few minutes then had an epiphany.

Chocolate Chunk Brownies. She liked the sound of that.

Yes, that would work. The name was perfect.

After typing it out, she sat back and pursed her lips as a fresh wave of emotion coursed through her, causing another batch of tears to erupt on the rims of her lower eyelids.

A sad smile tugged at the corners of her mouth as she remembered the night Mark had taught her the lesson of the chocolate chunk brownie. Who would have thought a reference to dessert would become the keystone to their entire relationship?

"Damn you, Mark," she said quietly. "Why did you make me fall in love with you." She knew it wasn't his fault, but it felt good to blame him and vent a little anger his way. If he hadn't been so damn perfect, she wouldn't be so miserable.

Satisfied with the look and title of her blog, it was time to lay out her heart, strip herself bare, and use the

Donya Lynne

blog for its intended purpose. To let Mark go.

They say you never forget your first true love...that one special person who touched your heart before anyone else, and who, with just a thought, can still set hummingbirds to flight inside your stomach. He will always be there, even though he's gone. He will always hold a special part of your soul. A part he ripped from your body — because it belongs to him now — and left an empty hole that rejects any attempt to fill it with a memory. A place that aches so acutely and with such intensity that you feel as though you will never be able to breathe deeply enough again.

I don't know who "they" are or how they came to know such truths, but I know they're right.

Last May, I met my first true love. I'll call him M. He was a consultant where I work. Dark brown hair, intense grey-green eyes, and a voice so rich and alive I could almost wrap it around me like a favorite sweater. One made of cashmere and the shade of buttered toffee, and just as delicious to hear. He was over six feet tall and who cares how many pounds? Every ounce of him was sexy. Ideal. Perfect in every way.

From the day I met him, I knew there was something special about M. But I never would have guessed just how special he would become or that I would fall in love with him.

But I did fall, and not just fall, but tumbled head over heels down a ravine so steep and deep that I don't think I'll ever be able to climb my way out. And, to be honest, I'm not sure I want to. I like remembering him. I like the memories we made together. If remaining in this hellish crack inside my heart, where all I have left is his memory, is the only way I can be close to him, then this is where I want to stay.

My dad tells me to "get over him." My friends urge me to "forget him and move on." They say that's the healthiest way to move forward. But I don't want to get over him. I don't want to forget him or be "healthy." I don't want to move forward at all. I want to go back. I want to reverse the clock so that I can relive every incredible, magical, unbelievable, erotic moment all over again. And when we reach the last day we spent together, when he made love to me for the last time and held me in his arms, raining kisses over my face, I want to freeze time. I want to stay in that moment forever. I don't want to fall asleep and miss those final precious hours. I don't want to watch him drive away for the last time, out of my life forever.

But my pain is partly my fault.

I let him go.

I could have seen him one last time. He gave me a chance to see him and I chose not to. Maybe...just maybe...if I hadn't responded to his text and had hurried home to meet him, things would be different now. Maybe I would have fought harder to make him see how right we were together. Maybe I would have convinced him that we could make it work. Maybe he would be here with me now, watching Home Alone, *his arms around me, if I had just made an effort.*

Maybe.

But now it's too late, and I'm brokenhearted.

Ask me what I wouldn't sacrifice to have that chance back. Ask me what I wouldn't give for just a few more minutes with him.

Nothing. There's nothing I wouldn't give to see him just one more time.

Karma slapped her hands over her face as her body shook from sobs. Reliving that last day was torture. She could still see him from her hiding place across the road, still remember in crisp detail the expression on his face as he read her last text. He had seemed disappointed, but he had honored the hidden meaning in her words. Beyond telling her good-bye, he hadn't tried to contact her again.

She thought that would have made moving on easier. Fail.

She grabbed a tissue, wiped her eyes and nose, then turned back to her blog.

What would have happened that day if I hadn't answered his text? Would he have come for me as he threatened to? I guess I'll never know, but I suppose it's not healthy to live in the past, wondering what could have been if only I'd done things differently.

Maybe the lesson in all this is I need to learn how to look forward instead of back. I need to take what M taught me and apply it toward my future. Believe me, I'm trying. It's just hard.

But then who ever said life was supposed to be easy?

Chapter 3

New Year's Eve

"Mark, this is Crystal. Crystal, meet my friend, Mark."

What the hell was Rob thinking? Mark was in no mood to be set up on a blind date.

Standing inside the entrance to Boka, one of Chicago's premier restaurants, Mark shot Rob an icy glare. Rob should have known Mark wasn't on the market and hadn't been for months.

Shifting gears, he cleared his throat and turned toward Holly's friend. "Pleasure to meet you, Crystal." He could at least play civil for a few hours. He would deal with Rob later.

"The pleasure's mine." Her gaze ranged his face as she smiled.

If Mark had known Rob and Holly had planned to fix him up tonight, he wouldn't have come. He would have stayed home to ring in the New Year alone. Not that he didn't think Crystal was attractive. She was gorgeous. Long black hair, bright blue eyes, full lips, slim waist. Crystal was the whole package.

She just wasn't the *right* package. There was room for only one woman in his thoughts right now, and

Crystal wasn't her. And he could already tell she was going to give him a headache. Not a good sign.

"Mark's a consultant with Carter Mitchell," Rob said when Mark didn't say anything further.

"Impressive." Crystal's perfect black eyebrow arched as if she approved.

Carter Mitchell was one of the top consulting firms in the country. He wondered if Crystal knew that or if she had just said "impressive" to make him think she did. The clueless sparkle in her eyes suggested the latter.

In his experience, a lot of women put on false pretenses because they thought that would make a man more interested. Such shenanigans didn't work on Mark. He liked women who were real. Who weren't ashamed of their lack of knowledge. If Crystal had simply said, "What's Carter Mitchell?" he would have been more impressed.

Mark shifted side to side and glanced away. Boka certainly was crowded. Then again, it was New Year's Eve. What did he expect?

Turning his attention back to his blind date, he said, "What do you do, Crystal?"

Maybe he didn't want to be there, and maybe Crystal was on the path of trying too hard to capture his attention, but he didn't need to forget his manners. He was nothing if not the picture of controlled politeness, even though what he really wanted to do was spin on his heel and walk out. But Mark had spent years putting on a false front. By now, he was good at it. Although, for the first time, being someone he wasn't felt more like a chore instead of a choice. It was just one more symptom of what he dubbed the *Karma Effect*. For months, he'd grown more ill at ease over habits that had once been ingrained behavior. His resolve to stay true to the past was slowly flaking away.

"I'm a pediatric nurse, but I'm also a Luvabull." Crystal flipped her hair off her shoulder and flashed a bleached, straight-toothed smile.

Luvabulls were the dancers who performed during Chicago Bulls games. She definitely looked the part.

"A nurse, huh?" Mark said. "That's a noble profession."

She stepped closer and touched his arm. "I just love working with children."

"I bet it can be hard, though, seeing them when they're sick." Blah, blah, blah. The last thing he wanted to talk to this woman about was children. He could already tell she was sizing him up as a potential sperm donor for her own, and he feared the more they stayed on the subject, the more hopeful she would become. He was not interested in becoming her stud. Let another man sire her offspring.

"Oh, yes." She touched his hand this time, leaning in so her breast brushed his arm. "But it's also rewarding when they get well. And of course there's…"

Mark tuned out as the crowd sucked Crystal's words into a vacuum. He nodded, only catching every third or fourth word. Off to the side, hand in hand, Rob and Holly smiled at each other like proud parents. Clearly, they thought tonight's surprise meet and greet was a success. Rob wouldn't be smiling later when Mark had a heart-to-heart with him about being blindsided.

A couple of local sports stars worked their way

through the crowd, causing a small murmur of excitement. Flashbulbs went off, and Mark spotted the local paparazzi hovering nearby. No doubt the media hounds would be busy tonight, scurrying from party to party in an effort to capture New Year's Eve in Chicago.

As distracted as he was, he didn't notice that Crystal had wrapped her arm around his until she gave him a tug. He turned to find their party had been called. Abandoning the crowded front entrance, he followed the others to their table.

During dinner, Crystal droned on and on, barely coming up for air. And when she did, Rob or Holly filled the blessed silence with another godforsaken topic that sent Crystal on another verbal crusade.

After dinner, the four climbed into Rob's rented limousine and headed to the Palmer House Hilton, then up to the fourth floor ballrooms. Chicago's biggest New Year's Eve party was already well underway, but all Mark could see was the way the room had looked eight months ago, when he had been there for the Chicago Arts Coalition's annual charity benefit.

His life had changed that night, but right now, he wasn't sure if it had changed for better or worse. He was in love, but he was alone. Not even the tattoo on his chest or a reminder that this was all part of the patient journey he had to take to find his way back to her made him feel better. He'd never felt such empty yearning.

That was his own fault, though. He'd walked away from Karma. He'd been the one to end the relationship. His reasons were well established and, at the time, rational. But now, as with so many other aspects of his life, he was beginning to question his motives, his rationale, and how emotionally closeted he'd allowed himself to become since his doomed wedding day seven years ago.

He hadn't counted on Karma. He hadn't counted on falling in love with her.

But as much as he loved her, the more time that passed the harder reaching out to her became. And after what Razor had said to him a month ago, he shouldn't try reaching out to her at all. *Let go. Have faith.* Talk about your rocks and hard places. On one side, he loved her so much it hurt to be without her. On the other, he feared reconnecting. What if she had moved on? What if she turned him away again the way she had that last day when he texted her. He had told her he would stop by her apartment if she didn't answer him. Her response had said it all.

Good-bye, Mark.

Her message had been clear. She was moving forward without him, and she wanted him to do the same. But he hadn't told her how he felt. Maybe that would have made a difference. Then again, maybe not. Because he still would have returned to Chicago and she still would have stayed in Indianapolis. The distance wasn't conducive to a relationship. So maybe it was better this way. But if that were true, why couldn't he stop thinking about her?

But there was a third side to his inner turmoil. He couldn't shake the feeling that she was better off without him. That if he did return to her, he would only let her down and hurt her again.

So yeah, he was between a rock and a hard place and couldn't move side to side. Triple whammy. If he put his heart on the line again and reached out to her only to be rejected, he wasn't sure he wouldn't fall back into the hell he'd gone through after Carol fucked him over. He couldn't live through that kind of agony again. Maybe the sign he was waiting for would never come. Maybe the sign he should be seeing was that he should just move on and let Karma do the same so he didn't destroy them both.

Strange how one life-shattering experience could alter his life so badly that he couldn't even trust himself or his own decisions. But he'd lived in fear for so long he couldn't see any other way. He realized that now. He admitted to himself he was afraid, but he kept that shit hidden and wrapped so tightly that anyone who met him only saw unshakeable confidence and power. His fear was his and his alone.

Unfortunately, he wasn't dealing well with it, because fear was winning in his battle to find a way back into Karma's life. One that didn't involve risking humiliation or failing to live up to her expectations.

Be patient.

But the more he tried to remind himself to be patient, the more *impatient* he grew. If the universe intended to reunite him with Karma, it was taking way too long. He could feel his innate need to regain control creeping in, but that could blow everything.

Why did this love shit have to be so damn hard?

He let Crystal navigate him through the crowd. She still hadn't shut up, and now she had her arm secured around his like she possessed him, making Mark's skin crawl. A headache threatened to explode any second from her nonstop chatter, which revolved around children, marriage, her manicure, and her search for compliments by degrading every aspect of herself. *Do you think this dress is too tight? I hate wearing short skirts because my thighs are a little too big. I need to lose another five pounds before I look good in those Luvabull shorts.* At one time, Mark would have been drawn to her need for reassurance, but now all he felt was irritation. She was beautiful, but she cut herself down like she was a grade school outcast. If she'd ever been an outcast, he was Santa Claus.

"Oh, look," she said, "a casino."

The Red Lacquer Room once again hosted a casino the way it had eight months ago, and he glanced in the direction where he had first seen Karma sitting in her dangerously red dress at a blackjack table. His heart flip-flopped all over again, just as it had that night. The image in his mind's eye was so real, so perfect, so vivid.

But that was all it was. A memory. She wasn't there. Why would she be? She was in Indianapolis, at home or at some party. With some other man holding her hand. Some other man dancing with her. Kissing her. Maybe even making love to her.

"I'm a sucker for blackjack, although I suck at it," Crystal said. "Maybe you can teach me." She gave Mark's arm a squeeze.

He met her gaze. That sickeningly fake smile beamed like the glare of lights from an oncoming jumbo jet. If he didn't get out of the way, the thing would run over him, smearing him into nothing more than a flesh stain on the runway.

A year ago, maybe he would have enjoyed teaching Crystal how to play blackjack and a whole lot more, but now…? He'd hung up his teacher pants the second he'd driven out of Karma's life. He didn't want this. He didn't want Crystal, the reminder of a past he had walked away from, or the pain that lanced his soul every time he remembered *her*.

What the hell was he doing here?

Frowning, he pushed Crystal's hand off his arm, spun on his heel, and marched out.

"Mark? Hey, Mark! Wait up." Rob chased him down and grabbed his arm. "What's wrong?"

Mark whirled on him, rage flashing in the depths of his soul as months of pent-up frustration found an outlet. "What's wrong? Really? You have to ask? Fucking *everything's* wrong, Rob!"

Rob's eyebrows shot high into his forehead, and his mouth fell open in dumbfounded silence.

"Look, when are you going to get it that I'm not interested in being fixed up?" Fiery fumes burned the backside of Mark's skin. "And to a woman like that?" He pointed toward Crystal, who stood beside Holly looking as flabbergasted as Rob. "You should know me better than that, Rob. You should know the type of woman I like."

Rob's face shaded pink. "I…" His mouth hung open, his eyes full of confusion.

"Never mind. I'm outta here." He slapped the elevator button, but when the doors didn't open within a couple of seconds, he shot toward the door to the stairs and threw it open. He so didn't want to be there, at the party, at the Palmer House Hilton. The place was too connected to his memories of Karma, and the last thing he wanted was to taint them with Crystal's incessant, on-and-on-and-on blabbering.

Once outside in the icy, crisp wind off Lake Michigan, it took what felt like forever to hail a cab. The chill diverted his attention from his aggravation, and by the time a taxi stopped and he settled into the backseat, regret had begun to ooze in. He'd lost it back there. Just snapped. Damn these mood swings. He was so frustrated and strung so tight that the tiniest irritations, which would have been mere inconveniences a year ago, now led to major outbursts.

But after three-and-a-half months of impatiently holding onto faith that a higher power was working on setting his world right, Mark was beginning to fray around the edges. He wasn't sure how much more he could take, or how much longer he could wait.

He dropped his head back, jaw clenched, angry over losing his cool. As irritating as Crystal was, she hadn't deserved Mark's reaction. And Rob had only been trying to help. Still, the guy needed to back the fuck off. Mark didn't want any help. The only thing he wanted was three hundred miles away, a fact made perfectly clear on Thanksgiving when he'd agreed to escort one of his parents' new European dance students to their annual holiday get-together.

His mom had probably hoped Mark would take a romantic shine to Annika, but he hadn't. Not that Annika didn't have her good qualities. He would have much rather spent New Year's Eve with her than Crystal, even if only as friends.

Annika was beautiful and talented, and she held

herself in an unpretentious, almost self-conscious manner that would have lit Mark's fire eight months ago. He'd always had a soft spot for the quiet ones. The ones who didn't realize how lovely they were. The ones like Karma.

And that was the problem. Like Crystal, Annika wasn't Karma. As gorgeous as she was, and with that alluring European accent that would have sent other guys' dicks skyward, Mark felt nothing but a professional interest in seeing her succeed as a dancer in Chicago, even after taking her to dinner twice.

Part of him had gone out with Annika as a test to see if she could awaken a spark of interest, even though deep down he'd already known he was wasting his time. But if he could feel even a glimmer of sexual arousal with Annika, then maybe it meant he would eventually get over Karma. He hadn't. So much for that.

The cab pulled up to his apartment building. After paying, he climbed back out into the cold and made his way inside to the elevators.

Thanksgiving returned to his thoughts. His mom had known something was troubling him. After dinner, while everyone else watched the game downstairs, he had slipped away to his childhood bedroom, where his mom tracked him down.

"There you are," she'd said.

Mark had turned toward the door to find his mother, her hand resting on the doorknob, her other arm lifted against the wall. She had stood in his doorway like that countless times in his childhood, and a whisper of nostalgia eased through him.

Dressed in black slacks and a mocha-colored mohair sweater that draped halfway down her thighs, his mom was, as always, the picture of grace and demure beauty. Her gaze drifted to the shelf of trophies he'd been staring at, and she smiled.

"Remembering your glory days?" She glided across the carpet and joined him.

She moved like the wind, silent and whimsical.

Mark regarded his trophies—some for dance, some for basketball—then glanced toward the cherrywood desk he used to do his homework on. "Something like that."

The glory days had been easy. What he was going through now wasn't. In less than six months, he'd gone from being a man in complete control of his life to not knowing which way was up. He struggled to smile. He fought through every day. His existence revolved around his heart now, which was a more unruly beast than his mind. Hearts can't be tamed, brains can.

In a word, he was a mess.

His mom touched his arm. "What's troubling you, honey?"

Of course she would notice.

"It's nothing, Mom."

She gave him the look all moms give their kids when they know they're being fed a lie. "Come on, sit down." She sat on the edge of the bed and patted the mattress. "Talk to me. Is it Annika? Is something wrong?"

"No." He sat down. "It's not Annika, Mom."

His mom wrapped her arm around his and squeezed. "Then what's wrong, honey? What's got you so upset?"

"I'm not upset." He forced himself to square his shoulders.

She uttered a quiet laugh. "Could have fooled me."

Mark relented and kissed her on the cheek. "No fooling you, is there?"

She smiled up at him. "You never could, and you never will." Just a hint of her Italian accent framed her words. "So, what's wrong with my little boy?"

Mark grinned and glanced to the floor. "I don't want to trouble you with my problems, *Mamma*." He fell into the Italian accent, which came so easily around his mother.

"Nonsense. That's why I'm here. It's my duty as your *madre* to take your problems as my own. Now, talk. Tell me what's got you so sad."

Even though his mom wasn't the stereotypical headstrong Italian matriarch portrayed in movies, she could be pushy, and it was useless to resist.

"I met someone." What an understatement.

"A girl?" Her eyebrows lifted into interested arcs. "That's good news, isn't it? Not something to be sad about." Her voice held a note of reticence, which was understandable. She knew what he'd gone through after Carol and how many women he'd dated and dismissed. She wouldn't want to get her hopes up too high that he'd actually met a keeper.

"A woman." He smiled, but the gesture didn't reach his heart. "I met a woman, *Mamma*, not a girl." And what a woman Karma was.

"Why didn't you bring her? Annika would have understood."

"I couldn't." He sighed. He'd never told his mom

about Karma. He'd never told anyone except Rob. "She lives in Indianapolis." Well, technically, she lived in Clover, but it was close enough to Indianapolis to generalize.

Awareness filled his mom's eyes. "Oooohhh, I see." A smile crept over her mouth. "You met her while working there last summer, didn't you?"

What his mom didn't know was that he'd actually met Karma in Chicago at the arts benefit last April, only to find out the following Monday that she worked for the Indianapolis company he'd been assigned to. Talk about signs. Maybe that had been one. He'd met the woman of his dreams in Chicago then saw her again two days later in Indianapolis. What were the odds?

Mark couldn't quite meet his mom's eyes. "She worked for the company where I was on assignment."

His mom wrapped her fingers around his. "You love her?"

He'd never admitted his feelings for Karma to anyone. Doing so felt too real. Once he revealed the words to another, they were out there. There was no taking them back. And if he couldn't take them back, they could cause him pain. But this was his mom. He couldn't lie to her, because she would see right through him.

He lowered his eyes then nodded once. "Yes." He cleared his throat and spoke quietly. "I love her."

"Does she love you?"

"I don't know." Karma had never told him she loved him, but then, he'd never told her, either. That hadn't been the type of relationship they'd had. At least it wasn't supposed to have been.

45

He'd gone into the affair with the premise that it would last only as long as his assignment at Solar. It wasn't supposed to have been anything heavy or long term. Falling in love with her had broken all the rules, and now he was paying the price.

"Did you ever think to ask her?"

He shook his head and squeezed her fingers. "*Mamma*, it wasn't that kind of relationship." He let go of her hand.

"And yet, here you are, sulking."

He gave her a good-natured smirk. "I'm not sulking."

"Like hell you aren't." She tapped his arm. "You look the same way you did after Rex died."

Rex had been his golden retriever when he was a kid. He'd loved that dog.

"*Mamma*, please. Let's not talk about this right now." He took her hand and stood. "Let's go back downstairs."

All this talk about Karma was making his heart hurt.

She pushed off the bed with a shake of her head. "You're hiding from the truth, Marcus." She rarely used his given name. "You can't run forever from what Carol did."

His mom never brought up Carol. The fact that she was now made Mark suck in his breath. "Mom, I—"

"Honey, I think of Carol as a daughter." She cupped his cheek. "You know that. She's the brightest dancer at the studio. But you're my son. I love you more. I always have and always will. What Carol did to you was…" She paused as if searching for the right word. "Some would say it was unforgiveable." She pressed her palm against the side of his face, and her rounded cheeks lifted as she smiled. "But I forgave her. You need to, as well. I fear that if you don't, you'll never be able to move on. You'll never be happy. And you'll never allow yourself to truly love again." She sighed. "You love this girl in Indiana, but something is holding you back from being with her. I think it's Carol." She pulled her hand away from his face and waved it toward the top of his head. "Or rather, the *memory* of what Carol did to you." She grew still again then sighed. "Your emotions always did run deep. When you were young, you wore them on your sleeve. Then you grew up, suffered a little heartbreak, and…" She paused and shrugged as if she were surrendering. "And now you hide your feelings like you're ashamed of them. Don't let what she did steal your happiness, Marcus. Don't let her actions prevent you from embracing love again. *Carol* has moved on. She's happy now. She just had her baby and is aglow with life." His mom's eyes danced toward the ceiling as her shoulders briefly scrunched upward. "But *you're* still stuck in the past. Don't you think you deserve the same happiness, Mark?"

Talk about punches to the gut. His mom held nothing back.

But maybe what she'd said held more truth than he wanted to admit. Was his reticence about contacting Karma more about feeling he didn't deserve happiness than due to his fear of rejection? Or was it a combination of the two? He'd beaten himself up after Carol left, taking full responsibility for her betrayal. But maybe he shouldn't have. He hadn't forced her to sleep with Antonio. He hadn't been the one to keep her affair a secret. Carol had done that. She had been the one to sneak around behind his back. But instead of laying blame where blame was due, he'd taken the onus completely on himself, feeling that he hadn't been man enough to keep her faithful.

For the first time in almost seven years, he considered that maybe he'd never been to blame at all. Perhaps Carol had just been too young to know how to tell him what she wanted, and perhaps he'd just been too busy with school to notice her unhappiness. Maybe neither one of them were to blame and the incident had been one giant mistake from the beginning. Even so, the aftershocks were hell on his heart. They *still* were.

But his problems with love extended beyond Carol. Every significant relationship he'd had, even in school, had ended badly. And each failed relationship shattered his confidence with the opposite sex a little bit more than the last. Carol jilting him had just been the breaking point, pushing him over the edge. Fighting his way back up the side of that jagged cliff was proving almost impossible.

But through all the broken hearts, his mom had stood by him.

"I love you, Mom." He kissed her cheek.

"I love you, too, honey. Now, come back downstairs. You haven't had dessert, yet, and Maria made the most incredible brownies. They're full of chunks of fudgy chocolate and covered with caramel and marshmallows. They're divine." His mom's eyes had rolled back dreamily as she wrapped her arm around his again and led him to the door.

Mark stared at the panel of buttons in the elevator as he remembered the feelings that had rolled through him at his mom's mention of Maria's chocolate chunk brownies.

They had felt like a sign. Maybe not *the* sign, but one the higher powers at work in the universe had used to let him know they were working on granting his wish.

Be patient.

Razor's advice whispered through his mind.

But his patience was waning. Sooner or later, he would reach a breaking point, and when that happened, all bets were off, despite Razor's words of wisdom.

The elevator doors opened, and a renewed sense of frustration fueled his steps as he marched to his apartment like a Navy SEAL about to open a can of whoop-ass on a terrorist encampment.

He unlocked his door, stalked inside, yanked off his tie, and whipped it onto the couch as he disappeared into the hall. Entering his bedroom, he wrangled off his jacket and flung it onto the bed as if it were a rock he couldn't throw hard enough.

All the aggression felt good. Like he was actually doing something for a change instead of sitting around on his ass like a useless lump. He unfastened the top buttons of his shirt as he stormed into the bathroom and flipped on the faucet.

"Fuck!" He cupped his hands under the cold, running water then splashed it on his face before lifting his gaze to the man in the mirror. A tormented ghost glared back from the reflection, a stream of water drizzling off his chin.

Donya Lynne

He didn't want to rush things, but the universe needed to get off its ass and start working on that sign he'd asked for, because his patience was running out.

Chapter 4

January 9

Karma sat on the couch across from Jan in her office, which felt more like a cozy living room than a clinical setting. Maybe that was the point, because it was a lot easier to relax in a home than in a sterile white room.

"How was your Christmas?" Jan said, situating her iPad on her lap.

"Difficult."

Jan's eyebrows ticked inward. "How so?"

Karma struggled to put her feelings into words. "I don't know. I just felt…" *Sad. Angry. Miserable. So in love it hurts to breathe, to get up, to move, to even think. All I wanted was to see him again. Talk to him. Hear his voice. Touch him. Slap him. Scream at him for leaving me alone.*

"Karma…?"

Tears sprung to her eyes. She tried to blink them away. "I thought a lot about Mark on Christmas." She sniffled and grabbed a tissue from the end table. "Everything seems to be getting worse instead of better."

The weeks of rehashing her relationship with Mark during these sessions, as well as writing about him in her blog, were mounting an offensive strike on her emotions that felt like an invasion. It didn't help that the self-doubting voices she'd endured since being bullied as a child had started whispering in her head again.

She'd been a fool to think that four blissful months with Mark would be enough to eradicate a lifetime of torment.

She turned pleading eyes on Jan. "Shouldn't I be getting better by now? I mean, we were only together four months. How could only four months hurt this much?"

Jan sat forward and spoke softly. "Because you loved him, Karma. And first loves are always the hardest to get over. Some people never get over them."

"But...but..." Karma finally gave in and let herself cry.

She just wanted her life to go back to normal. Problem was, she no longer knew what normal meant. After spending a glorious summer with Mark, he'd redefined what normal was.

For example, was *this* normal? All this heartbreak and sadness? Karma had never had a boyfriend before Mark, so she had nothing to compare to. All she knew was that the day Mark left, a whole lot of emptiness had invaded her life.

Maybe what Jan said about first loves was reason to hope, though. If first loves were the hardest to get over, maybe all this pain and misery *was* normal. Wasn't it true that the first time for anything was the hardest? The first kiss. The first time riding a bicycle without training wheels. Losing your virginity.

So maybe all this pain wasn't so much a normal reaction to losing a man she loved but a result of experiencing her *first loss* of love. The sorrow and despair were amplified not because it was Mark, but because she'd fallen in love for the first time. Mark just happened to be the one she'd fallen in love with. The good news was at least now she could check *this* first off her list so she never had to deal with it again. Next time, breaking up wouldn't be so hard. But this time? Yeah, this time sucked.

But the misery blistering her soul was caused by more than just losing him. With Mark, she had found herself. Really *found* herself. He had helped her uncover the woman she'd always wanted to be but had been too afraid of, right down to her sexuality. Talk about bringing someone out of her shell. Not only had Mark pulled her from the shell, but out of the ocean, up the beach, and deep into the mainland.

He'd been more than just a simple first. In four months, he had revolutionized her existence. No wonder she was so messed up without him there to guide her.

Without him, she couldn't stop herself from dragging her withered body back toward the only safety net she'd ever known: the shell she'd spent over a decade in. The mainland was too much for her to handle alone. The childhood taunts crept back in. Her fledgling confidence, which had flourished under Mark's tutelage, faltered. Getting back to the ocean and into her shell seemed the only way she would feel safe again.

And, damn it, that pissed her off.

She didn't want to lose the woman she had become. She liked who she'd been with Mark. Somehow, she had to find a way to recapture that woman on her own.

That was why she was in Jan's office now. As much as she still loved Mark, it was time to stand on her own. But she needed help to learn how. Jan could guide her back to the mainland and help her put Mark behind her.

"Are you okay to continue?" Jan said when Karma finally regained her composure.

She nodded and wiped under her eyes. "Yes, I think so."

Jan relaxed into her chair. "Be patient with yourself, Karma. This is only our fifth appointment. You're not going to get over him just like that." She snapped her fingers. "It takes time. Breathe through your sadness. Fully experience it. That's the only way you'll be able to understand it, learn from it, and eventually move on."

With her dad and her friends telling her to forget Mark, she had begun to think there was something wrong with her for continuing to think about him. That maybe she was defective since she couldn't just stop loving him and get on with the next big thing. Now, here came Jan, who wanted her to revel in her sorrow. Well, maybe not revel, but at least not discount it. Not just toss her sadness away like threadbare socks that no longer served a purpose. Jan was giving her permission to hurt and feel the pain losing Mark inflicted.

"Have you heard about the five stages of loss?" Jan set down her iPad.

Karma shrugged. "No."

"Many relate the five stages of loss to the death of a

loved one, but they can apply to any loss. Especially the loss of a relationship." Jan uncrossed her legs and sat forward. "The five stages are denial and isolation, anger, depression, bargaining, and acceptance." She ticked them off on her fingers. "The theory is, when we experience loss, we go through all five phases in one way or another, and everyone goes through them differently. Sometimes, the first emotion we feel is anger or depression. Sometimes it's bargaining."

"What's bargaining mean?"

Jan sat back and recrossed her legs. "Thoughts such as, 'if only he'd done this,' 'if only I had one more chance.' That sort of thing. Sometimes, a person might try to make a deal with God or turn things over to the universe: 'Please, God. If you give me another chance, I'll do such and such.' There's a lot of negotiating with a higher power you perceive has control over the situation, as if it's not *you* controlling your destiny but someone or something else. People make promises to God in return for Him to take things back to how they were before the loss occurred. Does that make sense?"

"Yes." Karma had done her share of bargaining after Mark's departure.

"Some people get stuck in the bargaining phase, mistaking fate for loss. They look for signs, which serves only to keep them rooted in place instead of moving forward. People stuck in bargaining often become angry or depressed. Sometimes both." She paused for a breath. "The other thing that can happen is that the person becomes intensely remorseful or guilty, which prevents healthy healing. In my experience, I've found that people who get stuck in the bargaining phase feel they've made a mistake or enabled the loss to occur, and oftentimes they feel as if their head is warring with their heart. Rationally, they understand the loss, but emotionally, they resist accepting it."

"I don't want to get stuck. I want to accept that he's gone and move on." Mark wasn't coming back. She needed to work through her emotions and let go.

Jan winked and smiled. "Don't worry. I'll help you." She clasped her hands in her lap. "So, how many of the five phases would you say you've been through since Mark left?"

"Obviously, depression." Karma's sadness had been what led her to Jan in the first place.

Jan offered a benign smile. "Obviously."

"Bargaining. I've definitely had a lot of *if only* thoughts." Whether or not she was stuck there, though, she wasn't sure, but she didn't think so.

"Okay." Jan picked up her iPad and made a note. "What else? Do you think you went through denial?"

Karma thought for a moment then shook her head. "No, not that I can think of."

"Any anger?"

She recalled blaming Mark and being mad at him for driving away without even trying to fight for what they had.

"Yes." Karma hadn't been excessively angry, but there were times if Mark had been standing in front of her, she would have slapped him.

Jan made another quick note then placed her tablet in her lap. "So it sounds like you're working through the five phases pretty well." She smiled and lifted her hand off her lap. "You might be a bit stalled in the depression phase—not stuck, but stalled—but that's pretty normal, especially for women. I've noticed that men tend to get stuck more often in anger or bargaining." She smiled as if amused. "I think it's a control thing."

This made Karma smile. "I can see that."

Jan's expression softened. "So, now we just have to work you through your sadness and help you move toward acceptance. Just remember that you can't force yourself to move on. That's why I said you need to breathe through the sadness and experience it. You need to pay attention to your feelings and let them teach you what they need to teach you."

"Does this mean I'll move into denial next?"

"Maybe. But more than likely, if you haven't experienced denial by now, you probably won't. Denial usually comes pretty soon after the loss, if not immediately after."

Karma remembered the way she'd reacted when her phone rang the evening after Mark's departure. She'd thought for sure it was Mark only to be disappointed when it was her friend, Lisa. Maybe she'd been in denial up to that point, hoping he would come back. But when she saw Lisa's name on her caller ID, all hope evaporated, and denial with it.

"You know, I think I did go through denial. For a few hours after he left, at least. But then I realized he wasn't coming back."

Jan made a note on her iPad. "Good. Then we just need to work through these last lingering feelings to find acceptance."

She made it sound so easy.

"And you'll help me?"

"Yes. That's what I'm here for, and it's why I asked you to start a blog. Writing your feelings will help." She paused. "I read it over the weekend. Your blog, I mean. Excellent stuff, Karma. Very evocative. I'm curious, though, why you named it *Chocolate Chunk Brownies*."

Karma knew Jan would ask, and she felt her face heat. "It was something Mark said to me once."

Jan's curious gaze implored her to continue.

Karma took a deep breath, willing her emotions to remain in check. "It's kind of silly." She briefly hid her face in her hands before taking a deep breath and diving in. "Before Mark and I had sex, he taught me…things." Her face blazed with embarrassment. She couldn't believe she was revealing such intimate moments. "One of the things he taught me was the difference between a clitoral orgasm and a G-spot orgasm. Before Mark, I never even knew there was a difference or that there were different types of orgasms."

Jan rested her chin on her hand and grinned as if hearing this story entertained her.

"Anyway, the analogy he used was that a G-spot orgasm was to a clitoral orgasm what a chocolate chunk brownie drizzled with warm caramel and vanilla sauce was to a piece of Dove chocolate. He said that while both were good, one made you moan while the other just made you smile. He said he was going to give me a chocolate chunk brownie."

And he had made good on his promise. Many times.

Jan's grin turned into a smile. "I like that. He has

quite a way with words." Using her stylus, Jan made another note on her tablet. "But so do you. What you wrote was very insightful and well written. Have you ever thought about being a writer?"

"My degree is in journalism."

Jan made another note. "I see. So, do you want to write?"

"Yes."

"Why don't you?"

Karma shrugged. "There weren't any jobs in my field after graduation."

"Maybe you could write a book. You don't have to work in journalism to write. You just need the desire, a pen, and a piece of paper. Or a blog," she added as an afterthought.

Mark had said something similar to her once. Perhaps they were both right. Maybe her new blog could ease her into the idea and help her figure out her writing future.

After several seconds of silence, Jan lifted her tablet again. "Why don't you tell me what you liked best about Mark. Why does it hurt so bad that he's gone?"

Karma dropped her gaze to her lap and picked at her thumbnail. "He was just different. He made *me* feel different."

"How so?"

She remembered the night Mark had stood behind her in front of her mirror.

"He helped me see myself with new eyes. When I was a kid, my brother, his friends, and a bunch of my classmates, teased me. I was a gangly, awkward kid. All arms and legs, no curves, especially where my breasts were concerned. I developed late. Kids made fun of me. Not a day went by that someone didn't say something about my small breasts or my body." She frowned as those old taunts echoed inside her mind. She no longer believed them, thanks to Mark, but now that he was gone, those naysaying voices crept back in to chip at her self-esteem. "After I told Mark about what had happened to me as a kid and how it still affected me as an adult, he took me to my mirror, stood behind me, and began ticking off all my features." She smiled as she remembered his words. "He told me I have beautiful skin, that my eyes were the most captivating eyes he'd ever seen, that my body was perfect. As I looked at my reflection, I began to see myself the way he saw me. He made me feel beautiful and sexy and desirable, and I'd never felt that way before."

"And are you any less beautiful, sexy, and desirable now that he's gone?"

Excellent point.

"No."

"So, Mark opened your eyes to who you really are. Is that what you're saying?"

"Yes." Fond memories of their time together played through her mind. "And it wasn't just the way I saw my physical body that he helped change. It was everything. Being with him made me feel more confident." She curled her feet under her and nestled against the arm of the couch. "I don't know how to explain it, but he empowered me. He taught me things about life, about sex, about me and what I want and who I want to be. I began standing up for myself. All my life, I let people walk all over me. I never stood up for myself." Karma grinned at the memory of when she let loose on that bitch Jolene at work and then again at her parents' house on Memorial Day. "After I met Mark, all that changed. I refused to take other people's shit, anymore."

"So, Mark helped you find your voice, too? And he helped you feel more confident, in general?"

"Yes."

Jan quietly eyed her then said, "Have you ever considered that maybe Mark's purpose in your life was simply to be a catalyst?"

"What do you mean?"

"It sounds like he brought out the best in you. He helped you discard old beliefs and old ways of thinking that weren't serving you. Maybe that was his purpose in your life."

Karma had benefited in so many ways from knowing Mark. She was a better person now than she had been a year ago, and it was all because of him. But if he had only been a stepping-stone for her, wouldn't that mean she had been the same for him?

"Well then, what was *my* purpose in *his* life?"

The tiny laugh lines at the outside corners of Jan's eyes crinkled as she smiled. "That's for him to find out. We're here to help *you*."

Karma's brow furrowed as she glanced out the window at the partially frozen pond. She felt like she was missing something. Some vital clue about Mark, his intentions, or maybe his purpose in her life

She didn't feel as if he'd been *just* a stepping-stone.

So then...what was he?

By the end of the hour, Karma felt both relieved and conflicted. As if a weight had been lifted and another, lighter weight, had replaced it. Recounting the details of her special times with Mark had ripped her heart open all over again...and yet healed a tiny piece of it at the same time.

"I want you to keep writing in your blog," Jan said, setting her tablet aside. "Every day, even if only a paragraph or two."

"Okay." Karma gathered her purse and dabbed another tissue on her damp cheeks.

"Also, before our next appointment, I'd like you to make a list of all the things you enjoyed before you met Mark. Besides writing, what were you passionate about? Think all the way back to when you were a kid. What gave you the most joy?"

Karma tossed the tissue in the trash can. "Do you want me to write that in my blog, too?"

"That would be perfect."

Karma's mind was already sifting through her memories, trying to come up with all the things she used to like. Had life really existed before Mark? Sometimes it didn't feel like it.

Jan opened the door and led her through the quaint reception area. "Great session today, Karma. You're already making big breakthroughs."

"Thank you." Karma pressed her fingertips to the puffy, heated skin under her eyes. She sure didn't feel like she was making progress. In fact, she felt like she was getting worse.

But then, maybe that was what Jan considered big breakthroughs. Maybe repairing her wounded emotions was like rehabbing an old house. She had to tear down all the walls and gut the place before she could rebuild. She sure felt gutted.

After returning home, Karma slipped into a pair of sweats and a sweatshirt, grabbed a bag of Doritos, trudged to the couch, and flopped down on the cushions.

She pointed the remote at the TV and turned it on.

Click...click...click...

She was becoming a pro at channel surfing. She stopped when she reached the Food Network. *The Barefoot Contessa* was on, demonstrating how to make French-style sole. Karma's mouth watered, and she scrunched her nose at the bag of Doritos before setting it aside. Then she turned up the volume and watched Ina Garten pour butter sauce over her lightly poached sole fillets and slip them into the oven.

Hmm, that looks pretty good. Simple, too.

She used to love cooking, not that she had a huge repertoire of dishes, but she made a mean homemade lasagna.

Thinking about the list Jan had asked her to create at today's appointment, she grabbed her laptop and pulled up her blog.

My therapist asked me today to make a list of everything that gave me joy before I met M. Maybe she thinks if I remember what made me happy before, I can get back in touch with those things and be happy again. No matter the reason, if this is what I have to do to get over M then I'll do it. I know it's time I move on. It's just hard, especially when I can't remember what it was like before I met him. What did I like?

What brought me joy? What made me smile, and what couldn't I wait to do?

The first two items on the list are easy enough:

1. *Writing - I've always loved writing. Packed away somewhere are notebooks filled with stories and poems I wrote when I was in school.*
2. *Cooking - I'm watching* The Barefoot Contessa *now, and she's making this yummy French fish dish that I think I'll try. It looks really simple.*

Other things that bring me joy:

3. *My cat, Spookie, even though I can't have her at my apartment. Stupid apartment management and their no-pets policy. Spookie stays at my parents' house, but when I was in high school, she was my little pal. She would sit on my desk while I was doing homework and play with my pencil as I was trying to do my math. She's always been my baby. Maybe it's time to start shopping for a new apartment now that I got that raise.*
4. *Running. In high school, I was on the cross-country team and really enjoyed that. Running was always kind of an escape for me.*
5. *Yoga – duh.*
6. *Pilates – double duh.*
7. *Hanging out with my friends (no names since I'm keeping this anonymous, but they know who they are).*
8. *Music. When I was a kid, I taught myself how to play the guitar and used to be pretty good. But nowadays, I enjoy listening to music more than playing it.*
10. *Sports. In addition to cross-country, I played*

basketball in sixth and seventh grade. And I've started playing softball on the company team. Other than that, I love to watch all kinds of sports. Dad and I try to get together once a week to catch a game.

11. Beaches. I've never seen the ocean, but I have this picture of a seascape at sunset hanging on my bedroom wall. I often fantasize that I'm standing on that beach, staring out at the ocean. I'd love to stay in a beach house. I'd live on the deck when I wasn't walking along the edge of the water.

12. Reading. Before M, I read all the time. Romance mostly. But then M had me read a bunch of books on sex and sexuality, and now I just find it hard to read. My poor Kindle hasn't been charged in months. Maybe I'll go charge it right now and download a bunch of books. Perhaps that will help get my mind off M.

Her hands hovered over the keyboard as she reread her list. Then she hit publish. Funny, but just writing that list made her feel better. For the first time in months, she wasn't dwelling on how alone she was and actually considered getting off her ass. She hadn't been to a yoga class in ages, and her Pilates instructor had probably forgotten what she looked like.

She checked the time. If she hurried, she could just make the class before it started. She prayed they hadn't changed the schedule.

She shut her laptop and glanced at the flat screen as Ina served scrumptious sole fillets on yellow plates. With a resigned nod, she stood and headed toward her bedroom. She snagged her Kindle, plugged it into the charger, gathered the stacks of sex books off her dresser — where they had resided for months — and carried them into her spare room, where she packed them into one of her bookcases. Returning to her room, she quickly changed into yoga pants and a tank top, pulled on a cable-knit sweater, shrugged into her coat, grabbed her purse and gym bag, and headed out. First stop, the gym. Second stop, the grocery store.

She was having French-style sole for dinner to celebrate taking her first real step toward recovery.

Chapter 5

January 15

As Mark pounded the ever-living crap out of the weighted bag, sweat poured down his body. And this was his cooldown. He'd already spent an hour banging out reps in the free weights. His muscles were screaming.

"Hey."

Mark's gloved fist smacked the bag as he pulled up and glanced over his shoulder at Rob. They hadn't talked since New Year's Eve. Partly because Mark was still angry with him, but also because he was still too pissed off at the world to make a genuine apology for blowing up at Rob. It seemed as more days passed, the more agitated he grew. He'd never experienced feeling like this...a blend of helplessness, sorrow, impatience, and rage. What a destructive cocktail.

"Hey." Mark steadied the swinging red bag and rubbed the back of his wrist across his dripping forehead.

"Happy birthday." Rob set down his bag. "I know I'm a few days late, but..."

Tense discomfort settled between them. Mark had

never gone longer than a few days without talking to Rob or joining him for a game of hoops, but ever since Rob met Holly, and especially since New Year's Eve and Mark's cataclysmic meltdown, they had grown further and further apart.

"Thanks." Mark took a step back then turned for the bench where his half-empty water bottle rested. He popped the cap and swallowed a healthy gulp.

"Mark, look…" Rob sighed. "I'm sorry about New Year's Eve. Holly and I shouldn't have sprung Crystal on you like that."

"You think?" Mark winced at the harshness in his voice. Shit, but his fuse was impossibly short. Why the hell did he have to snap at Rob every time he saw him? If anything, he should be apologizing *to* Rob, not getting an apology *from* him.

Rob's brow dug into his eyelids. "Hey, give me a break. I'm trying to say I'm sorry here."

Mark set his bottle on the bench. He wasn't being fair to Rob. "I know." He turned and offered Rob a crooked grin. "I know you are, and I'm sorry for being such an ass. I—"

"You miss her."

Mark's blood ran cold for a split second as he met Rob's gaze.

"You. Miss. Her." Rob said again. "I get it."

"I don't want to talk about it." Mark returned to the bag and shot a vicious jab-cross into the red leather. Just the mention of Karma sent a shock of frustration down his spine. He'd promised to let fate decide his future, but the longer he waited, the harder it became. He was beginning to think he was going to have to renege on his deal with the universe, say to hell with patience, and take matters into his own hands.

Rob remained silent for several seconds then said, "I'm going to ask Holly to marry me."

Mark halted in mid-jab. Ice plunged into his blood again. He'd known months ago that this moment was coming, but Rob's announcement still caught him off guard. "I figured."

Deep down, he was happy for Rob, but seeing Rob and Holly thriving was a painful reminder of how alone Mark was and what he'd lost when he walked away from Karma. Right now, the mental smack in the head was too much for Mark to handle.

Rob's brow crinkled. "You 'figured'? How about 'Congratulations, Rob'? Don't you think that would be more appropriate?"

Mark lowered his gaze. The blue mat under his feet was dappled with sweat. "Congratulations." Then he faced the punching bag again, turning his back on Rob. He didn't need to see someone else's happiness when he'd squandered away his own like a dumb shit.

"You know what, Mark? Fuck you." Rob swiped his bag off the floor. "Fuck. You." He turned on his heel and headed for the exit.

Mark steadied the bag with one hand, glaring at Rob's retreating back. As Rob disappeared around the corner, Mark blew out a frustrated breath as his shoulders sagged. What was he doing? He was chasing everyone away. Karma. Crystal. Now Rob. He was isolating himself. He hadn't even seen his parents since Thanksgiving. He'd stayed home alone on Christmas. He'd bailed on Rob and Holly on New Year's Eve.

Now, dreaded Valentine's Day loomed on the horizon, and before he knew it, the one-year anniversary of the night he met Karma would be upon him.

This was not the time to be alienating everyone.

Snatching his bag and water bottle, he took off after Rob and caught up to him in the parking lot after blowing through the locker room to yank on his sweats and grab his coat.

"Rob, wait. I'm sorry. I was an asshole." The biting Chicago wind stung his sweat-streaked face.

Rob spun and jammed a finger against Mark's chest, making him ricochet backward. "You know, I got why you did what you did after Carol walked out on your ass, but I don't get this. I don't get why you're so pissed off when you're the one who said you had to walk away."

Mark hung his head. "I know, I know. I'm sorry." As usual, Rob pegged him.

"If you like Karma so damn much then call her. Tell her you miss her. Tell her you made a mistake."

"I can't." Even as he said it, he wasn't sure how much longer he could hold out, despite his tattoo artist's words of encouragement to do just that.

"Why the fuck not?"

"Because that's not how it's supposed to work. I set her free."

"Jesus Christ!" Rob began marching toward his car again. "What is this obsession you have with staying locked in misery, Mark? For God's sake, if you love her, fight for her. It'd be better than this shit. You're imprisoning yourself in some kind of self-imposed torture. And for what? Because you set her free? What is that, Mark? What's that all about? You're making no sense!" Rob tossed his bag in the backseat of his car and slammed the door.

How could Mark make Rob understand this? He barely did himself, but he'd made his deal with the universe, and he didn't want to fuck that up by being impatient, even though impatience was all he was feeling. "Haven't you ever heard the saying that if you love something, set it free?"

Rob's head bobbed up and down and side to side as if he were an angry bobblehead. "If it comes back to you, it's yours forever. If it doesn't, it never was. Yeah, so?"

"That's why I can't call her. I set her free. Do you get it now?" Mark raked his fingers through his hair, more agitated than he should have been. "I set her free, goddammit. If it's meant to be, and when I'm ready, God or the forces at work in the universe that control this shit will bring her back to me. They will. I have to believe that."

Have faith. Let go. Don't force it.

Razor's words had become a mantra.

Rob sighed heavily and jacked his hands on his hips. For a long moment, he said nothing. "Man, Carol really fucked you up, didn't she?" Compassion filled his voice, as well as his eyes.

Mark dropped his bag by the back tire of Rob's car and parked his ass against the rear quarter panel. His shoulders sagged. "Ya think?"

Rob joined him, and for a long, silent moment, they stood together, leaning against Rob's car, not speaking a word as the binding threads of their friendship sewed themselves back together. Mark relied on Rob in so many ways. He hadn't realized until just this moment how much. Rob was his conscience, his sounding board, the kick in the ass he needed every once in a while.

"This isn't like you, Mark." Rob spoke gently. "I've never seen you like this."

Maybe that was because Mark had never felt so lost. Until he met Karma, he'd been in total control of every facet of his life. He'd had a plan and he'd never deviated from it. Then came Karma. She'd shot enough holes in his scheduled, orderly life to leave him feeling like Swiss cheese. And the harder he tried to fill the craters, the larger they grew.

Karma had changed him as much as he had changed her. He didn't look at women the same way now. In fact, he hardly looked at them at all. None of them could hold a candle to Karma. Other women were merely posers trying to fit into a glass slipper much too small and dainty for their big, clunky feet. The only foot capable of wearing such an exquisite shoe belonged to Karma. And what lovely feet she had.

Beyond that, she had shown him he could trust again. Their last night together, right before she blindfolded him, she had asked if he trusted her. With anyone else, the answer would have been no, but with her and only her, he knew without a doubt that, yes, he did.

That night, his heart opened to hers more than it had ever opened to anyone. But at the time, he'd been too mired in the battle between emotion and logic to see how right she was for him. As a result, he'd denied his heart's only wish—to stay with her. Instead, he had appeased his mind by walking away.

Fool.

Only when it was too late, after she'd told him good-bye and he was driving back to Chicago, did he realize the gravity of his mistake and struck his deal with a higher power.

"Stay with her or leave her?" Mark shrugged. "It was a decision I couldn't make, man. My head wanted one thing and my heart wanted another, so I'm letting fate decide."

"Should've gone with your heart."

Mark scowled out of the corners of his eyes. "Hindsight's twenty-twenty. And when you've lived your whole life making decisions with your head, switching to the heart isn't easy."

"So…what? You gave the decision over to God?"

"God, the universe, fate, a higher power. Whoever or whatever controls this kind of thing…but yeah, since I couldn't decide what to do, I took a leap of faith and made a deal. I turned her loose. I let her go. If Karma and I are meant to be together, we'll find our way back to one another."

Rob glanced toward the sky between the tall Chicago buildings. "Sounds like a pussy move to me."

"Fuck you." But there was no punch to Mark's words.

"I think you're scared."

Mark blew out a derisive puff of air. "Me? Of what?" But Rob was right. He was terrified, which was probably why he was as moody as a bipolar patient off his meds.

"I think you're scared of getting hurt again." Rob kept his voice neutral.

Mark frowned and looked away.

"Hey, I get it," Rob said. "I know what you went through with Carol, and I get why you'd be scared of going through that again. But, Mark, like I said before, life isn't always going to give you roses. Sometimes it throws shit on you. It's up to you to wash it off, pull yourself up, and flip life the middle finger and try again. You don't just give up. You don't just relinquish control." Rob chuffed. "Man, you just can't find the middle ground, can you? First, your self-control was so rigid you refused to even fathom giving Karma a chance. Now you've given complete control over to fate. Meanwhile, Karma's between the two, waiting for you to get off your fucked-up ass and find the middle ground and take what you want. And you *want* her. I know you do."

"I'd probably just mess up her life." Mark sighed. "She deserves someone who isn't afraid of commitment. Who won't go into an emotional hemorrhage and physical meltdown at the idea of marriage." He shifted against the car and glanced at his feet. "Besides, she's probably moved on by now, anyway."

"Now you're just making excuses."

"Damn, Rob, I'm trying here."

Rob shook his head. "No you're not. You're dying. Every day you don't reach out to her, a small part of you withers and dies. If you're not careful, you'll end up cold and heartless, with no feeling whatsoever."

Mark frowned and screwed up his face in a dubious

smirk. "Aren't you just full of good cheer today."

Rob offered a flippant shrug. "Just keeping it real."

"Sometimes I wish you weren't so damn honest."

Rob gave him a light shove. "I'm awesome like that. And you know I'm right."

Mark smiled. His first smile in days, if not weeks. "Have I ever told you how modest you are?"

"Once or twice."

He and Rob stared at each other for a long moment.

"Do you realize I bought her a Christmas gift?" Mark knew how pathetic that sounded. Why would you buy someone a gift you may never be able to give?

"Who? Karma?"

Mark nodded. "Yes. A scarf. It's in a gift bag on my credenza."

Rob blew out a heavy exhale, his cheeks puffing out. "My man, you've got it bad. What are we going to do about you?"

"There's nothing to do. I committed to this, and come hell or high water, I've got to see it through. Is the waiting around driving me crazy? Hell, yes. But this is the deal I made. I have to live with it."

"No, you don't. You just think you do." Rob's earnest gaze scratched something deep inside Mark's soul, awakening a niggle of discomfort.

He looked away and shuffled his feet against an icy patch of snow, letting silence consume the uneasiness for a long moment. "By the way. Congratulations." He hesitantly met Rob's eyes again. "Really, I'm happy for you. Honestly, I am." He waved toward the gym. "I'm sorry I was such a douche in there."

"Don't worry about it." Rob fist-bumped him, bro

code for *I forgive you.*

"When are you going to pop the question?"

"Valentine's Day."

A tremor of pain throbbed inside Mark's heart. For so long, he'd been the hopeless romantic. Big tough guy like him, and all he'd wanted was a wife to give flowers and a heart-shaped box of chocolates to on Valentine's Day. To take dancing, kiss, and make love to on a bed covered in rose petals. That had been his dream for so long. He'd thought Carol would be the fulfillment of that dream, but then she'd destroyed everything. Now he wasn't sure he would ever see his dream fulfilled.

"Be my best man," Rob said.

Mark's pulse kicked up a notch at the idea. "Rob—"

"I *want* you to be my best man, Mark. I know how you are with churches and weddings, but you're my best friend. You have to stand up with me."

Mark dropped his gaze to the snowy pavement.

"Please." Rob's voice implored him.

He knew he couldn't bail on Rob. Doing so after being best friends for twenty years would be a betrayal.

"Okay." Mark met Rob's gaze. "I'll do it. For you, I'll do it."

Rob was his brother from another mother. No way could he let Rob down and not be there for him on the most important day of his life. Hopefully, Rob's big day would go better than his had seven years ago.

"How about a beer?" Rob said.

Mark nodded. "Yeah. I'd like that. I could *use* a beer right now." Maybe the alcohol would dull the rampage of despair and frustration inside his head. At least for a little while.

Rob pushed away from the car and grabbed the handle of the driver's side door. "What you could *use* is a shower. I think your sweat is freezing to your hair. Jeez, how long were you at it in there?"

"Over an hour." More like ninety minutes.

Rob sighed. "Well, at least all this anger is getting you ripped." He opened his car door.

Mark picked up his duffel. "Let me run by my place and get cleaned up. I'll meet you in an hour?"

"I'll see you then."

Mark waved as Rob pulled out of the parking lot. Then he climbed behind the wheel of his BMW.

Before putting the car in gear, he grabbed his phone and pulled up Karma's contact information. For about the hundredth time since returning to Chicago, Mark typed her a text message.

I miss you. Can't stop thinking about you.

He stared at the message, his thumb hovering over the send button. One of these days, when enough time had passed, and when he no longer felt like his heart would self-destruct if she didn't reply — or did reply and told him not to contact her again or that she had gotten married — he would actually grow the balls to send one of his texts.

But that day wasn't today. As with all the other messages he had typed to her, he backspaced this one out, too. Then he leaned the back of his head on the headrest and stared up at ceiling.

God, what's taking you so long? I need her. I need her now. Before I self-destruct.

Chapter 6

Valentine's Day

Karma pulled open the door to Single Servings and stepped inside. At least a dozen pairs of eyes turned toward her. Last year at that Chicago benefit where she met Mark, all the attention had excited her. Now it just made her self-conscious.

Keeping her head down, she wandered toward the back corner of the room.

Why had she let Jan talk her into this?

"Have you ever heard of Single Servings?" Jan had said during their last session.

"No."

"Well, it's a cooking school catered toward single people. Singles meet up, cook, eat, have a good time. Sometimes they organize meet-ups at restaurants or do other activities. I have a couple of other clients who attend the Single Servings events and really enjoy them. Maybe you should give them a try now that you're cooking again."

Karma balked, holding up one hand, palm out. "I don't think I'm ready for something like that." Cooking in the privacy of her home was one thing, but teaming up with other singles in a meet-and-greet-let's-hook-up kind of place was another.

"Oh, I don't know about that," Jan said. "I think you should give it a try. It sounds like something you would really enjoy." Jan crossed her legs. "You've been doing a lot of cooking since Christmas, and even if you don't meet anyone, if nothing else, you'll add a few more recipes to your pantry. It's a win-win any way you look at it."

Jan had clearly wanted her to get back into the dating public.

So, here she was, anti-mingling at her first Single Servings event. The front half of the space was set up like a restaurant, with small tables and booths. Most of the other guests congregated around the bar stretched along the opposite wall, but she and two other obviously timid types hovered alone in the shadows, sipping cocktails.

In the back, behind a low wall, a large kitchen area was set up with multiple stations. Apparently, that was where the cooking took place.

"Hi there."

Karma turned and found a tall, not-quite-unfamiliar man standing next to her. She could swear she'd seen him before but couldn't remember where.

"Hi." She took an automatic half step back.

He smiled. "You don't remember me, do you?"

Karma's gaze met his chocolate brown eyes. "You do look familiar, but I can't quite…" She squinted as if that would help.

"I met you last summer," he said, still smiling. "At the bookstore."

Karma's mouth fell open. Flirt Quest. Oh God, this was the man she'd unknowingly flashed her *Blow Him* book at. After making a complete fool out of herself, he had hunted her down and asked her to dinner. Or was it coffee? She couldn't remember. But she did remember him giving her his card.

"Brad, right?"

His face lit up. "Yes. And you're...wait...don't tell me." His eyes narrowed for a couple of seconds before he said, "Karla?"

"Close. Karma."

"Ah. One letter off. Damn." He snapped his fingers.

His gaze danced over her face, and for a long moment, neither of them said anything.

"Is this your first time at Single Servings?" he said.

"Yes." She glanced down into her cocktail glass. How awkward that she actually knew someone there.

"So, I guess you're not still *sort of involved* with someone?"

It took her a second to understand what he meant, and then she remembered that was what she'd told him when he asked her out for coffee or dinner or whatever. That she was sort of involved with someone else. Mark. She and Mark had made an agreement that while they were together, neither would get involved with anyone else. That's why she hadn't taken Brad up on his dinner offer. Well, that and her gut had told her Brad really wasn't her type.

But here they were, meeting again. What were the odds? Maybe it was a sign.

"No, I'm not sort of involved with someone anymore." Saying the words sent an echo of pain through her chest, and a lump briefly formed in her throat before she washed it down with a sip of her drink.

His grin grew bigger, making the skin around his eyes crinkle. "Well, lucky me then."

He was an attractive man with thick, black hair seasoned with a touch of grey and kind, brown eyes that appeared a little wary, as if they'd seen their share of heartache. His forehead was lined with shallow creases, but in an outdoorsy, weathered kind of way. How old was Brad? He looked older than Mark. Brad had to be at least thirty-six, if not older. That was quite an age difference between them. Maybe that was why her gut had shied away from him last summer.

"Yes, lucky you," she said, lifting her drink.

Brad glanced toward the kitchen. "So, do you know how this works?"

"How what works?"

"Single Servings?"

She shook her head. "Not really. Just that cooking's involved. Why? Do you?"

"I've been coming to these things for a while, so yes, you could probably call me an expert."

"How long is a while?"

"About six months." He sipped from what looked like a glass of scotch. Mark had been drinking scotch the night she met him. Brad's choice of drink felt like a sign, too.

The slender, blond hostess chose that moment to step into the center of the room and tap a spoon on her glass. "Excuse me, everyone." She brushed her hair off her shoulder and waited until the guests quieted. "My name's Natalie." Her gaze swept the room. "I see a lot of familiar faces this evening, as well as quite a few new ones." Her bleached smile was so white it looked fake. "For those new to Single Servings, welcome." She briefly raised her glass then proceeded to go around the room for introductions.

Karma felt her face heat when it was her turn to speak. "My name's Karma Mason."

"And what brings you to us, Karma?" Natalie said.

She nibbled her bottom lip and glanced toward the floor. "Um, well…" She didn't think explaining that her therapist had suggested she come would make a good impression. "I'm single and like to cook, so I thought this would be a good way to meet new people."

That was evasive enough.

"You came to the right place," Natalie said.

Out of the corner of her eye, she could see Brad watching her.

The last two guests introduced themselves, then Natalie explained how things worked. There were eight stations in the kitchen, plus one for the instructor. The sixteen guests—eight women and eight men—were to pair up with a member of the opposite sex and take a station.

Brad turned to her. "Would you like to be my partner?"

He was the obvious choice. At least she knew Brad. Well, sort of. Could she really count a ten-minute encounter at the bookstore, where she had royally embarrassed herself by revealing her stack of sex books, as knowing him? Still, they had talked, and he seemed genuinely nice. And he was more attractive than she remembered. Kind of sexy in his maroon sweater and charcoal grey slacks.

"Okay, sure." She followed him into the kitchen where they claimed a station with the number three painted on the wall over the stove. A bevy of dessert ingredients lay neatly on the island facing toward the front of the room.

"Everyone, put on your aprons." Natalie stepped behind the teaching station then tied her apron around her waist.

Karma did the same, casting Brad a sideways glance. He had a nice profile. He caught her eye and smiled. She quickly looked away.

"In honor of Valentine's Day," Natalie said, "we're going to make *decadent chocolate truffles*." She emphasized each word. "In front of you, you have the recipe and all the ingredients you'll need."

Karma picked up the six-by-nine card and followed along as Natalie relayed the ingredients and instructions. Then Natalie demonstrated the first few steps before turning everyone loose.

Brad poured cream into a saucepan and set it on the stove while Karma unwrapped the chocolate.

"So, have you read any good books lately?" Brad asked.

"No." Karma snapped the bar of chocolate in half and set the pieces on their wood cutting board. "I've been kind of busy."

Busy mourning the loss of the greatest man ever to happen to me.

Brad picked up one of the two chef's knives and helped her chop the chocolate. His forearm brushed hers. "Me, too. My office picked up a new project and things have been a little crazy. Lot of long days"

"You're an engineer, right?" Karma remembered that from the business card he'd given her.

"Yes. And I'm the office director, too, which means I oversee all our projects." He looked genuinely impressed...as if he figured she hadn't given him a second thought after meeting him but was glad to hear she'd paid enough attention to remember what he did for a living. "What do you do?"

"I'm an executive assistant for a company that manufactures lawn care products and does landscape design."

"Sounds interesting."

"It can be." She scooped up shards of chocolate and dropped them in a glass mixing bowl. "My degree was in journalism, though. I'm hoping to move back into that someday."

"Ah, a writer, huh?" Brad checked on the cream, making sure it wasn't boiling.

She shrugged and chopped up the last of the chocolate. "Maybe someday."

They worked in silence for a couple of minutes, and the sounds of the others talking and laughing filled the empty space.

"I think the cream's ready," Brad said, removing it from the heat.

He set it on the counter.

Karma checked the recipe. "We need to let it cool for about twenty seconds then pour it through the sieve into the chocolate."

"So, you enjoy cooking?" Brad picked up the sieve

and watched the clock.

"Yes. You?"

"Some." He picked up the pan. "I'm usually so pressed for time, though, that I don't cook as much as I should."

Karma grabbed the whisk. "Pour it slowly," she said as he began pouring the cream into the chocolate.

As he poured, she stirred.

"Do you have any kids?" Brad asked.

Kids? How old did he think she was? "No. You?"

"One. A daughter."

That was a surprise, but then it really shouldn't have been. Brad looked old enough to be divorced with a kid.

"How old is she?"

"Twelve going on twenty."

Karma laughed at the tired, I've-already-had-enough-of-her-drama way he said it. "That bad, huh?"

He tossed the sieve aside and opened the bottle of Grand Marnier while she continued slowly stirring the hot cream into the chocolate. "Oh, it's not that bad, but sometimes I can't keep up with the mood changes. Everything's a crisis or unbelievably 'awesome.' I'm praying for the end of puberty."

Memories of Karma's own childhood crept into her mind. Her life had been a wreck when she was twelve. If not for her dad's steadying influence and encouragement, she might not have turned out as emotionally healthy as she had. And that was saying something, because she still carried a lot of baggage into her adult life from the bullying she'd endured. She could only imagine that life for a preteen girl these days was even harder.

"Give it time. I'm sure everything will work out. Just be there for her, and I'm sure she'll grow up well adjusted." She frowned at what looked like lumps in their cream and chocolate mixture.

"I hope so." Brad poured a tablespoon of Grand Marnier. "You ready for this?"

Scowling at the lumpy consistency of the ganache, she nodded. "Sure." Hopefully, the rest of the chocolate would melt by the time they scooped it into balls.

Brad added the liqueur, coffee, and vanilla then set aside the bowl. It had to sit at room temperature for an hour.

While they waited, they cleaned then wandered into the front of the room with a few others to grab hors d'oeuvres and chat. After making small talk about books and work, Brad told her he'd been married for eleven years but that they'd gotten divorced when his daughter, Jade, was nine.

"What happened?"

"We just grew apart." He wiped his fingers on his small, square paper napkin. "I think we got married too young, before we knew what we wanted. As the years passed, we seemed to have less and less in common." He shrugged. "After a while, all we did was argue. It wasn't a healthy environment for Jade."

"Your ex-wife has custody?"

"Yes, but I see her on the weekends and get her for a month every summer and for a couple weeks during the holidays. She may be a diva in the making, but she's my angel."

Karma liked how he talked about his daughter. Brad

sounded like a good father.

After an hour passed, they returned to the kitchen, scooped out balls of ganache, and refrigerated them for thirty minutes while prepping the garnishments for their truffles. Then they rolled their balls of ganache into perfect spheres and coated them with crushed almonds, powdered sugar, or chocolate sprinkles.

"Do we dare?" Brad said as he picked up a finished truffle and held it toward her.

"Why not?" She grabbed one covered in powdered sugar and held it out for him.

At the same time, they leaned in, took the truffles in their mouths, and watched each other eat.

The chocolate was still lumpy, so fail on the ganache, but the flavor was good.

"Well?" she said, covering her mouth with her hand.

He nodded and licked powdered sugar off his lips. "Not perfect, but not bad for a first attempt."

Karma had been at Single Servings for over three hours. And she hadn't died. Honestly, she'd had a good time. Maybe even a great one. She'd only thought about Mark a couple of times, but for the most part, she'd kept herself in the moment. And Brad was nice. She was glad she'd come and bumped into him.

As the evening wound down and everyone filtered out—some in pairs or groups, others alone—Brad helped her into her coat.

"I'm glad you came tonight," he said.

"Me, too." She started for the door, carrying her container of truffles.

"Do you think you'll be back next week?" He followed her into the chilly night. The interest in his voice was unmistakable.

Was she ready to embark on another journey with a man other than Mark? If she did this, she would be taking her first step toward walking away from Mark for good...really saying good-bye this time. Not like before, when she'd said good-bye but hadn't meant it.

She glanced at Brad, and he smiled hopefully.

Brad didn't seem afraid of commitment. He'd been married once, and even though he'd been divorced, he was out here trying to meet someone else, daring to try again despite past failure, unlike Mark, who had never recovered from being jilted and a lifetime of letting go of his heart only to have it squashed. If she sat around waiting for Mark, she would only meet disappointment. Mark wouldn't come back. And if he did, he would never marry her. He would never want a commitment. Brad seemed more than ready for both.

"Yes," she said. "I'll be back next week. What about you?"

His smile lit up his whole face. "I will be now." He walked her to her car. "Good night, Karma. Happy Valentine's Day. I'll see you next week."

"Happy Valentine's Day to you, too." A tiny bubble of excitement gurgled in her heart.

As she drove home, she silently thanked Mark for everything he'd taught her. Without his help, she wasn't sure she would have met Brad, and she wasn't sure she would have felt enough confidence to talk to him.

Maybe Jan was right. Maybe Mark's purpose had merely been as a catalyst. A stepping-stone from one phase of her life to another. She would still need time to get over him, but tonight had been a good first step.

Chapter 7

February 25
Karma's Blog
"I'm Insane"

What am I thinking? I must be insane. How do I let my therapist talk me into these things?

I just signed up to run this year's Mini-Marathon the first weekend of May, which means I have only two months to prepare.

Sure, I ran cross-country in high school and did a little running in college, but that's been almost three years ago. I guess I'll find out soon enough if this decision is a colossal fail or the best idea I've ever had.

To help prepare, I finally used my bonus money and bought a state-of-the-art treadmill and spin bike this week, and they'll be delivered this afternoon. My friends are coming over this morning to help me clean out my second bedroom so I can turn it into my training room. The treadmill and bike will go in there, along with a few pairs of dumbbells I purchased for cross-training.

M would be proud. I'm actually going to weight train.

Dad would be proud, too. I've actually put on a couple of pounds now that I'm eating again.

I'll be eating a lot more, too. I need to feed my body as I

Donya Lynne

embark on this intense training schedule. Luckily, my new friend B is going to help. He's running the Mini, too. We talked about it during this week's cooking class. So, now that the weather is starting to break for spring, we'll meet a couple times a week at the gym to help each other cross-train, although I think he'll be helping me more than I'm helping him. Once I'm able to run distance, we'll start hitting the trails. The race will be here before I know it.

B's a nice guy. Not M, but really, there will never be another M. But B is a good guy. I like him. I have no idea where things will go, but I guess it's time I moved on, and B seems like a good man to do that with.

A knock at her door drew Karma's attention away from typing. She quickly hit *Publish* then darted into the living room.

"Hey, guys!" Her best friends, Daniel and Lisa, stepped inside.

Daniel hugged her. "You look good, honey."

"Thanks. So do you. How's that hubby of yours?"

"Zach's sexy as ever."

"You two make me jealous, you know." Karma gave him another squeeze before letting go.

"Why's that?" He peeled out of his coat.

"Because your relationship is perfect." She would give anything to have the kind of relationship Daniel and Zach had. So full of passion and love.

Daniel winked and meandered into the kitchen, leaving her with Lisa.

"You do look a *lot* better, sweetie." Lisa draped her coat over the arm of the couch beside Daniel's. "The question is, do you feel as good as you look?"

Karma nodded, albeit slowly. "I think so." She'd been spending more time with Brad, and while he didn't blow her mind the way Mark had, she liked him. "I think I'm finally making a turnaround."

Daniel reappeared with a glass of iced tea. "When are they delivering your *torture device*? I can't believe you're taking up running again." He led everyone back to the spare bedroom.

"Hey, don't dis my passions, Daniel." She lightly shoved his arm. "And the delivery guy said after one o'clock. They're supposed to call thirty minutes before they arrive." Karma pulled her auburn hair into a ponytail. She really needed a haircut.

"What's this?" Lisa said, pointing to her computer. "*Chocolate Chunk Brownies*? Karma, is this—?"

"It's nothing." She quickly closed her laptop.

The looks on Daniel's and Lisa's faces indicated they weren't buying it.

"Fine." She slumped into the chair and reopened her laptop. "I started a blog about him, but it was my therapist's idea."

"Why?" Lisa parked her butt on the corner of the desk, concern etched in her face.

"She thought it would help me process my emotions or something." She glanced at the screen. "I promise I'm not dwelling on him or anything like that."

Daniel and Lisa exchanged glances. They knew how hard Mark's departure had been on her. They'd worried about her for months. Now that she seemed to be turning her life around and moving on it was understandable her writing a blog about him would unnerve them.

"Well..." Daniel glanced into his glass then met Karma's gaze, his eyes filled with concern.

"What?" Karma didn't like his expression. He looked like he had bad news. Scary bad. "What is it, Daniel?"

He set down his glass, dug into his back pocket, and pulled out a folded sheet of glossy paper. "I get *Chicago* magazine. I finally got around to reading last month's issue and saw this." He unfolded the paper and handed it to Karma.

She scanned the title on the page then inspected the picture. It was an article about New Year's Eve. The picture was of two Chicago football players at some party.

"So?" She shrugged and turned confused eyes on Daniel then Lisa. "Am I missing something here?"

Lisa sighed, and the sound held as much foreboding as Daniel's expression. "Look in the background."

Karma glanced at the picture again and her heart stopped. "Oh." A lump formed in her throat when she saw Mark standing arm in arm with a tall, beautiful, busty woman who was clearly smitten with him. "How nice for him." She handed the ripped-out page back to Daniel.

"I'm sorry," he said.

"But we thought you needed to know." Lisa touched her arm.

"It doesn't matter." Karma shook her head and aimed her gaze into the hallway as if searching for something that wasn't there.

So, Mark had replaced her already. And with a woman who couldn't have been more opposite from her. She wasn't sure what hurt worse, that he was gone, or that the next woman he'd moved on to had boobs the size of cantaloupes when hers were merely kiwis. She cleared her throat and glanced back at her blog. "Well, at least I have something new to write about in my next post, right?"

Daniel and Lisa nodded warily.

"That's one way to look at it," Daniel said. "You sure you're okay?"

Karma pushed a smile onto her face. "I'm great. Really. I'm seeing someone, too. Did you know that?" She and Brad hadn't actually been out on any dates, but she knew he wanted to ask her. And when he did, she would say yes. Absolutely. No question about it this time around. And it was time she let her friends know she had another suitor.

"I didn't know you were dating again." Lisa appeared relieved but surprised. "When did this happen?"

Karma gave a flippant shrug and sat back. "I met him on Valentine's Day. He's going to help me train for the Mini-Marathon, too."

"Oh my God, really?" Daniel's eyes flew open. "You're running a marathon? I thought you were just using the new treadmill for exercise. How about that? You're running competitively again. I take back my jab about the torture device." He lightly tapped her knee.

"Yep, so see, I've never been better. I've got a new guy, a new hobby, and I'm cooking again. Life's great."

"So I guess the blog's been helping then, huh?" Lisa gestured toward her laptop.

"Yep, it's been a great help." The image of Mark

with that woman scored her mind like a knife as she turned back to her computer screen. There was definitely a venting blog post in her near future.

"How so?" Daniel sounded cautious, as if he wasn't quite buying her show of cheerful confidence. Then again, Daniel knew her better than anyone and could probably tell she was putting on a happy face when inside she was hurting.

"I don't know..." She waved at her computer screen. "It's just helping me work through everything. Writing about him and where I am now is giving me perspective."

"And you called it 'Chocolate Chunk Brownies?'" Lisa gave her a tight smile as she glanced at her laptop.

"I thought that was as good a name as any."

"With significant meaning, too." Lisa arched one brow.

"Yes. But it's also ambiguous. The blog is anonymous, so you guys can't tell anyone about it, okay. I want to keep it a secret."

Lisa and Daniel both crossed their index fingers over their chests, silently swearing their allegiance.

Daniel pulled a giant beanbag chair out of the corner and plopped down. "Can we read it?"

Karma almost laughed at the beggar-boy expression on Daniel's face. "Can I stop you? I mean, now that you know the name of the blog, you can read it pretty much any time you want."

Daniel grinned as if he'd just been granted three wishes.

Karma pointed a finger at him. "But you can't tell anyone, and I don't want any commentary from the peanut gallery." She hardened her stare on Daniel then turned toward Lisa. "And you two are the peanut gallery."

Lisa held up her hands, giggling. "Hey, I'm down with keeping my mouth shut if motormouth over here is." She nodded toward Daniel.

Daniel held out his hands, palms up. "Why are you looking at me? I can keep a secret."

"Okay, fine." Karma relaxed into her chair. "But seriously, guys, this blog is deeply personal. I reveal everything. Talk about baring your heart and soul." She cast a sideways glance at the screen. "Some of the things I write about are incredibly painful. Others are more heartfelt. Either way, I've cried a lot of tears into what I've written here."

And she would cry a few more when she was alone and had a chance to fully process that Mark had moved on without her. All the more reason for her to do the same with Brad.

"But as long as it's helping, it's all good, right?" Daniel glanced from Karma to Lisa and back again.

Karma considered the question. Admittedly, she felt stronger now than she had two months ago. At least until she'd seen that picture. But overall, she was in a much better place physically, mentally, and emotionally. How much of that was from the passage of time, and how much was from her sessions with Jan and the "homework" she gave her.

Funny how she was once more doing homework to make a change in her life. First Mark, now Jan. At some point, she needed to learn how to apply her lessons without someone watching over and guiding her.

"I think so." She nodded. "I'm feeling better now." She hadn't cried in over two weeks. "And..." She glanced toward the window. Pellets of sleet tapped the glass, and rivulets of rain ran down the pane.

"And what?" Lisa said.

"And...I kind of like this Brad guy."

"That's great." Lisa's smile lit up the room.

"So where did you two meet, anyway?" Daniel leaned forward and chucked her knee.

"I actually met him last summer at the bookstore, but I met him again at this place I've started going to called Single Servings."

"I've heard of that," Lisa said. "Cooking club for single people, right?"

"Yes."

Daniel gave her a sly look. "And I bet you two can *cook*, sister." He snapped his fingers.

Warmth shot into her face. "It's not like that."

"Not yet." Daniel cocked his head to one side. "But give it time and a little tumble in the sheets, and you'll be saying, 'Mark who?'"

Karma didn't think she would ever say "Mark who?" The man was permanently imprinted on her soul. He was her first love. He'd been the first man to give her an orgasm. He'd altered not only her perception of herself but also her reality. Without Mark, she wouldn't be the same woman she was today.

"I don't know, Daniel. I'm not sure—"

"You like Brad, right?" Lisa said, cutting her off as if she didn't want to let Karma go down that path.

"Well, yeah. Of course I do."

Daniel leaned in. "Is he hot?"

"Why does it always have to be about looks with you?" She didn't feel right saying that Brad was hot. He was attractive, but he was no Mark, who had struck her breathless at a glance.

"Honey, it's always about the looks. Most people just don't want to admit it. So, is he? Hot, I mean?"

Karma giggled. Daniel could be such a breath of vibrant yet incorrigible air. "He's attractive."

Lisa jumped back in. "How old is he?"

Daniel waved his hand. "Who cares, sister? He sounds fine."

Karma shook her head at Daniel's exuberance then turned back toward Lisa. "I don't know, but older. Maybe mid- to late-thirties. He has a twelve-year-old daughter."

"Oooohhh." Daniel sucked his tongue between his teeth, making a sound between a chirp and a tsk, and then exchanged cautious glances with Lisa.

"What?" Karma said.

Daniel gave her a compassionate look, his eyebrows upturned over his nose. "A man with a kid. You are going to have to win that young thing over if you want to be with her dad. I hope you know that."

Karma huffed. "He hasn't actually asked me out, but I know he will. And when he does, I'm sure it will be a while before I meet Jade."

"You already know her name?" Lisa's mouth curled into a knowing grin.

"Yeah, so?"

"So, that means he's already asked you out, you just don't know it, yet."

"I think I would remember if he'd asked me out,

Leese."

She held up her hand. "He may not have actually asked, but in his mind, he already has. Mark my words, he wouldn't have told you about his daughter and given you her name if he wasn't planning on asking you out."

True. Brad had told her quite a bit about Jade. Would he really have done that with just anyone?

"Enough about my social life." Karma waved her hands as if clearing a swarm of gnats. "We need to work. This stuff isn't going to move itself, and we only have..." She checked the clock. "Two hours."

She didn't want to get any deeper into the discussion about her and Brad. They'd only seen each other twice at Single Servings and once at the gym to discuss training for the Mini. She liked him. He was nice. He made her smile. But right now it was time to work.

Chapter 8

St. Patrick's Day

Sweat poured from Mark's body. He was drenched, but he refused to stop.

"One more set," Rob said, poised behind the bench press.

Since Mark's global meltdown in January, he and Rob had made amends, and Rob was doing his best to be down with Mark's plan to give fate time to work through the red tape of bringing Karma back to him.

Mark lay back on the bench and gripped the bar.

Rob stood ready to spot him through his last grueling set. "How many?"

"Eight."

"Got it."

After taking a series of deep breaths to oxygenate his muscles, Mark pushed the weighted bar off the rack and balanced it above his chest.

Inhaling on the way down and exhaling on the way back up, he worked through the first four reps without much distress. But on number five, his fatigued muscles protested. By rep seven, he was straining. This may have been his lightest set of eight, but after five hardcore sets, the eighth rep wasn't coming easily.

Holding the bar over his body, Mark took several rapid, deep breaths as Rob moved in and placed his hands under the bar.

"You've got this, Mark." Rob was using his personal training voice. The one edged with grit and determination. "Come on. One more. Don't you puss out."

His arms burned. His shoulders and chest screamed. But he was doing this for *her*. In the beginning, his brutal workouts had been about trying to forget Karma. About pushing her from his thoughts. But now the grab-him-by-the-balls beatings he gave himself five times a week had morphed into an almost meditative practice where his determination to be with her again overtook everything else. Instead of using this time to clear his head, he used it to visualize the two of them together. One way or another, he was going to make that happen.

Taking one final breath, he lowered the bar then growled, straining as he pushed it back up. Rob began to help.

"No!" Mark would see this through by himself. He would complete this set without needing Rob to save him.

Slowly, he ground out the last rep and dropped the bar back on the rack.

"Good job." Rob blew out an exhale as if he'd been the one pounding it out instead of Mark.

"Fuck." Mark swung himself upright and rested, legs on either side of the bench, elbows on his knees.

His hair had grown out and hung over his face as he

stared down at the floor. Droplets of perspiration trickled down his neck and back.

I will get her back. Damn it, I will.

After allowing him to rest another thirty seconds, Rob tossed him a towel and his water bottle. "Break over. Let's hit the pads."

This was what made Rob the most popular personal trainer at the gym, even if he only worked there part time. The guy was ruthless. He built a program and made his clients stick to it. Which was why Mark had told Rob to build him the most insane program he could. He needed the challenge, not only for his body but also for his mind. And it was working. The gym sessions were so intense that it was no wonder they felt more like meditation than a workout. With the shit Rob threw at him, Mark definitely had to get down with the idea of mind over matter. Otherwise, matter would kick his ass.

"How much weight have you lost?" Rob said as they made their way to the boxing area.

Mark killed his second bottle of water and screwed the cap back on before chucking the empty container in his bag. "Since January?" Mark thought a couple seconds. "About ten pounds, I think."

"You look it. Shit, but you've leaned out."

"Thanks to you and this killer workout you've got me doing."

A couple of gym bunnies on their way to the stair climbers smiled at him and Rob and giggled as they passed. A year ago, Mark would have given them a second look. Maybe even a third. But not now. Karma consumed one hundred percent of his interest. There

Donya Lynne

wasn't room for anyone else. In fact, the last time he'd had sex was with Karma last September. Talk about a drought. But at least this was self-imposed. There had been plenty of opportunities to wet his wick. He just couldn't stomach the thought of doing so with anyone other than her.

Rob helped him tape up his hands. It was time for punching practice. As Mark flexed and fisted his fingers, Rob grabbed his pads, strapped them to his hands, then raised them out to the sides.

Mark was no boxer, but playing one in the gym sure helped cut his body fat percentage. And it gave him another outlet to both vent his frustration and build his fortitude. The universe was taking way too long to get its act together and show him the door that would lead Karma back into his arms. As the weeks passed, he grew more and more determined to take matters into his own hands.

He cross-jabbed and his fists popped against the leather pads. The exertion felt good. Again, he crossed then jabbed, then jabbed again. *Pop-pop-POP!*

"Good." Rob clapped the pads together then held them up again as he stepped to the side.

Mark followed, keeping his eyes on the targets.

Pop-pop!

He never should have left. He should have turned around on the way back to Chicago.

Pop!

Rob circled him, moving the pads, turning one so it faced the floor and holding the other out to the side.

Mark hooked then sent an uppercut into the downward-facing pad.

Downward-facing. That made him think of yoga, which made him think of *her* again. Did she still do yoga?

Maybe he should take up yoga. Maybe that would help clear his mind even more.

Rob sidestepped and backed up. Mark stayed with him.

Pop-pop!

He envisioned the red leather pads on Rob's hands as representations of fate.

POP! He laid into the right pad with a fierce jab. *Take that, fate. Maybe that will get you off your ass and pick up the pace.*

It had been seven months, for God's sake. How long did it take to create a goddamn sign?

One thing Mark knew for sure, he was on his last legs of waiting around.

One way or another, he was getting back his precious Karma, even if he had to do it himself and ditch his promise to the universe.

Come hell or high water, she would be his again.

Chapter 9

March 27

"I like your hair," Jan said as she settled into the chair across from Karma.

"Thank you." Karma ran her hand down her shorter tresses, which hit just below her shoulder. She hadn't cut her hair this short in...well...ever. She felt refreshingly lighter. Her stylist had also added some burnished highlights, bringing out the red tones.

Jan crossed her legs and rested her tablet on her lap. "How's training for the Mini-Marathon coming along?"

"Slow, but good. I might end up walking part of the marathon, but it won't be for lack of trying."

Karma had been interval running three times a week since getting her treadmill. On the days she didn't run, she rode her spin bike and lifted weights, and two or three times a week, she met Brad at the gym. They usually grabbed a quick bite afterward.

That first week had been brutal. Not a night had gone by when at least one muscle group or another hadn't protested the new routine.

"How are things going with Brad?" Jan held her stylus over her tablet.

"Good."

"Has he asked you out?"

"Not officially, but we've been spending so much time together that it feels like we're already dating." The time she spent with Brad did actually feel more like dating than two training partners preparing for a marathon together. Still, going out on a real date, where he asked her out and they got dressed up, would be nice.

"And how do you feel about that?"

Karma shrugged one shoulder. "I'm ready. It's time for me to move on."

Jan made a note on her tablet. "And you want to move on with Brad?"

"Yes. I guess. Maybe." Admitting that she wanted Brad to ask her out made her feel like a traitor. "But I feel guilty."

"Why?"

"Because..." Karma glanced down at her hands then out the window.

"Because it makes you feel like you're not being loyal to Mark?"

She met Jan's gaze again and nodded. "Yes. I know it's stupid, especially since I know he's moved on." She'd told Jan about the New Year's Eve picture of Mark with that woman. "But I still feel like I belong to Mark. Like he's just away on business or something and that any minute he'll be back and will expect me to still be here waiting for him. I don't want to hurt him."

Jan's expression softened. "First of all, it's not stupid. It's human. Nothing you think is stupid, especially where your feelings for Mark are concerned. With that said, it's my job to help you explore why you're feeling this way about a man who has clearly moved on...who told you from the start he didn't want a commitment and would leave...and did exactly what he said he would."

Karma had thought the same thing a hundred times, maybe more. But Jan hadn't been with Mark like she had. Karma had seen the glint in Mark's eye. She had heard the love in his voice and felt it in his touch. Mark might have done exactly what he said he would do, but she would bet her last dollar that he had grown to see her as more than just some random woman with which to kill time.

Which made the picture of him spending New Year's Eve with another woman that much harder to understand. Maybe she'd never understood him as well as she'd thought.

"Despite what Mark said, I feel like he fell in love with me, too."

Jan's eyebrows raised. "Maybe he did."

"Then why did he leave?"

Jan pursed her lips and drilled her gaze into Karma's as if she'd just latched on to a key piece of evidence. "You tell me."

Karma searched her mind for several seconds, not seeing what Jan apparently did.

Jan uncrossed her legs and sat forward. "Why would a man who's in love with you leave you behind, Karma?"

She lowered her gaze, searching her thoughts. Then, "Oh..." She met Jan's gaze, and her breath rushed out of her as if she'd been hit. "Because he didn't love me enough to stay. His fear of commitment was stronger than his love for me."

Jan's expression shifted into one that said she'd hit the nail on the head.

Karma's shoulders fell as she looked back down at her hands resting on her lap.

"Mark might have fallen in love with you, but the demons of his past were apparently too big to overcome. He may never get over what his fiancée did to him."

"And it would be a waste of time to put my life on hold and wait for him to come back when that's not going to happen."

Jan grinned like a proud mother. "Very good."

There was no way Karma could compete with Mark's painful past. He would always bow down to what had happened, unable to put Carol's jilting behind him and move forward.

At the end of the session, Jan set aside her iPad. "So, you're seeing Brad again tonight?"

It was Tuesday. Single Servings night.

"Yes."

"And what if he asks you out?" Jan walked her to the door.

There was no reason why she shouldn't go out with Brad. Maybe her heart still felt loyal to Mark, but in time, it would come around.

"I'll say yes."

Jan smiled. "Glad to hear it. I'll see you next week."

From Jan's office, Karma drove directly to Single Servings.

Brad was already there and greeted her as she

entered. "Hi there. How you feeling after Sunday's run?"

The weather had been nice enough that he'd persuaded her into jogging with him. His pace had been fast, but she'd managed to keep up...just barely.

"I felt great Sunday, but last night? Let's put it this way." She hung up her jacket. "I was in bed by eight. Must have been delayed exhaustion. That run really took it out of me."

She'd slept a full nine hours, too, but when she awoke this morning, she'd felt great. She was living proof that there was something to the exercise endorphins theory. The more she exercised, the less depressed she felt. The post-Mark funk dissipated a little more every day, even if he still haunted her heart.

For the next three hours, she and Brad laughed and chattered their way through boning and roasting a duck inside a layer of pastry dough. By the time they sampled their efforts—delicious!—and boxed up the leftovers, which Karma planned for lunch the next day, it was after nine.

The evening was unseasonably warm.

As usual, Brad walked her to her car.

"I was thinking," he said as she set her take-home bag in the passenger seat and walked around to the driver's side.

She turned and noticed the pink color in his cheeks. His smile was the same one he'd worn when he'd tracked her down in nonfiction at the bookstore last summer.

"Yes?" She hesitated beside her door. He was going to ask her out. She could just tell.

"Well…" He glanced toward the windows of Single Servings as the lights shut off. "Maybe next week instead of coming here and making dinner we could go out. Just you and me. What do you say?"

Karma felt Mark's specter fade a little further, even though her heart still beat for him. *He's not coming back. He's moved on.* Brad was a nice man. He really was. Any woman would be honored to go out with him.

"Are you asking me out on a date, Brad?" She palmed her keys but made no move to get in her car.

He smoothed his lips together then nodded as a warm smile broke over his face. Such a lovely smile. "Yes, I am. I'm asking you out on a date. A real, bona fide date." He gestured toward the Single Servings building. "I mean, heck, I already feel like we've been dating every Tuesday night anyway. Why not break away from the herd and see how we do on our own?"

The ache in her heart beckoned her to say no, but the voice in her head demanded she say yes. Logic over emotion. As much as she still loved Mark, he was her past. Brad was right here, right now, wanting to be her future. In the way she knew winter would turn to spring, she knew Brad was looking for more than just dinner. A lot more. He was a man who clearly wanted to get married again. She'd learned as much from their talks over the past several weeks. He was willing to try for forever one more time despite his first marriage falling apart. He was prepared to risk his heart in the pursuit of love and happiness. Mark wasn't capable of that. Didn't she want someone to pursue her? Didn't she want a man to give her his heart?

In a way, she felt as though she'd passed some kind

of romantic audition for Brad to ask her out on a real date...as if the past month and a half had been a way for him to feel her out to make sure she would fit into his world.

She met Brad's gentle brown eyes and smiled. "I think I'd like to strike out on our own next week for a change."

His chin rose a little higher, and his skin appeared more radiant as he held her gaze. It looked like he was breathing a silent sigh of relief. "Well, uh..." He nodded, his smile widening. "I'll call you."

"And I'll look forward to it." She climbed behind the wheel and glanced at him as he waved and took a couple steps backward.

She waved back then put the car in gear and slowly pulled away.

As she drove home, she warred with her emotions. Part of her clung desperately to Mark's memory, as if warning her she was making a mistake by moving on, but the other part eagerly anticipated this new journey. Brad seemed like the ideal guy.

But would he be ideal for her?

Chapter 10

April 7

Mark finished his run as he approached Millennium Park. Slowing to a walk, he breathed heavily, hands on his hips.

Winter was finally breaking, and even though the air still held a chill, there were a lot of people in the park today.

He stopped and stretched for a few minutes before wandering farther into the park, past the colossal silver "kidney bean" sculpture and into the courtyard, which was decorated with huge pastel-colored eggs. Tomorrow was Easter, and there was a giant Easter egg hunt planned. Children and their families would descend in droves, squealing with laughter, stuffing plastic eggs into baskets and bags, gorging on cotton candy, jelly beans, marshmallow Peeps, and chocolate bunnies. Afterward, they'd probably go home and collapse into a post-sugar high coma the way he had when he was a kid.

Fond memories touched Mark's thoughts as he found a bench and took a seat, content to sit back and watch a little boy dart up to a giant, white bunny holding a basket full of flyers as it made its rounds to promote tomorrow's festivities. The little boy was maybe three years old, toddling in sneakers and a puffy red jacket, pointing his tiny finger at the bunny as he looked over his shoulder at his mom and dad, who strolled up behind him. His dad knelt and pointed at the bunny, too, and it looked like they were having an animated conversation about how special tomorrow was. Then the dad lifted the little boy as he stood and set him on his shoulders. The boy screeched and laughed, hugging his arms around his dad's head, which made the mom laugh.

Mark smiled as he watched them. He wanted that. He wanted what that man had.

Bowing his head, he nodded to himself. Maybe he was going about this all wrong. Perhaps he didn't need the universe to give him a sign. What if fate was simply waiting for him to act?

Could it really be that simple? Maybe instead of sitting around waiting for the universe to pull a miracle out of its ass he should take a more active role in making his own dreams come true.

He glanced up and watched the family meander away, the little boy still on his dad's shoulders, rocking back and forth in time with his father's footsteps.

Being a dormant bystander wasn't getting him anywhere. It was time to take back control of his life.

But talk about poor timing. Mark was starting a new assignment in Wisconsin on Monday. If not, he would drive to Indianapolis this weekend to see her. But just when he was ready to leap, his job interfered. For the next three months, he'd be eyeballs deep in work. But that didn't mean he couldn't start making plans. In the little down time he *would* have, he could formulate the perfect way to reenter Karma's life. Something grand. Something that conveyed just how much he loved her and how serious he was about making her a part of his life. This was something he definitely didn't want to do over the phone.

So, the universe had three more months, and maybe not even that long if he finished his assignment early. If the powers that be didn't produce a sign before his assignment in Wisconsin was over, he was taking matters into his own hands. Karma belonged with him, and he would have her.

As he stood and glanced back toward the family in the distance, the first flicker of hope he'd felt in eight months flared inside his chest. He stood a little taller, feeling a bit of his old swagger reemerge.

If that wasn't a sign, he didn't know what was.

Chapter 11

Karma pulled her keepsake box from the top shelf of her closet and carried it to the bed. Was this really a good idea? Brad was picking her up in an hour. Now probably wasn't the time to go through old memories.

Even so, she pulled the top off the box and closed her eyes. Until last September, she hadn't put much in her keepsake box, but after Mark, she had damn near filled the thing up.

His scent captured her first. She could still smell him on the sheets and the pillowcase he'd used that last night in her apartment. When she opened her eyes, she inhaled heavily. There he was. Mark. All she had left of him, anyway.

The sheets that still smelled like him, the red scarf he'd used to blindfold her, which she had turned around and blindfolded him with their last weekend together in Chicago. And the gold brooch that started everything.

Digging under the folded sheets, she found the case of dildos he'd given her. And the Ben Wa balls. She smiled as she remembered the night he helped her remove one that got stuck. Then the smile faded and tears took its place.

"I don't want to say good-bye." She sniffled and wiped her eyes on the sleeve of her sweater. "Not again. Why couldn't you be what I needed you to be?"

Talking to the things that reminded her of Mark was as close as she could come to actually speaking to him. Sure, she could call him. She assumed he still had the same number. But what good would that do? Calling him would only exacerbate the pain and reawaken the heartache she'd managed to compartmentalize. At least until she'd opened the box. Now all the sorrow rushed back and hurt her heart, and the ghost of last fall's depression threatened to consume her once more.

Then the edge of a journal caught her eye. She dug it out from the bottom of the box. "Karma's Poetry" was scrawled in permanent marker over the worn, brown cover.

She flipped it open and read the first page, which was a poem she remembered writing in eighth grade.

The Caterpillar
By Karma Mason

I look in the mirror
What do I see?
A tiny worm
Staring back at me.

She's sad and plain
And a little grey
And I have to wonder
How she got that way.

Was it the jokes, the teasing,

The ruthless jeers
That hurt her heart
And fed her tears?

She wants to sing
And wear a grin
But the pain she bears
Feels like a sin.

Is this how life
Will always be?
With a worm in my mirror
Staring back at me?

Or will someday
I wake to find
That all this time
I was only blind?

Will I fall asleep
One day soon?
Tucked away,
In a cocoon?

And when I wake
Will I finally see
A beautiful butterfly in my mirror
Staring back at me?

Karma blinked back the tears and closed her notebook. She no longer saw herself as a tiny caterpillar or a worm. She had become a beautiful butterfly, all because of Mark. He had given her this gift. The gift of true sight. Like a guardian angel sent to sweep away anything that dulled her confidence, he had helped her see through the filmy cobwebs that had tainted her self-vision since childhood.

Her laptop summoned from her desk, which had been transplanted from what was now her exercise room back in February.

Taking a seat in her chair, she pulled up her blog and began a new entry.

M,

I love you. I'll always love you. You're the best thing to ever happen to me. You've given me so much.

Even now, eight months after you've left, all I have to do is open my keepsake box, breathe your scent on the pillowcase I folded and tucked away there, and I'm back in bed beside you. I'm back in your arms, tasting your kisses, listening to your heartbeat as I rest my head on your chest.

But you're not really here. I can't really feel you, or taste you, or listen to the beating of your heart. It's all an illusion. I'm remembering you the way I want to remember you, not the way you are.

My intuition tells me you love me as much as I love you, but that your fear of failure and heartache is greater than that love. I want more. Like Julia Roberts in Pretty Woman, *I want the fairy tale, and I want my prince to climb up to my balcony, even though he's afraid of heights, and claim my heart. I want the man who isn't afraid to risk his heart to win mine. Who is strong enough to rise up against heartache, look it square in the eyes, and say, "Fuck you, heartache. I won't let you keep me from what I want. I won't let you keep me from the woman I love."*

I've met someone new. He asked me out, despite

previously going through a divorce. Our first date is tonight. Maybe he's exactly what I need. He's certainly willing to put himself out there, even though he has every reason not to. But here I am, sifting through memories of you, hurting, wanting you so badly I could kick myself. I don't want to love you, anymore. I want to move on. I want to move on with B. I want to give him a chance.

It's time for me to let you go, M. I love you, and I'm grateful for everything you've shown me, but I have to learn how to tell you good-bye.

She published the post, shut down her laptop, then sat very still. Eyes closed. She willed herself not to cry anymore. Deep breaths, one after the other. She drew the air in through her nose then slowly blew it out her pursed mouth as if she were meditating.

Mark was in her heart, but he would never be in her life again. She had to accept that. She had to find peace with the knowledge that sometimes love isn't enough. Sometimes the pain of the past bears more weight, controlling those who can't let go and move on. And there was nothing—absolutely nothing—she could do about it.

Finally she stood, replaced the lid on her keepsake box, returned it to its place in the back of her closet, and finished getting ready for her date.

When Brad arrived a half-hour later, she opened the door with a smile on her face and hope in her heart.

"You ready?" Brad asked, his brown eyes gleaming.

Karma took a moment to breathe and say a final good-bye to the past. "Yes. I'm ready."

Chapter 12

Despite wearing a heavy jacket, Karma was still cold as she stuffed her hands into her sleeves. To make matters worse, it was beginning to rain. Thank goodness the game was almost over.

What had possessed Brad to think their first real date should be a minor league baseball game? It was April. Not the warmest time of year in Indiana.

"Sorry." Brad pulled out his umbrella and opened it. "I hoped the rain would hold out until after the game."

"No such luck." She forced a smile. Hopefully, this wasn't a bad omen for their relationship, but she couldn't quite shake the feeling that something wasn't right.

She dismissed her jitters. Her hesitancy was just a symptom of her still getting over Mark. That was all. Once she gave Brad a chance, she would see how silly all her worries were and that Brad was really the perfect guy.

When the game ended with a loss for the home team—under such nasty conditions they could have at least won to make enduring the cold and wet worthwhile—Brad took her hand and led her toward the exit.

"Your hand is freezing." He wrapped his more securely around hers.

"I forgot my gloves."

The rain began coming down harder, and they huddled under the umbrella as they scurried down the sidewalk in the direction of the parking garage.

"Wow, it's really coming down." He was practically jogging now.

Thankfully, she could keep up.

By the time they reached the parking garage, they were breathless, and their sneakers and pant legs were drenched.

He helped her into the car, shook out the umbrella, tossed it on the floor of the backseat of his Camry, then hustled around to the driver's side and hopped behind the wheel. Within seconds, he had the engine started and cold air blasting from the vents.

"It'll heat up in a few minutes," he said, putting the car in gear.

Karma's teeth chattered for a couple of miles before the engine heated up enough to shoot out warm air. She finally began to thaw.

"Are you hungry?" Brad glanced across the seat at her.

She shook her head. "No." She was cold and soaked. There was no room for hunger right now.

Twenty minutes later, he pulled into her apartment complex and drove around to her building. The rain was still coming down hard, so he snagged the umbrella from the back and came around the car to help her out and shield her from getting even more soaked.

Once inside, he set down the umbrella and stood beside her at her door.

"Sorry about tonight," he said. "I guess going to a baseball game wasn't the best idea after all." He offered her a sheepish, almost defeated grin that tugged at her heart.

"It's not your fault." She faced him more fully. Maybe if she showed she was still interested he wouldn't feel so bad about the disastrous date.

He took a tentative step closer. "I promise to do better next time." He placed his hands on her hips, and his cheeks shaded pink.

She bit her bottom lip and rested her hands on his arms. "Will there be a next time?" She tried to sound flirtatious but felt like she was forcing it.

"I'd like there to be a next time. Would you?" His gentle gaze caressed hers.

A quiet ache vibrated in her chest, longing for the man who was no longer a part of her life and never would be again. She shoved past it and took a trembling breath. "Yes." Brad deserved this chance, and she deserved to find happiness. If Brad could make her happy, why not push forward with him?

"Then how about dinner tomorrow night?"

"Tomorrow's Easter. Won't you have Jade?"

He shook his head and pressed a little closer. "Her mom has her this weekend."

Karma could tell he was going to kiss her. Any second, he would press his lips to hers. Did she want that?

"Okay then," she said. "Dinner tomorrow night."

He grinned. "And maybe a nice safe movie indoors.

No rain this time."

She giggled. "Yes…dinner and a movie. Inside. No rain."

"I'll pick you up around six." He began to lower his face to hers.

"Okay." She practically held her breath.

When his lips brushed over hers, she felt…well…there was a little tingle of warmth that shot down her spine, but the sensation was nothing like what she'd felt when Mark kissed her. Mark's talented lips had nearly blown off her toes. Brad's simply warmed her. But Mark's lips were blowing off another woman's toes now. Karma needed to learn to be happy with what was right in front of her, not yearn for what had once been.

And maybe Mark had simply affected her the way he had because he'd been her first real lover. Perhaps fireworks weren't supposed to go off every time a guy kissed her. Maybe the way it felt with Brad was normal.

Running her hand up Brad's arm to the back of his neck, she opened her lips and licked her tongue against the seam of his mouth. She could use what Mark taught her to increase the fire. Maybe that would help.

Brad moaned and exhaled through his nose as he opened and slid his tongue against hers. His arms eased around her back and pulled her closer.

Closing her eyes, she could almost envision he was Mark. Almost. But it was enough to let her get a little lost in Brad's more excited good-night kiss and to feel a tiny burst of arousal bloom between her legs.

Brad finally pulled back and took a heavy breath. Karma opened her eyes and blinked up into his, which were glazed yet smiling.

"Good night, Karma." His hold loosened.

"Good night."

He pressed a lingering, chaste kiss against her mouth. Then he released her and pulled away, clearing his throat.

"I'll see you tomorrow night." He backed toward the stairs.

"See you then." She pushed open her door and waved as he started down the staircase.

Inside, she draped her jacket over the arm of the couch and set her handbag on the floor before peeking out the window at his retreating taillights as he drove away, the same way she'd done when Mark drove away that last time. Only this time, she knew Brad would return. This time, she didn't have to worry about Brad leaving her.

Maybe his kisses hadn't pushed her toward cardiac arrest the way Mark's had, but they were safe kisses. They still simmered even if they didn't boil. Brad was a keeper. He wouldn't run away from commitment.

She glanced back out the window just as Brad turned the corner and disappeared from view.

This would be good. It would.

Finally, she could say a last good-bye to Mark. She had a new boyfriend, and she was moving on.

Part II

Together Again

Chapter 13

Five months later

September 4

In her car in Solar's parking lot, Karma stared at the diamond ring on her finger. She had never seen the proposal coming, and yet, yesterday, at her parents' Labor Day cookout, Brad had asked her to marry him.

Everyone had just finished chowing down on burgers, baked beans, and potato salad while sitting around the large patio table when Brad addressed her dad.

"Mr. Mason, I'd like to ask you something."

"Please," her dad said, "call me John."

Dad liked Brad. At least he acted like he did. Karma thought he was just happy that she'd finally moved on from Mark, which was why he was overly welcoming when she'd shown up at the cookout with Brad. Her dad had heard about him for months, but this was the first time they'd actually met.

Brad offered a deferential smile. "John then, I'd like to ask you something."

"Sure, ask me anything."

Across the table, her brother Johnny, whose behavior was much improved from last summer, bounced his one-year-old daughter on his knee. Johnny's wife, Estelle, looked on. Both had been surprisingly quiet and polite, but Karma knew the peace could only last so long. Johnny would eventually show his ass again.

Brad took her hand and squeezed. "John, I've been dating your daughter for six months." He paused as she turned and gave him a quizzical look. What was he doing? "I love her, and, with your permission, I'd like to ask her to marry me."

Thud! Marry him? Where had this come from? She'd never seen this coming.

Her mom uttered a soft squeal and covered her mouth as her eyes lit up. Johnny stopped bouncing his baby. A slow grin spread over her dad's face as he clasped his hands under his chin.

"Brad, I can think of *no one better* to marry my daughter." He pointedly met her gaze, his meaning clear. He was ready for the Mark Strong chapter of her life to be officially over. Marrying Brad would guarantee that.

Brad pulled a diamond ring from his pocket, scooted back in his chair, and got down on one knee. "Karma, with your dad's blessing, and in front of your family…" His whole face beamed as he poised the ring at the tip of her finger. "Will you marry me?"

She stared at him, her hand in his. Everything about this moment was perfect. Wasn't it? She glanced around the table at her family. This was what she wanted, right? She wanted to be married. She wanted a husband, a family, and a life where she was no longer alone.

As she took a deep breath and nodded, a tiny burst of alarm resonated in her soul. She brushed it aside, forcing herself to leap forward rather than stay rooted in the past. Even after a year apart, Mark's memory still rested in the back of her mind. She was beginning to think she would never completely get over him. But the Mark she still thought about from time to time was the Mark she wanted him to be, not the Mark he really was. She had to keep reminding herself of that. And she couldn't let her life stall out on a fantasy.

Case in point. Brad was offering her the future she wanted. She would be silly to refuse.

"Yes, Brad. Yes, I'll marry you." She was striding forward, furthering herself a little bit more from her memories of Mark.

Brad had slid the diamond onto her finger and hugged her. Even her brother had congratulated her. Surprise, surprise. Maybe there was hope for him to grow up yet.

Karma broke from her thoughts when her phone chimed, planting her back inside her car. She quickly gathered her purse and bag and hopped out. She'd sat so long reliving Brad's proposal she was now officially late.

Oops.

She rushed up the sidewalk and into the lobby as her phone began ringing again.

"Good morning, Nancy." She rushed past the receptionist.

As she took the stairs to the second level, she fished through her purse for her phone. At the top of the stairs, she finally pulled it free and checked the screen.

Lisa. Why was Lisa calling her?

Darting down the hall to her desk, she slapped her phone to her ear. "Lisa, what's up? Sorry it took so long to answer. I'm running late. God, I need to talk to you." She had yet to tell Daniel and Lisa that Brad had proposed.

"Karma! Will you shut up! I need to tell you something."

Sheez! What was up with Lisa?

Karma dropped her bags on the floor at her desk and booted up her computer. "Fine. Sorry. What?"

At that moment, the door to Don's office opened.

"Ah, there she is," Don said, gesturing toward her.

Lisa was still talking in her ear. "Karma, don't freak out, okay, but…"

Everything fell into slow motion. The earth dragged to a near standstill on its axis. Lisa's voice sounded like she was talking through a layer of cotton. And Karma was sure her chin hit her desk as her mouth fell open.

"Mark's here!" Lisa hissed. "In Don's office. Right now."

Karma almost dropped her phone as her gaze met Mark's for the first time in a year.

"I know," she murmured and hung up.

And just like that, in the time it took for a light to come on once the switch was flipped, all her hard-fought efforts to get over him vanished.

He was back. Mark was here.

And didn't her wildly beating heart know it.

Chapter 14

Mark had to fight the urge to scoop Karma into his arms and kiss her. She looked good. Different but the same. Her hair was shorter, a little redder from the brown he remembered from before. But gorgeous nonetheless. And she looked leaner, more sleek, like she'd put on muscle but not weight.

He'd been prepared to come back for her two months ago, on the Fourth of July, when the sign he'd been waiting for finally came. How ironic was that? Just when he'd wrested back control of his own fate, the universe had come through. How did that saying go? A watched pot never boils. The phrase was spot on in this case, because he'd all but given up on the universe bringing him a sign when Don called him out of the blue at the end of June.

Mark had been in Wisconsin, finishing his assignment, making plans to come to Indianapolis and win back Karma's heart when he had received a call. He had been on a conference call with Carter Mitchell's management team at the time, but when he saw the name on his caller ID, a zap of awareness shot through his body.

Don Jacoby? Why would Don be calling him after all

this time?

He let the call go to voice mail but struggled to concentrate on the remainder of his conference call. Don was a connection to Karma.

After the call with his boss ended, he checked his messages.

"Hey, Mark. It's Don Jacoby from Solar Industries. I hope you're doing well. But hey, I'd like to discuss an opportunity with you. Give me a call back on this number." He rattled off his digits. "Call any time. I'll be around. Thanks, Mark."

Not wanting to get his hopes up that the universe was finally delivering, Mark got up, shut the door to the office, and paced behind his chair as he collected his thoughts. This could all be nothing. Just an acquaintance calling to check in. A colleague and former client seeking advice.

Then again, Don's call could end up changing his life. This could be *it*. He took a deep breath and dialed his number.

"Mark. Hi. Thanks for calling me back so quickly," Don said.

"Sure. No problem. What's up? Everything okay at Solar?" He already wanted to ask about Karma. How transparent.

"Yes, yes. Everything's great. We're up almost ten percent over last year, thanks to you."

"Good. I'm glad to hear it." *How's Karma? Is she seeing anyone? God, I hope not.* And how selfish was that? He should be hoping that she was dating again. That had been the whole purpose of their time together, to set her up to find her one true love. But more and more over their months apart, he'd thought that maybe, just maybe, *he* was her one true love, because it was clear that she was his.

Don chuckled. "Took our guys a few months to get used to that new software, but now they can't live without it. They're getting almost twice as much work done now than before, and the customers have really taken notice. We've secured two large accounts we'd been after for years but who were always wary to commit."

To Mark, it was all *blah, blah, blah,* which was awful. He should have been happy to hear Solar was doing so well. And, really, he was, but that wasn't what he wanted to talk about. Still, he forced himself to say, "That's great, Don. Glad to hear it's turning around." He paced to the window and glanced out at a pair of geese drifting over the surface of the retention pond behind the office building, knowing Don hadn't called to give him a company update. The man had something on his mind, and all this chatter was just ice breaking kind of stuff. "So, how's everything else? Everyone doing well?" *Karma? Is she doing well?* "The family?"

"Yes, everyone's great. Better than great, actually."

"Oh?"

"Yes. And that's partly why I'm calling."

Now they were getting down to it.

"Mark, our COO is retiring, and I've been offered the position."

"That's great news." The geese tittered out of the water and shook their tail feathers. "I know you had your sights set on that position."

"Yes, it's what I've been working for. But now the director of operations position is open, and..." Don paused, and Mark could hear what was coming. "You're the first person I thought of as Phil and I discussed who would replace me."

Mark closed his eyes and turned his face toward the ceiling.

Thank you.

Even though nothing was set in stone, this was the sign he'd been waiting for. He could feel it. Yes, he would need to get the details. Yes, he would need to negotiate salary and give notice at Carter Mitchell. Yes, he would have to make arrangements to move. But in his heart, he knew that somehow, some way, he would end up taking the job.

That had been over two months ago. And now, here he was. It was a done deal. After weeks of discussion and negotiating, he had signed the paperwork last night. He was Solar's new director of operations, and Karma was his assistant. Of course, that would have to change now that he was back. She couldn't work for him if they were romantically involved. Mark wasn't sure how that would all work out, but he'd gotten his sign, so the rest would fall into place.

Mark had it all figured out. He would reenter her life and they would pick up where they'd left off last year. After a few months, she would move in with him, which was why he was looking at family homes instead of bachelor pads. He wanted enough room for them both...and anyone else who came along later. Because he definitely saw children in the cards.

"Hello, Karma," he said. "It's a pleasure to see you

again." Maintaining a professional demeanor while the woman he loved stood less than six feet away was nearly impossible.

Her brow crinkled as she glanced between him and Don. "What's going on?"

Okay, so that wasn't the reaction he'd expected, but then, maybe she was just trying to hide how intimate they'd once been with one another so as not to let the cat out of the bag. He really needed to discuss this with her in private. Maybe he *should* have called her first. He'd thought about it, but then decided against it, preferring to surprise her instead. Suddenly, his plan didn't seem like the best idea.

"Mark's joining us," Don said, clapping him on the shoulder.

"J-joining us?" Karma's luminous, green eyes opened wide. "What do you mean?"

"He works for Solar now. We're making an announcement at the company meeting this morning. Mark's our new director of operations."

The color drained from Karma's face, and she looked like she might be sick.

"You okay?" Mark realized this had to be a lot for her to take in. The decision not to call and warn her seemed to be backfiring. He'd only wanted to surprise her, not give her a stroke. Now it was obvious he hadn't really thought things through. He'd been too excited to get back than to actually formulate a plan on how to reenter her life.

"Yes, I'm just tired. I had a…um…" She exhaled and lifted her fingers to her brow as she glanced down. "It was just a long night."

Donya Lynne

That's when he noticed the ring.

Whoa. That wasn't supposed to be there.

The fat, sparkling princess cut diamond on her left hand glared like a magnified explosion he was viewing through a telescope. And for all the destruction obliterating his heart that very second, it might as well have been an H-bomb.

She wasn't supposed to be engaged. That hadn't been part of his plan.

"Karma?" Don reached across the counter and took her hand. "Is this what I think it is?"

Color rushed back into her cheeks as she met Mark's gaze and gulped. "Uh, yes. Brad asked me to marry him yesterday." Her eyes never left his as she spoke.

"Well, congratulations. That's good news."

Yeah. Great news. Just fucking great.

He cleared his throat. "Yes, congratulations." Shit, but he felt like *he* was going to be sick now.

The universe hadn't given him a sign, after all. It had slapped him in the face, and now it was sitting back laughing its ass off.

So much for putting his faith in invisible entities.

Chapter 15

In a stupor, Karma plopped into the chair beside Lisa in the large, downstairs conference room. The rest of Solar's employees filtered in. The company's president, Phil, along with Don, Mark, and Barrett, the chief operating officer, stood in a cluster at the front of the room, engaged in conversation.

Seeing Mark again had nearly made her faint. He looked better than she remembered, his features sharper. He'd also let his beard and mustache fill in, giving him a distinguished yet welcoming appearance. She'd thought he looked good clean-shaven, but this look was just as hot, if not hotter. And, damn him, he'd worn that navy pin-striped suit she loved so much. Seeing him in that suit had always turned her on, and now was no different. She wanted to run her hands up the lapels and stroke his beard with the tips of her fingers as she took his lips against hers.

Except now, everything *was* different. For starters, she was engaged. Second of all, she'd put him behind her months ago. Or at least she thought she had.

What was he thinking taking a job with Solar? Don's job, no less. Was he insane? With their history, he'd been crazy to even consider the position, let alone accept it.

"When did this happen?" she said quietly, catching Lisa's eye.

Lisa hunkered down and leaned closer so no one would overhear. "From what I can tell, they've been talking to him at least a couple of months, maybe longer. He just accepted yesterday."

A couple of months! And he hadn't called to warn her? He hadn't thought this was something she should know, or that he should at least discuss it with her?

"What am I going to do, Leese?" This was a colossal train wreck.

"We'll figure it out. But, hey, maybe this means the two of you can finish what you star—"

"I don't think so." Karma held up her left hand, flashing her engagement ring.

"What!" Lisa's eyes bugged out as several pairs of eyes turned toward them, including Mark's. She instantly lowered her voice. "Oh my God, Karma. Brad proposed? When?"

"Yesterday. In front of my family."

"And you told him yes?"

Karma nodded and glanced down at the ring as she lowered her hand to her lap. Brad's proposal and their pending nuptials suddenly lost some of their luster. She just couldn't find the excitement she'd felt yesterday.

"What about his daughter? Jade? How's that going to work? From what you've told me, she hates you."

Karma pressed her lips together and rubbed her chin. Jade was a sensitive subject where Brad was concerned. "I don't know. We'll figure it out."

She never would have guessed that Brad's daughter

would be such a thorn in her side. After she and Brad had been dating a couple of months, he finally introduced them. Karma had looked forward to meeting his daughter only to find that Jade didn't feel the same way. In fact, Jade made no secret that she couldn't stand Karma and only tolerated her presence to appease her dad. And now Karma had just signed up for a lifetime with Brad...*and* his daughter. Hopefully, things would get better between her and Jade, because being around that twelve-year-old bundle of hostility and disrespect for an hour left her frazzled and near the end of her patience.

And now, to make matters worse, she had to contend with Mark. How was this going to work?

Mark lifted his gaze to hers from the front of the room, and her heart skipped a beat. In that split second, she knew without a doubt that she still loved him, but damn it, she didn't want to. Mark could never give her what she wanted. What she *deserved*. She'd worked so hard to forget him. For her efforts, she had won an engagement ring from a stable, good-hearted man who wouldn't flake out at the mention of commitment. Who welcomed the idea of eternity with her. Maybe Brad wasn't the most passionate man, and maybe he wasn't as sexually adventurous as Mark, but he was emotionally solid and promised security. Karma couldn't let Mark get in the way of that, because she knew where that road led. Straight back to heartbreak.

Lowering her gaze, she turned away.

"Damn him," she whispered to Lisa. "Damn him for coming back." Her tone held more aggression than she intended.

"Are you okay?" Lisa touched her wrist.

"No." Anger rose in her blood. Why now? Why come back now? After a year away? Mark hadn't tried to call her once. After leaving last September, he hadn't called, and he hadn't e-mailed or texted. He hadn't even written a fucking snail mail letter or sent a generic Christmas card or wished her a Happy New Year or a Happy Birthday or bothered to keep in touch at all. And now, here he was. And from his hopeful expression when he'd walked out of Don's office and met her gaze, he thought everything could go back to just how it had been before.

Well, screw that. She wasn't going back. She wasn't the same person she was last year, and she had no desire to return to that state of existence. She was with Brad now. That was where she belonged. Mark needed to get that through his commitment-phobic skull pronto. There would be no walks down memory lane, holding her hand, kissing her, sweeping her into his bed. That shit wasn't going to happen. Karma refused to allow it.

"Karma?" Lisa nudged her arm. "What's wrong."

"Just...I..." She huffed. "I'm so mad at him for doing this to me. Now, of all times, when I've finally moved on and found the man I'm going to spend the rest of my life with. Who does he think he is? He had no right to—"

"Calm down, Karma. Just keep your cool." Lisa gently waved her hand in a downward motion to indicate she needed to take deep breaths and chill. "We'll go to lunch after the meeting, and you can unload then, but hold it together during the meeting."

Karma crossed her arms and threw one leg over the other, tapping her foot in the air. Fine. She would keep her emotions under control for now, but once she and Lisa left for lunch, she wasn't going to hold her frustration in. She had a thing or two to say about Mark reinserting himself into her life when she had only just gotten over him.

Chapter 16

Karma fumed through the entire meeting. Why did Mark have to be so fricking hot? So delectably sexy? So magnetically gorgeous? Shouldn't someone allergic to long-term relationships have an egg-sized wart on his nose? A missing front tooth? No teeth at all?

But his sex appeal didn't make up for his audacity.

Unable to meet his gaze, she kept her eyes on Don, Phil, and Barrett—the traitor. Barrett was retiring. How dare he retire and leave an opening Don needed to fill. Now she was stuck with Mark, because Don would move into Barrett's upstairs office and inherit *his* assistant.

How was she expected to work with Mark given their past? She would just have to lay down the law immediately and make Mark understand she was with Brad now. She wasn't interested in getting caught up in any more of his "lessons." She no longer needed him to teach her how to be with a man, or how to talk to one. She no longer needed him to boost her confidence and make her feel beautiful. Been there, done that.

After the meeting, she bolted out of the conference room before Mark could stop her, rushed upstairs to grab her purse, then met Lisa outside by her car.

"What is he doing here?" She thumped her fist on the door panel as Lisa pulled out of the parking lot.

"Taking Don's job," Lisa said matter-of-factly.

"It's not that simple. Nothing was ever that simple with Mark. He's up to something." She crossed one arm over the other and nibbled her thumbnail. What angle was he playing?

"Maybe the opportunity was simply too good to pass up." Lisa turned up the air.

"Huh-uh. I'm not buying it. He came back for me. He came back to mess with my head."

"Karma—"

"No, Lisa. I know him. If he thinks I'm just going to fall back into his bed, he's got another thing coming." She smacked her fist against her thigh. "Damn it, Lisa. You know how long it took for me to get over him."

"Sounds like you're still not," Lisa said under her breath.

"What? What did you say?"

Lisa took a left into the parking lot for Café Nine. "Listen to yourself, Karma. Would you really be this upset if you were honestly over him?"

Karma ricocheted back. "Are you serious?"

"Yes, I'm serious." Lisa parked the car, shut off the engine, and turned toward her. The look in her eyes made it clear Lisa was about to give her a reality check. "You're not over him, are you? Tell me I'm wrong."

"You're wrong."

"I'm not buying it.

"Why not?"

Lisa's jaw clenched as if she didn't want to say what was about to come out of her mouth. Then she took a deep breath, held it for a second, then blurted, "Because if you were really over him, you'd be happy to see him." Before Karma could protest, Lisa held up her hand. "Look, it's okay if you're not over him. The two of you shared an amazing summer and you fell in love with him. I've read your blog. I know what he meant to you. You have a right to be angry right now, but—"

"But what? But maybe I should cut Mark some slack? Is that what you think I should do?"

"No." Lisa sighed. "But you're being irrational."

"Damn straight I'm being irrational." She pointed in the direction of the office. "That bastard just blew my entire world apart back there. I've moved on, and now he comes back and saunters out of Don's office like everything's the way it was between us, and all I wanted when I saw him was to..." She met Lisa's gaze as the wind blew out of her sails. In her tirade of tumbling thoughts, she'd been about to say that when she saw Mark all she'd wanted was to kiss him. The moment he emerged from Don's office, her heart skipped a beat then unfurled as her body instantly heated. Arousal flooded her lower belly, and all she'd wanted was to touch him, be touched by him, and taste his skin. Mark still had that effect on her, but she couldn't bow to it. She had to resist.

Lisa tilted her head as if she'd read Karma's thoughts. "You know, all this time I was worried you were just frontin' with Brad. That you'd latched on to him because you thought he was your only shot at happiness after Mark left." She paused. "I think you just confirmed I was right."

"I love Brad," Karma said a little too defensively.

Lisa smirked like she didn't believe her then got out of the car.

"I do." Karma hopped out and followed her into Café Nine. "Do you think I don't?"

"Oh, I'm sure you love him." Lisa stepped up to the counter to order then looked over her shoulder and said, "I just think you love Mark more."

The words hit her like a shot to the gut, rendering her speechless. But really, hadn't she realized during the meeting when Mark's gaze met hers that she was still in love with him? Lisa was only stating the obvious.

After ordering, Karma sat down across from Lisa at a patio table. "Fine, maybe I'm not over him, and maybe I do still love him, but, Lisa, he's never going to be what I need. He's never going to be able to commit, let alone marry me. If I learned nothing else from our four months together, I learned that much."

"Maybe he's changed." Lisa sipped her tea.

"Yeah, and I've got swamp land in Iraq I can sell you." She wadded up her straw wrapper and tossed it on the table. "That man will never—and I mean *never*—get over what his ex-fiancée did to him. And I can't sit around waiting for something that will never happen." She eyed her engagement ring. "Brad's good for me. He's not afraid to put his heart out there and make what we have permanent." But in the past five months she'd learned that Brad wasn't the most passionate bedmate, and she'd hinted as much to Lisa in a few of their "girl talks."

"Is that enough?" Lisa fixed her with a skeptical stare.

"It has to be."

"It doesn't *have* to be, Karma. You *can* have both, you know. Both the passion and the commitment."

Karma shook her head. "In my experience, that's not how it works. You get one or the other. And what I want is the commitment. Passion is nothing if there's no certainty it will still be around in a year."

"But, Karma, come on. You've been dating Brad what? A whole five months? And you're already engaged? Why the rush? I think you're taking things too fast. I don't think Brad's the guy for you, Karma."

Karma shook her head. No way would she let Lisa talk her out of this. "He and I started hanging out in February, almost eight months ago. We were friends before we dated." They'd made good friends, too. And a good friendship was a solid foundation for a good relationship. "I'm not going back to Mark."

Mark was a flight risk. Even if he said he wanted a commitment, he could still flee when the heat turned up too high. She would be stupid to walk down that road again, only to have her heart obliterated the same way it had been a year ago.

Lisa huffed. "I didn't say you had to go back to Mark. Just that I don't think Brad's the right guy for you. First, there's Jade. She hates you. How will that work? And then there's the stuff you told me about...you know...the way he's just not very *imaginative* in the bedroom."

She wished she'd never told Lisa about that. Then again, who would have thought her words would come back to haunt her?

"I've got this, Lisa. I've made my decision."

Lisa gave her a resigned nod. "Okay, okay. You're right. It's your decision. Just know I'm here for you if you ever need to talk."

"I know."

As their food arrived, Karma glanced back at the diamond on her finger. Brad was enough. She could make Brad be enough.

Chapter 17

After returning to Solar, Karma fumed at her desk while Don and Mark spent the afternoon in his office. Don asked her to make travel arrangements for him and Mark to fly to the East Coast location next Monday then down to the Atlanta office. They would return to Indianapolis on Friday. *Tour de Mark.* She finalized their itineraries and e-mailed them—and, oh, how efficient, Mark already had a company e-mail.

Around four o'clock, Mark exited Don's office and flashed her a wary smile on his way to the conference room. Good, he could tell she was angry. Good for him. He needed to know she wasn't going to be a pushover and allow him back into her bed.

Her phone dinged, and she glanced down to see a text from Mark.

Why are you angry?

Oh, *now* he could text her. Where had he been a year ago? Hell, where had he been a month ago to warn her he was returning. Talk about being tardy.

She refused to look at him, turning away from the conference room.

Her phone dinged again.

Please answer me.

Her heart melted just a little bit at the *please*, but then she set her jaw and squared her shoulders.

A member from IT stopped by Don's office and began dismantling his computer, preparing the space for Mark.

Finally, she typed out a response. *If you want to discuss this with me, schedule a meeting.*

She pulled out the hard copy of last quarter's presentation and began marking it up.

"Hi."

Karma lifted her gaze to find Mark standing at her counter, and every bone in her body melted. Up close, he was even more stunning. In addition to letting his beard and mustache grow in, his hair was longer. A tuft hung over his forehead and curled inward toward his eye. And his face was even more chiseled than it had been a year ago, as if he'd spent several hours a week in the gym. Probably to look good for all his ladies back in Chicago.

His grey-green eyes captured hers and held on, forbidding her from looking away.

She blinked and bit her bottom lip before recovering from the shock to her system his mere proximity created. "What can I do for you?"

"I thought we might take a minute to get reacquainted…now that we're going to be working with one another, I mean. Is now a good time?"

She glanced at the clock then at the open door to Don's office, where she could hear the sounds of equipment being moved around.

She wasn't looking forward to this discussion but might as well get it over with. "Fine. Sure." She stood and grabbed her notebook.

She followed him into the conference room.

He closed the door. His gaze stroked the wall where they'd fucked one another last July. Then he cleared his throat and gestured to one of the chairs.

"Have a seat." He sat in *his* chair.

Instead of taking the chair beside him—the one he had offered—Karma walked around to the other side of the table and sat across from him. She would make it clear from the get-go that she made her own decisions now and would set the tone for this new dynamic in their relationship. She was no longer the compliant, easily manipulated little girl he had met last year.

He pressed his lips together and narrowed his eyes under a wrinkled brow before glancing toward the window.

Silence stretched between them, but Karma refused to speak first. Her dad had taught her that he who speaks first loses. So, she crossed her hands one over the other, making sure her left hand and its sparkling diamond rested on top, and waited.

After several long, quiet seconds, Mark exhaled. "You're engaged." His voice fell flat.

Using that as his opener shouldn't have surprised her, but it did.

She raised her chin. "Yes."

His head bobbed up and down shallowly, and he looked away again. "Well, congratulations. You're happy?"

She squared her shoulders. "Yes. Very."

Another nod, a little bigger this time. "I'm…glad to hear it." His words sounded like he was squeezing them through a strainer.

More silence. It was unnerving, but Karma forced herself to remain composed. Part of her ego relished that he seemed disappointed she was no longer available. That meant he *had* thought about her during the last year. Oh well, too little too late.

Mark blinked and glanced down at his hands. "I, uh...I didn't expect..." His brow furrowed as if in frustration or maybe confusion.

This was not the Mark she remembered. That Mark had been full of confidence and bold. He had commanded the room. This Mark seemed...disoriented. Maybe even a bit timid. As if he were a small child facing a room full of strangers on his first day of school.

"What? You didn't expect me to be engaged?" She blew out a derisive puff of air. "You probably expected to come back here and find me still pining over you...sitting around like a spinster waiting on you to save me from becoming an old maid."

His gaze snapped to hers, and he frowned. "Of course not. I'm glad to see you're happy, Karma. That's all I'm—"

"Are you? Really?" She crossed her arms.

The scowl on his face said otherwise. It deepened. "Yes, your happiness was all I ever wanted." The words sounded like he was forcing them out with a chisel and hammer.

"Which was why you called me every week after you left." She tapped her finger on her forearm.

He tilted his head to one side. "Why are you so angry at me? I never lied to you. I told you up front how things would be. I thought you understood — "

"Fine. I get it." She held up her hand. "You were only doing what you said you would. It's not like you loved me or anything, right?"

But she knew in her heart that he did, and the way the skin around his eyes ticked and his mouth twitched confirmed she was right. And yet that love hadn't been enough. He'd abandoned her, anyway. That shit hurt like a kick in the shin. He was saying that she wasn't worthy of his love. That she wasn't enough to pull him from the funk of his past.

"Karma. I'm sorry. I never meant to hurt you."

With a sigh, she leaned back in her chair. "I've heard all this before, Mark." He'd told her repeatedly that he'd never meant to hurt her. "It's getting old."

They stared at each other for a long, silent moment.

Then he cleared his throat and looked away. "My apologies. I simply thought — "

"What are you doing here, Mark?" Being near him was becoming painful. Just remaining across the room was an exercise of willpower she wasn't sure she could sustain much longer. Every part of her wanted to touch every part of him so badly it was excruciating.

"I thought you'd be happier to see me than this." He pushed away from the table and sat forward in his chair. "Well, hoped. I'd *hoped* you would be happier to see me." He stood and walked to the window, where he sat on the ledge. "I guess I was wrong."

She shrugged and forced herself to keep a stoic face. "Well...I suppose it's a good opportunity for you. Don's job, I mean."

"It is." He crossed his arms. "But I didn't intend to

upset you when I took it. I was hoping—"

"What? You were hoping we could go back to the way things were? That I'd fall to my knees and thank my lucky stars that you were back?"

He closed his eyes and pinched the bridge of his nose. "No. I didn't expect that." He straightened and squared his shoulders. "But I didn't expect such animosity, either. I was hoping you and I could work together more peacefully than this."

She looked away, suddenly feeling ashamed of her behavior. Maybe she had misread his intentions and he hadn't come back for her, after all. The hot air fizzled out of her. "I'm sorry. I'm just—"

He held up one hand. "No. I understand. I deserve everything you want to throw at me."

"I was just shocked is all. I wasn't expecting..." She waved her hand toward him. "This. You. Here."

"I know."

"You could have at least warned me."

"You're right. I should have. I'm sorry. I misjudged the situation and handled things poorly."

Mark was nothing if not a gracious apologizer.

"So, are we going to be able to work together?" he said.

Wow. That was a quick about-face. One that shot a dose of reality into Karma's blood. She didn't want to lose her job simply because she held a grudge against Mark for doing exactly what he'd said he was going to do last year. Besides, she was in a better place now, right? She had Brad.

Lisa's words from lunch came back to haunt her. *If you were really over him, you'd be happy to see him.*

She *was* over him, and she would prove it.

"I can work with you," she said, "but I want to make very clear that it's just work. I'm with someone else now. I need to make sure you understand that. And even if I weren't, I wouldn't feel right getting involved with my boss, especially given our past." In particular, his unwillingness to let go of *his* past to embrace a future with her.

"I understand. I wasn't expecting anything like that from you, anyway." But his words didn't match the expression of wistful yearning on his face. "My reasons for returning are strictly professional."

Why didn't she believe him? "I'm glad to hear it."

He slowly approached the table and sat back down. "I promise to do what I can to make the transition easy for you."

"Same here."

"Great."

"Good."

"I'm glad we got that out of the way then." He set his palms on the table.

"Me, too." She stood, ready to get out of there before she did something she would regret, like rush into his arms and suck off his face.

"I'll need your help quite a bit in the coming weeks," he said, standing and joining her as she walked toward the door.

He smelled good. Spicy and manly. Just the way she remembered. "Sure. What can I do?" Controlling the way her heart beat harder from just standing so close to him would be a good start.

His smile damn near did her in. "I'm house hunting

and was hoping you could lend a hand by finding properties for me to look at."

"Sure, absolutely."

"I'll e-mail you the specifics and my agent's contact information." He lifted his arm, and for a moment, she thought he was going to wrap it around the small of her back the way he used to. Then he seemed to think better of it and dropped his hand back to his side as he opened the door.

"It's good to see you again, Karma. I'm looking forward to working with you."

"Same here." She hurried away to her desk. When she turned back around, he had already closed the door. She hadn't even heard the latch click. He had shut the door as silently as a thief slipping away in the night.

She sat in her chair and stared at the door. He'd said all the right words, but his actions wove a different tale.

Coming back to Solar was as hard for him as it was for her.

So then, why had he done it?

Chapter 18

Why was God making such a mockery of Mark's life? Once again, his plans for the future were thwarted, the same way they had been with Carol. He'd come all this way. He'd endured months of hell then ridden what he'd thought was a sign that Karma was coming back to him, only to find that she belonged to another. But he couldn't jump off the ride now. He'd already bought the one-way ticket.

He picked up his phone and dialed Rob.

"Hey, buddy," Rob said upon answering. "How's your first day? You engaged, yet?"

"No, but she is."

Silence answered for a split second, then, "Wait...what?"

"You heard me." Mark combed his fingers through his hair and paced toward the window. "She's engaged."

Rob groaned. "I told you that you should have called her."

"Not now, Rob." Mark planted his hand on his hip. "I don't need to hear 'I told you so' right now."

"Gotcha. I'm sorry." Rob hesitated. "Now what? What are you gonna do?"

"Not much I can do. I'm here. I've taken the job."

"Hey, maybe this is just how it has to play out. Did you consider that?"

Mark chuffed. "To hell with that. I asked for a sign. I didn't get it. I was so sure. I was ready to come here and be with her again. Really *be* with her. I had it all planned out."

"Maybe that's your problem. Stop planning everything out. Didn't you learn that lesson with Carol?"

He had planned his entire future with Carol before she'd even said "I do," only for her to leave him at the altar. The resulting cataclysm of being shackled without a backup plan damn near put him in an alcoholic grave. If not for Rob, he might not have found his way back to the land of the socially functional.

And now he'd done the same thing with Karma. Before he'd even talked to her, he'd planned their reunion all the way to the point where they had kids.

"I don't know any other way to be, Rob," he said honestly. "I can't help myself." Planning his life — and the lives of those around him — to the minute detail was in his hardwiring.

"*Try.*" Rob exhaled into the phone. "Jesus, Mark, just relax. Stop living for years down the road. Try living for the moment, for Christ's sake. Stop trying to dictate your future and everyone else's. Just *be.*"

"Easy for you to say. You've already found *your* future." Rob and Holly's wedding was the week of Thanksgiving.

Mark thought it was an odd week to get married, but Thanksgiving was Holly's favorite holiday. She said

Thanksgiving was all about family, and what better way to commemorate family than by starting her own the same week. Rob liked that it would make remembering their anniversary simple.

"If you would stop being so OCD, you would, too," Rob said. "So, who is this guy she's engaged to?"

"I don't know. I've only seen the ring." And what a ring it was. Nice and big. Garish, if Mark was being honest. Not Karma at all. She wasn't the garish type. She was more the brilliant diamond type. Simple, elegant, round. The princess cut was too angular for her slender fingers.

"Was she at least happy to see you?"

Mark rubbed his palm over his face. "That's the thing. She's angry—I mean, really angry—that I'm back."

"How so?"

"Just really pissed off. I swear, Rob, if I'd known she'd react this way, I'm not sure I would have accepted the job."

"It's a good job, Mark. It's a step up for you. Even if you and Karma don't hook up, that job is a move in the right direction. You were made for that job, and it's one step closer to you running your own company. That's why you took it. That whole 'it's a sign' thing with Karma was just a sideshow to the main event."

"Yeah, yeah. Believe me, if I'd thought this wasn't a good position, I wouldn't have taken it. But, Jesus, I hope she and I will be able to work through what's got her so mad at me."

"Think about it, Mark. You broke her heart."

Mark closed his eyes. He hated thinking about that.

It hurt to remember their last night together, how she'd cried, how she'd clung to him. He'd felt it, too. He'd been just as heartbroken at leaving her behind as she had been to be left there.

"But, hey," Rob added, "if she's really that angry, that's a good sign."

"How do you figure?"

"Anger is a sign of strong feelings, buddy. If she's angry at you, she probably still has feelings for you. If she's *really* angry, then those feelings are probably *really* strong. Exploit that."

"She's. Engaged."

"So?"

"Carol was engaged to me. Would you have said the same thing to Antonio?"

"You didn't belong with Carol."

"And that makes it okay?"

"Mark, do you want this woman or not?"

Yes. He wanted her. Despite his words to the contrary, she was the real reason he'd taken the job at Solar. The director of operations position just happened to be the perfect professional fit. He'd thought it was a win-win, but now, he wasn't sure.

"It doesn't matter if I want her. She's taken."

"Yeah, by the *wrong* guy. Now, do you want her or not?"

"Yes, I want her. I wouldn't be here if I didn't. But I won't steal another man's fiancée." He wouldn't do to Karma's fiancé what had been done to him. That would make him a hypocrite. Besides, he knew how bad that shit hurt.

"Why not? He stole yours."

"I didn't put a ring on Karma's finger."

"You should have." Rob sighed. "Mark, she belongs with you."

"How do you know?"

"Because I've never seen you like this about a woman. Not even Carol." Rob gave him a second to let that sink in. "Karma's *it* for you. She may be engaged to some other guy right now, but people break off engagements all the time. Women get involved with men who aren't right for them every day. He's a rebound that got out of hand. That's all. She *should* be wearing your ring. You *should* have staked your claim when you had the chance. But you were too caught up in hell to see the forest for the trees. So, really, this guy is engaged to *your* fiancée right now. Are you going to let that shit happen? Are you going to let him take your happiness the way you let Antonio take Carol? Sure, Carol wasn't right for you, but you changed. You became a better person because of that nightmare. A person who deserves to finally be happy and get what he wants, goddammit."

Damn Rob. The guy was one hell of a rah-rah artist. Still, going after a woman who belonged to another man wasn't his style. Shit, why did this have to be so hard? A sign wasn't supposed to be this much work. Or at least it shouldn't be. Then again, he wasn't fluent in signs. Maybe this was simply part of the program.

"I don't know, Rob. I'll see how it goes. I just…shit…I just thought I'd come back here and we'd be together. Now I just don't know."

"Well, I'm here for you. You know that. I'd like nothing more than to see you show up at the wedding in November with her on your arm, but the ball's in your court. You've got to make it happen."

"Yeah, yeah. Look, I've gotta get off here. I'm viewing a house tonight and need to meet the agent in thirty minutes." He didn't think any of the houses he'd received info on would be right, and right now he had lost the ideal frame of mind to house hunt, but he had to start somewhere. Hopefully, with Karma's help, he could find the perfect home. Preferably one she'd want to share with him someday.

"Good luck. Talk to you later."

Mark hung up and looked out the window. Funny the twists and turns life throws at a person. Another man had stolen his fiancée from him seven years ago. Now he was considering doing the same thing to someone else.

Chapter 19

One Week Later

Jan sat across from Karma, head at an angle, eyes attentive, chin resting on her index finger. Karma had spent the last forty-five minutes spilling her anger over Mark's abrupt reappearance.

"This was last Tuesday?" Jan said.

"Yes."

"And how have things been since?"

Mark had returned to Chicago last Tuesday night to give notice to his employer and pack up his apartment. "He's traveling with Don this week, so it's not bad. But he calls me and asks me for things. I'm helping him locate homes to view. And I'm doing his footwork in the office, coordinating with other departments to get him added to meetings, e-mail groups, stuff like that. It's a lot of administration at this point." She made a fist. "But I'm just so damn mad. I don't get it. Why am I angry about this?"

After her discussion with Mark last week, she'd briefly felt better. Then she began obsessing over his return and got angry again. Her life had finally reached a level of contentment, and then here came Mark to throw a wrench into what had become a well-oiled machine.

"Remember before how we talked about the five stages of loss?" Jan asked.

Karma nodded her head a little more aggressively than normal. Then again, she was still reeling. "Yes." A sudden realization struck her. "Do you think this is my anger phase? That seeing him again has finally made me experience anger?"

Jan shrugged while making a note on her tablet. "I don't know. Do you think it is?"

"It could be." But Karma wasn't convinced. Her anger toward Mark felt more like a defense mechanism than a rational reaction. Then again, her response to him could have been as strong as it was because she had repressed her anger for months instead of experiencing it. That argument held merit, too.

But she thought she'd worked through the five phases and found acceptance months ago. If the anger she felt now was part of the five stages of loss, did that mean she still hadn't found acceptance?

As she processed the last six months to see how they fit into the five stages, her mind returned to the night of her first date with Brad and she sucked in her breath.

"What?" Jan tilted her head to the side. "What just came to you?"

"I think..." Had she used Brad to force Mark out of her thoughts? And if she had, wasn't that a form of denial? God, she hoped that wasn't why she'd started dating Brad, but the more she considered it, the more likely it seemed.

"What, Karma?" Jan prompted her to go on.

She told Jan about how she'd tucked all the things that reminded her of Mark into the back of her closet the night of her first date with Brad, as well as how she'd made her final decision to go out with Brad right after seeing the picture of Mark with that woman on New Year's Eve.

Jan's face remained serene.

"What if that was denial?" Karma sighed and looked down at her hands. "What if I used Brad to force out the pain of Mark's memory?" If that's what she'd done, then she'd circumvented the grieving process and hadn't allowed herself to fully work through her feelings. "By tucking away everything that reminded me of Mark, I denied what I was still feeling for him and channeled my energy toward forcing him out of my mind by replacing him with someone else."

Jan set down her stylus. "And now you're worried that you delayed the healing process by removing the necessary stimuli. Is that what you're thinking?"

"Yes. I didn't allow myself to fully reach acceptance because I shut off my anger and depression." Karma shook her head at herself. "And now both have shoved themselves front and center."

Karma glanced out the window. The days were growing shorter and colder. Soon, it would be autumn. The leaves would begin to change within weeks, and then it would be the holidays again.

She smirked to herself. It had been a year. Almost exactly to the day. Mark had been gone an entire year. She'd just made the connection.

"You know," she said, turning toward Jan. "It's been exactly one year that he's been gone." She looked down at her hands...at the square diamond sparkling on her finger.

In the beginning, it had been hard to go about her day-to-day activities, but after she started working with Jan, she'd begun to get back out there. She'd started cooking. Then she took up running again. Next came cross-training. Before long, she'd been filling all her spare time to the point that she often collapsed in an exhausted heap every night only to get up and do it all over again the next day. Of course, Brad was in the picture by then, too. Hell, he'd been involved in most of all that busy stuff. And Jade. She couldn't forget Jade. That girl gave Karma nightmares.

"You know, I met Brad and things got crazy. I thought I had moved on." She shrugged. "I thought I'd reached acceptance, but I was only fooling myself."

Jan scrutinized her. "Why do you say that?"

"Because, clearly, I haven't accepted that I'm over Mark. Otherwise, why do I feel the way I do? Angry...sad...all-around upset." She clucked her tongue. "I've been hiding behind Brad. Using him to keep my mind off Mark."

"And now Mark's back, and you can't ignore him anymore, can you?" Understanding flashed across Jan's expression.

"Exactly. I can't ignore him anymore. I have to face him. And I have to face what he did and how it made me feel."

Sweeping him under a rug had been easier when he wasn't around. Now it was time to lift the rug and face the dirt. A nagging voice inside her head told her that would be easier said than done and that there was a lot more to Mark's reappearance and her reaction to him than she wanted to admit.

Patient benevolence projected from Jan's expression. "Maybe this is what you need to finish working through your grief."

"Maybe."

Either she would finally find true acceptance...or Mark was about to turn her world on its head again.

Why did she fear it would be the latter?

Her session with Jan still echoed through Karma's thoughts two hours later as she climbed out of Brad's shower. She and Brad had gone running tonight, which left her drenched in sweat. September in Indiana was notorious for stagnant heat and humidity. The dog days of summer, as they say.

She dressed in capris and a T-shirt and joined him in the kitchen. His hair was still damp from his shower, and he smelled like Dial shower gel, which always made her sneeze.

"Whatcha making?" she said, stepping up beside him at the stove as her nose tickled.

An empty spaghetti sauce jar sat to the side.

"Spaghetti and salad." He grabbed the colander from the cupboard.

She gazed at the pan of generic sauce bubbling on the stove. Mark had made her spaghetti once. With homemade sauce and meatballs that had rocked her world. They'd made love the first time that night.

Brad wasn't the best cook in the world, but as a single man he did the best he could, and when it came to cooking for Jade, he bent to her tastes. Jade was a picky eater. The girl ate out of a jar or a box for every meal.

"All those cooking classes at Single Servings, and we're eating jarred sauce?" She gave his arm a good-natured nudge.

"I'm doing the best I can, Karma." His voice clipped.

Sometimes she never knew what to say around him. He got so short-tempered when his work stressed him, but she never knew when that was until was too late.

"I was just joking," she said defensively, shying away. She took plates out of the cabinet as he drained the spaghetti.

Mark never would have snapped at her like that. Even when his job at Solar had reached intensely stressful levels, he'd always shown Karma nothing but tenderness and patience. He'd always been able to separate work from life. Brad got short with her at least a couple times a week. Would that worsen once they were married?

Brad sighed. "I'm sorry. I didn't mean to snap." He set the colander in the sink and took her hand. "I'm just tense over work. We're behind on a couple of projects and corporate's putting on the pressure."

Brad didn't handle stress well. He liked projects to run smoothly but had a couple of problem employees who notoriously dragged their feet and let projects fall behind. He needed to cut them loose. Instead, he took on more of the burden and worked longer hours, which enabled the slackers to continue dropping the ball. Mark never would have allowed that to happen, but then, this was Brad. Her fiancé. He had a golden heart and believed in second chances. And third chances. And fourth. Okay, so the guy was a pushover at the expense of his own mental and emotional limits, as well as hers, because longer days in the office usually meant a shorter temper at home.

She wrapped her arms around his waist, feeling a sneeze well up in the back of her nose. "Well, after dinner, maybe I can help take your mind off it."

He patted her hand. "I'd like that, but I really have to work. Rain check?"

Another rain check? For sex? They'd been engaged a week and hadn't had celebratory sex, yet. This was the third rain check this week. She was beginning to resent those damn slacker employees of his. Not that the sex was stellar. Brad was an engineer in every sense of the word, including in the bedroom. He was methodical, always following the same script. First came kissing then heavy petting. Then they went to the bedroom— sex always took place in bed—and got undressed. Most of the time, he was on top, but occasionally, he let her be on top. But he never took her from behind, and he couldn't come unless they were in missionary.

The straight and narrow sex was her own fault, though. She'd never spoken up about what she wanted. She'd never suggested they try other things or experiment with other positions. Maybe she would have to do that next time they had sex. If and when she got the chance to cash in her rain checks.

"Sure, okay." She let go of him, sniffled back her sneeze, and carried the plates to the table while he mixed the sauce and spaghetti together.

"I was thinking," he said. "I've got Jade this

weekend. Why don't we all go to the zoo?"

"Ah-choo!" What a perfect time to let loose, because she could swear she was allergic to Jade as much as to the smell of Brad's soap.

"Bless you."

"Thanks."

"So, how about it. Us. Jade. The zoo this weekend?"

Karma's heart rate spiked at just the mention of Jade's name. If she and Brad were going to make it as a couple, she really needed to find a way to get along with that girl. Maybe now that she and Brad were engaged and it became clear Karma wasn't going anywhere, Jade's cold shoulder would warm and she would stop being such a brat. Then again, in light of tonight's session with Jan and all the surprising revelations she'd had, maybe Jade was a symptom of a far bigger problem. Maybe she and Brad didn't belong together and she was forcing something that wasn't meant to be, all in the name of denial.

"Sure," she said, pushing her concerns aside. She wasn't ready to deal with the possibility that she and Brad weren't meant to be together. "Sounds like fun." *It sounds like a disaster.*

"I want to tell her about us." He unceremoniously dumped a clump of spaghetti on her plate then his.

Announcing their engagement to Jade would either bring peace or go over like the coming of the Antichrist. As much as Karma hoped for the former, she feared it would be the latter.

"Good idea." Bad idea, but they had to tell that devil child sooner or later.

Brad set the pan back on the stove and took a seat. "I

know things are tense between the two of you, but sooner or later she has to accept that we're together." He took her hand. "And I can tell you're trying."

Yes, Karma was trying, but her patience was wearing thin. Jade was so damned hardheaded. Observing Brad with Jade, and hearing how he talked about her after the divorce, made it clear that he was overcompensating for no longer being a full-time dad by giving in to all Jade's demands. And it sounded like Brad's ex had tried to make a contest out of who could show Jade they loved her more by buying her tons of toys and accusing Brad of ignoring their daughter and laying on the guilt any time he got involved with another woman. Was this what Karma wanted to sign up for? Did she really want to be forced to deal with this uncomfortable, dysfunctional dynamic every day for the rest of her life? She already struggled to keep her own emotions and behavior in check when it came to Jade and Brad's ex, and they had only officially been together less than six months. What would happen after a year? Two? Five?

Brad's and his ex's behavior had already led to one very angry, very spoiled, and extremely entitled little girl who didn't have a brain-to-mouth filter. What Jade thought, no matter how rude or disrespectful, Jade vocalized. Was Karma setting herself up for failure right out of the gate?

And since Jade was preteen, Karma was going to get to experience Jade's rebellious teenage years immediately after saying, "I do." This could end up being an eight-year migraine in the making.

After dinner, she helped Brad clean up then went

home so he could work.

Back inside her apartment, she plopped down on the couch, clicked on the TV, and snagged the bridal magazine off the coffee table.

All her life, she had dreamed of being a bride. Of wearing the white dress, walking down the aisle, and taking vows with her soon-to-be husband. Of starting a family and living the proverbial happily-ever-after.

And here she was, finally engaged. Her dream was coming true. She should be happy. But as she flipped through the magazine, admiring one dress after another, she felt like the dream was slipping away. There were so many arrangements that needed to be made, but instead of excitement, she felt apathy. It was as if the last thing she wanted to do was plan her wedding.

She closed the magazine and tossed it on the coffee table. Feeling weighed down, she pushed off the couch and went to her bedroom, where she flicked on the light in the closet, crossed her arms, and leaned against the doorframe. Her keepsake box stared back at her from the back corner.

Damn Mark. He'd come back and wrecked everything.

She snapped off the light then flopped down on her bed and stared up at the ceiling as she tried to imagine herself walking down the aisle. Maybe imagery would help get her head straight and help her find the excitement she'd felt right after Brad proposed.

But as she imagined herself walking toward the front of the church, to where her groom waited for her, it wasn't Brad's face she saw on her husband-to-be. It was

Mark's.

She didn't need Jan to tell her she was in trouble.

Chapter 20

Three weeks later, Mark officially started at Solar as the new director of operations. The time in Chicago—all the packing, preparations, reassigning his projects at Carter Mitchell, the good-bye dinners with his coworkers, friends, and family—helped sidetrack his mind from dwelling on his Karma dilemma. But the moment he turned the corner and saw her as he began the familiar walk down the hall, which led to his new office, his desire to have her rushed back.

"Good morning, Karma."

"Good morning." She met his gaze then quickly glanced away.

They had a meeting first thing this morning to discuss expectations and his schedule.

"Give me five minutes and we can get together." Maintaining a measure of professionalism was challenging when what he really wanted to do was sweep around her desk and plant a kiss on her heart-shaped mouth.

He settled into his new leather chair behind the L-shaped mahogany desk he'd inherited from Don and pulled up his e-mail and calendar, which was already packed with meetings. Personalizing his new space would have to take a back seat. Work first.

Karma knocked a few minutes later. "You ready for me?" She sounded like she was forcing herself to remain professional, too.

"Yes." He swiveled around and gestured for her to take a seat.

In her cream-colored pencil skirt and peach, short-sleeved sweater, she looked good enough to lick. The diamond flashing like lightning on her ring finger killed the mood, though.

She entered, leaving the door open, and approached his desk to set a mug of coffee on the coaster beside his left hand. "One sugar, right?" She averted her gaze and sat across from him, her cheeks flushed.

He glanced at the coffee then back at her. "Yes, thank you." He hadn't asked her to get his coffee. And she remembered how he took it. One sugar, no cream.

She met his gaze in the silence, and her cheeks burned a deeper shade of crimson when she caught him staring. He knew exactly what that pink-cheeked expression meant, as well as her flustered demeanor. Maybe Rob had been right about her. Maybe her anger masked something more profound, something deeper, emotions she didn't want to acknowledge let alone allow him to see. In a blink, she'd revealed everything, and his observant eye missed nothing.

Karma was still attracted to him. And not just a little, but a lot. The truth lay in the telltale flutter of her eyelashes as she blinked away from his gaze, in the way she smoothed her palm down her thigh, the way she tucked her auburn hair behind her ear and licked her lips. It was in the fact she had brought him his coffee without him asking.

How interesting. He wondered if she was even aware of her own response to him. Perhaps he wasn't out of the game just yet.

"What?" she said a moment later, fidgeting under his gaze.

He grinned and broke off his stare, turning back to his calendar. "Nothing. I just..." Instinctively, he knew he couldn't let on that he'd caught her foible. That would send her running and throwing up her defenses. "I'm just happy to be getting back to work."

She tapped her fingers on her notepad and glanced around his office as if trying to look at anything but him. "Are you all moved out of your apartment?"

He forced himself to keep a straight face when what he really wanted to do was laugh. A few weeks ago, she had vehemently denied she felt anything for him. She had sat across from him in the conference room, seething, insisting in her own way that she had moved on, and yet, it was becoming clearer by the second that nothing could have been further from the truth.

"Everything's in storage," he said. "All I need is a house to put it in." For the time being, he had signed a short-term lease for a modest, two-bedroom apartment.

"Well, I found a few more listings for you. I'll e-mail them when I get back to my desk."

She had been feeding him home listings for the last three weeks. Some hadn't appealed to him, but he had asked her to set up appointments with his realtor for several. He was set to view them this weekend.

"I'd appreciate that." He inhaled and snagged his Montblanc pen from beside his laptop. "If it's not too much to ask, I'd really like your opinion. Would you mind joining me this Saturday as I view the properties?" Asking her to join him in viewing houses was a risky nudge to see if she would respond as more than just his assistant, but he couldn't help himself.

"I can't." She glanced down and ran the tip of her delicate index finger across her eyebrow. "Brad and I are spending the day at the zoo."

Disappointment clouded Mark's previous good mood. "That sounds fun."

"Yes, we're finally going to tell his daughter about the engagement. We were supposed to go a few weeks ago, but…" She paused and took an unsteady breath as if she were suppressing an uncomfortable thought. "Brad's been busy."

"His daughter?" He hadn't meant to say that out loud, but the fact that Karma was involved with a man who had a daughter surprised him. "How old is she?"

"Twelve." There went the jaw clench again.

What was Karma holding back? Clearly, she and Brad's daughter didn't get along, and from her reaction, the rift between them was more like a chasm. Mark's gut told him that Karma was entering into a situation that would make her miserable if it wasn't already.

He sat forward and folded his arms against his blotter. "You two don't get along?"

Karma released a sharp sigh. "I don't want to talk about this with you. Can we get back to the meeting?"

Straightening, Mark shifted back in his chair. Whatever frustrations Karma had with Brad's daughter would remain hers. At least for now. But if he had any chance of winning her back, eventually he would need to get her talking about her relationship. That was the only way he would be able to convince her she was making a terrible mistake.

Thirty minutes later, Karma returned to her desk with a lengthy to-do list to help Mark get set up and hit the ground running as Don's replacement.

But one thing had become clear during their meeting. She needed to start putting out feelers for another job. No way could she continue to work at Solar if Mark was going to be her boss. There was too much history between them. Just being alone with him in Don's—his—office had caused old feelings to stir in her heart. Feelings of longing, desire...love.

God, she didn't need to fall in love with him again. That was a one-way ticket to heartache. Hell, screw that. She already *was* in love with him. Being around him simply reminded her of that. Her one-way ticket was already punched. *Heartache, here I come.*

But wasn't she happy now? With Brad? They were engaged. She should have been happy. She had a future with Brad. What would she have with Mark? Nothing.

Oh sure, with Mark she would feel alive again. Desirable. Mark wouldn't make her take a rain check for sex. If nothing else, she had learned from her time with Mark that he was an exceptional lover. A connoisseur of sensuality and foreplay. He would always factor in sexual playtime. Even if he had to work, he would set the stage to pique her arousal so that when he finished whatever task required his attention, he could come to her with the breathtaking intensity of a spring thunderstorm...to wash her away on a deluge of heavenly stimulation so mind-blowing, it could bring her to tears. And it had once. Her first time with Mark had moved her beyond any emotional capacity she had ever experienced, leaving her crying cleansing tears of joy.

And Mark didn't come with snarky adolescent children, either. After enduring Jade's rude behavior for months, being with a man who she could share the experience of becoming a first-time parent sounded appealing. Refreshing even.

However, Mark had plenty of other baggage that set off warning sirens in her head, and right now, those bells and whistles were the only things keeping her from marching into his office that very second, shutting the door, and climbing onto his lap.

Which was why she simply couldn't see a future at Solar. How could she do her job and work for a man who tempted her heart? Every day would be a test of wills. An exercise in self-control. How long could she last against such temptation? She'd begun to think she and Brad were making a mistake, but she wasn't giving up what they had without a fight, and she refused to jeopardize her relationship with Brad for a man who could give her nothing but a euphoric roll in the hay. If she and Brad didn't make it, it wasn't going to be because of Mark.

Resolved to update her résumé and begin sending it out, she turned to her computer and e-mailed Mark the property listings she had promised him.

Around three o'clock, as she was compiling data from the project managers for Mark, Jasper swung by her desk on the way back from a meeting with his team. As the others continued on to the war room, Jasper made a beeline for her desk. She had gone out on a couple of casual dates with Jasper last fall, but nothing had come of them. She hadn't been ready to date. A few weeks later, Jasper had met his current girlfriend, a physical therapist, after the last softball game of the season.

"Hey, do you think Mark would want to join us for softball tonight?" Jasper set his iPad on her counter. "We need a second baseman. Tom can't make it."

The fall softball season had started last week. Finding players in the spring and summer was easier than in the fall, when parents had to tend to their kids' after-school events. Tom had three kids, and Karma had no idea how he kept all their activities straight. From the moment the school year started until the second it ended, those children were more active in sports and extracurricular activities than she thought was humanly possible. When Tom's kids did homework, ate, and slept, Karma had no idea.

"Um..." The last thing she wanted was for Mark to join the team. Brad already played as their shortstop, and she really didn't want Brad and Mark to meet, least of all in the field. Talk about awkward.

Mark took that moment to come out of his office, coffee mug in hand, heading toward the coffee station.

Jasper flagged him down. "Hey, Mark. How's it going?"

"Hey, Jasper. Everything's good? How are you

doing?"

They shook hands.

"Great. Just had a meeting with my team. Looks like my top customer is going to be giving us another project soon. A big one."

"That's good news. Sounds like you're doing good things on that account."

They chattered about business and projects for a couple of minutes as Karma looked on. *Please don't ask him to play. Please don't.*

But God wasn't answering her prayers today.

"So, do you play softball?" Jasper said.

Karma cringed inwardly. *Please don't let him say yes.*

"I've played a little softball. Not much, but enough. Why?"

"Solar has a team in a local league and we need a second baseman. Tom usually plays, but now that school's started, I think he's going to drop out."

Wait a minute. Karma thought this was just for one game. Now Jasper was making it sound like he wanted Mark to play in Tom's place for the rest of the season. Not cool.

"Sounds like it could be fun." Mark set his mug on her counter. "Are we talking fast-pitch? Slow-pitch? How serious are we talking here?"

"Oh, we're not that serious." Jasper gestured toward Karma. "We're a co-ed team. Slow-pitch. Just for fun."

Mark turned toward her. "You're on the team? How did I not know that?"

She didn't like the mischievous gleam in his eyes.

Before she could answer, Jasper did for her. "Yep. Karma's on the team. So is her fiancé. So, if you have a girlfriend or anything, she's free to come, too."

Mark's mouth curled into a benign smile. "I'm not currently dating anyone, so it'll just be me."

So, Miss New Year's Eve had been dismissed, too. *Welcome to the long list of Mark Strong heartbreaks, sister.*

"So, you'll come?" Jasper sounded hopeful.

Mark lifted his shoulders. "Sure. Why not. Sounds like fun."

"Great." Jasper turned back toward her. "Can you give him all the details? I've gotta jump on a call with a customer."

"Uh..."

"Thanks, Karma." Jasper darted off.

She turned and looked up into Mark's sexy, dark gaze. "I'll e-mail you the details."

He only stared back at her, saying nothing, but Karma could see his wheels turning. After a long pause, he said, "I'm looking forward to meeting your fiancé." With that, he grabbed his cup and disappeared around the corner.

Damn Jasper.

At five forty-five, Brad pulled into the softball complex. Mark's BMW was already there, causing an odd, conflicted yearning to overtake her. Part of her—the part who wanted to take Mark into the nearest storage closet and strip him bare—perked up in excitement. But her practical side—the one devoted to Brad and all things reasonable—scowled. That side of her detested the intrusion on a physical outlet that had helped distract her mind from her depression last year. And now, here he was, infiltrating and inserting himself into yet another facet of her life.

"It's a little chilly tonight." Brad grabbed his duffel from the backseat.

Karma hefted hers over her shoulder, thankful she'd brought a sweatshirt. It was the end of September and the weather was growing cooler. Soon, it would be sweater weather. She loved sweater weather. Or, rather, she loved the *idea* of it. The thought of snuggling into a soft, fluffy, oversized sweater on a trip to the local orchard to buy homemade apple butter, cider, and search the pumpkin patch for the perfect pumpkin to make a jack-o'-lantern filled her soul with warmth and left a nostalgic grin on her face. Unfortunately, the reality was that the trip to the orchard would be on a dreary, rainy day too bone-chilling cold for just a sweater. If late September's weather was a temperamental mix of hot and cold, October's was notorious for overcast, drizzly autumn days.

As they approached the softball diamond, Karma spied Mark warming up with Lisa and frowned. Her best friend was consorting with the enemy. Lisa should know better than that. They tossed a ball back and forth, and Mark looked as at ease with softball as he had playing basketball when she'd visited him in Chicago last summer. The guy was built for sports. And damn, his arms were ripped. Looked like Mark had been seriously working out in his year away.

Jasper and several other members of the team were already warming up, too. As usual, she and Brad were the late arrivals. Brad could never seem to pick her up on time. There was always some last-minute crisis at work he had to tend to.

"Hey, Karma!" Lisa waved.

Mark turned, caught her eye, and then his gaze quickly jumped to Brad.

Let the awkwardness begin.

"Hi." She waved back at Lisa, briefly met Mark's gaze again, then knelt beside her bag along the dusty sideline.

She fished out her mitt, grabbed one of the balls from the equipment duffel, then she and Brad trotted out to the field, setting up a few feet away from Mark and Lisa. Standing about twenty feet from Brad, she tossed the ball his direction.

The white ball landed in his leather mitt with a familiar *thwack*.

Back-and-forth, they tossed the ball, getting a good, easy rhythm going. *Thwack…thwack*.

For five minutes, she focused on the flying white orb, forcing herself not to look at Mark. But she could feel him. He was right there, barely ten feet away. It was like the guy had invisible tentacles, and they were caressing her from head to toe, sending her awareness into the stratosphere.

With only a couple more minutes until the game started, all the players made their way to the bench.

"Looks like tough competition." Mark nodded toward the opposition.

"They're from Methodist Sports Medicine." Jasper dropped his mitt on the bench and grabbed his water.

"That explains it." Mark glanced at her and held her gaze a second longer than necessary as he sat beside her.

Brad sat on her other side. He reached across her body, hand outstretched toward Mark. "By the way, I'm Brad."

Mark hesitated for a fraction of a second as if sizing up his competition. "I'm Mark. I'm Karma's new boss." Karma didn't miss the possessive tone in his voice, even if it passed right over everyone else's head. But she knew him more intimately than the others, and right now, he was a rooster strutting around the hen, trying to intimidate the other roosters.

"Karma didn't tell me she had a new boss." Brad gave her a quizzical look.

She felt her cheeks flame to life and waved her hand dismissively. "It just happened. Besides, it's no big deal, and you've been busy." She rubbed her arm against his affectionately. Probably too affectionately. "Mark worked at Solar last year as a consultant, so it's kind of like he never really left." She shot Mark a pointed glance. Because, clearly, he *had* left. And when he did, he'd given up any right to stake a claim over her, which he was clearly trying to do now by preening his feathers in front of Brad.

"I'm here to stay this time," Mark said, his gaze boring into Brad's in a way that sent all kinds of my-dick-is-bigger-than-yours vibes.

And, honestly, Mark's dick was bigger than Brad's, but jock size wasn't how she measured the worth of a man.

Brad looked between her and Mark then narrowed his eyes and smiled. "I see. Well, it's too bad my *fiancée* hasn't mentioned you."

Uh-oh. Sounded like Brad had picked up on the

verbal challenge. The way he slid his hand into hers and wove their fingers together proved it. Brad wasn't into displays of public affection, but faced with what he perceived as another suitor vying for her attention, he must have cast aside his aversion to make clear exactly who she belonged to.

Thankfully the umpire called the first batter to the plate, ending the covert cock fight she was smack in the middle of. The first two up to bat got base hits, then Jasper got a double. Then three outs in a row. But they had scored two runs. Not bad for a first inning at bat.

Karma grabbed her mitt and jogged out to right field. The testosterone coming off Mark and Brad was almost like another player. Hopefully neither of them would do anything stupid. Such as actually whip out their penises and argue about which was bigger.

The first batter for the other team knocked a hit into left field, which Jasper caught for an out, but the second batter looked like a pro. What were these sports med guys doing playing in the slow-pitch league? They looked like minor leaguers.

He hit a grounder right toward Brad. He scooped it up and tossed it toward first base, but not before the runner was called safe. The next batter popped one into center field, which sailed over Lisa's head. By the time she retrieved it and threw it toward second, the first runner was rounding for home. Mark reached to catch the ball, but Brad jumped in front of him to catch it instead.

What the hell?

Mark flung out his arms in obvious exasperation as Brad turned, adjusted, and threw the ball toward home plate. But he couldn't get the ball there fast enough. The other team scored while the runner rounded second to third.

"What the hell was that?" Mark shouted. "I could have gotten two outs."

Brad shrugged as if he didn't care then bent and rested his hands on his knees in anticipation of the next hit.

This was a side of Brad Karma had never seen. It was one thing to be competitive and to want to show Mark who she belonged to, but what he'd done just now had cost them not only a run, but also an out. Mark was justifiably upset, as were the rest of the members on the team.

"Shake it off!" she yelled. "Come on, shake it off. We'll get the next one."

The next hit beamed straight for Mark. Easy out. Except…Brad ran for the ball.

No, Brad! No! Karma cringed and threw her hands in the air as if that would be enough to make Brad stop. No such luck.

Brad flung himself toward the ball. It grazed the front of his mitt, deflecting away from both him and Mark.

Mark rushed after it, leaving second base uncovered, which meant Brad should have covered the base. When Mark jumped around to throw him the ball, Brad had returned to shortstop. Mark had to double clutch and dart back to the base, but not before the runner got there first.

Appearing frustrated, Mark shot her an exasperated glance as if this was all her fault then tossed the ball back to the pitcher.

God, this was turning into a nightmare. Brad was behaving like a six-year-old, and from the frustrated expression on Mark's face, he was only just barely holding his tongue.

Somehow, they managed to get three outs, but not before the other team scored five runs.

At the bench, she quickly pulled Brad aside. "What was that all about?" she whispered hotly, pointing toward the field.

He scowled and turned away. "Nothing."

"Nothing? You cost us at least three runs, Brad. *At least.*"

"I don't like that guy." He glowered at Mark, who was sitting on the bench, drinking from his water bottle.

"What?" Karma tried to sound confused even though she knew exactly what Brad meant. "You just met him."

"Yeah, well, I don't like how he looks at you."

Karma pulled back. "How he looks at me?"

"Yeah. He looks at you like he owns you."

She forced herself to laugh. "You're imagining things." She had never known Brad to be the jealous type, but here he was, wigged-out over another man. Yes, she and Mark had a history with one another, but she had made her choice, and her choice was Brad. Seeing him so jealous was unnerving.

"Am I?" Brad gave her a hard look then marched past her to warm up. He was next in the batting lineup.

She plopped onto the bench.

"Your boyfriend needs to learn how to play ball,"

Mark said under his breath.

"He's not my boyfriend. He's my fiancé, remember?"

"Yeah, I remember, but he still needs to learn how to play."

She glanced around to make sure no one was within earshot. "What he needs is for you to stop showing your ass."

"Me?"

"Yes, you." She glared at him. "You and your macho bullshit. Don't think I don't know what you're up to."

"Hey, I'm just here to play ball."

"Then play and quit trying to wave your dick in Brad's face. I'm with him now. *Him.* Not *you.* I've made my choice. And you…aren't…it." She pushed off the bench and left him to stew on her words while she grabbed her favorite bat and took a few practice swings.

For four more innings, nothing further was said about Brad's incompetent playing, but he did begin to play more sensibly. Karma took her place in right field and chattered at the batter with her teammates.

"Hey batter, batter, batter…swiiiing batter!"

And swing he did, dinging one into right field, straight for her. That's what she got for taunting. The hit wasn't just a pop fly. It was more like an arcing missile. She ran up on the ball but couldn't get to it in time. It hit the ground and bounced like a laser-guided bullet right toward her face. She saw the damn thing coming but couldn't duck in time, taking a hit right in the eye.

Pop!

She flew backward and fell, covering the left side of her face with her mitt as pain erupted in her cheek and nose. She rolled to her side in the grass, instinctively shielding her injury from further harm.

"Karma!" It was Mark's voice.

Within seconds, the rest of the team surrounded her, abandoning the ball and letting the other team score.

"Are you okay?"

She blinked through stinging tears at Mark's concerned face. Genuine worry coated his expression.

"Karma? Hey, you all right?" Brad practically shoved Mark out of the way and took her hand.

Mark took off for the sidelines, and Jasper called an injury time-out.

"Yes. I think so. Just...hurts." It felt like her face was swelling and pain throbbed like a heartbeat in her cheek.

"You took quite a hit." Brad helped her up, wrapped his arm around her waist, and led her toward the bench.

Mark approached holding a cold pack from the team's first aid kit. "Here. Put this on your eye."

She took the pack and pressed it against her tender face, wincing.

"You should go to the hospital." Mark reached for her arm.

Brad knocked his hand away. "Don't be silly. She's fine. Right?" He turned toward her. "You're fine. Just a little bump."

Mark frowned. "She could have a concussion or a broken nose." Anger splashed over his words. "She needs to get checked out."

Brad ignored him and guided her to the bench.

"How's it look?" She lowered her mitt to reveal the battered side of her face.

Brad blinked and raised his eyebrows. "Well…"

"Like you need to go to the hospital," Mark said, kneeling in front of her.

Brad huffed. "She doesn't need to go to the hospital. It's just a little black eye."

Mark scowled at Brad, shaking his head. "It might be, but it'd be better to find out for sure."

Brad was probably right. It was probably just a black eye. But Mark was also right. He was clearly worried. Did her face really look that bad?

"Let me take care of my own fiancée, Mark," Brad said, glaring. "I think I've got this."

Karma needed to defuse the situation. She held up her free hand between them. "If it gets worse, I'll go to the hospital, okay?" She glanced from Brad to Mark and back again. "But I think I'll be okay. It's just a little bruise."

Mark glanced from Brad to Karma. What appeared to be frustration mixed with hopelessness crossed his face, and then he grabbed his mitt and stood. With his jaw clenched, he backed away then tore his gaze from hers and returned to the field.

Brad scowled after him then returned his gaze to Karma's as he placed his hand over hers on the ice pack. "It looks fine. A little swollen. You'll probably have a black eye. But you're still sexy."

Sexy? How could a swollen, blackening eye be sexy? Really, Brad shouldn't try so hard to one-up Mark. The machismo didn't look good on him.

"Can you play?" Jasper asked.

"Of course she can't play," Brad said. "Look at her eye."

She pushed out of Brad's hold. She didn't need him speaking for her. "I'm fine. We've only got a couple more innings. I can play." She turned toward Brad. "You can nurse me after the game."

The injury really wasn't all that bad. Her pride was more bruised than her face, which probably looked worse than it felt. But hey, if she played her cards right and milked her battle wound and Brad's guilt for all they were worth, she might be able to cash in on a rain check or two tonight.

Chapter 21

Karma sat beside Brad at the Stacked Pickle an hour later, a half-eaten burger and fries in front of her and a Ziploc bag of ice wrapped in a towel pressed to her cheek. Half the team, as well as most of the players on the opposing team, had stopped in after the game for food and drinks.

Brad stuck to her side like glue. Apparently, he didn't want to leave her alone where big bad Mark could swoop in and steal her away. The attention was nice but left Karma a little discombobulated. She'd gotten used to Brad's standoffish, I-don't-like-displays-of-public-affection demeanor, and now she had to shift gears to keep up with his change in direction.

But he really needn't have worried about Mark. He'd taken up flirting with a lean, busty brunette from the other team. They were sitting together at the next table over, laughing and sitting much too closely to one another. The brunette reminded her of the woman in the picture with Mark on New Year's Eve.

What did he see in that woman? Her boobs were obviously fake, her skin tanned from a can, and her laughter sounded like something forced through an exhaust pipe. It was more like a cackle than a laugh.

And apparently Mark was the newest comedic sensation to hit the circuit from the way that woman cackled nonstop.

But she was a looker.

Maybe Karma shouldn't have been so quick to shove Brad in Mark's face. Seeing him with that woman was as painful as being popped in the eye, especially when he paid the bill, stood, placed his hand at the small of the woman's back, and guided her toward the exit.

"How's your eye?" Brad asked a couple minutes later as he removed his arm from around her shoulders.

Now that the enemy was gone, Brad could loosen his guard.

And she'd just started to enjoy the attention.

"Better." She'd gotten a look at her new shiner in the ladies room earlier. The swelling felt like it was going down, but she had a feeling when she woke up in the morning, that thing was gonna hurt like a bitch. Or a slap in the face, which was what had just walked out the door. But hey, maybe the black eye would keep Jade from being a total drag on their trip to the zoo. Then again, Jade was more likely to ask who'd given it to her so she could send a thank-you note.

Which reminded Karma she needed to get up early in the morning to make a batch of truffles. She really wanted to get along with Jade, and what better way than through a peace offering of chocolate? After all, what girl didn't like chocolate?

One who is trying out for the part of the Wicked Witch of the West.

Now, now. She needed to stop thinking that way. Jade was just a troubled little girl. Once she realized

Karma was an okay gal with a big heart who knew how to make truffles, everything would work out fine. Positive thinking here.

"You ready to go?" Brad asked a few minutes later.

"Absolutely." She shifted the ice pack on her face and let Brad help her to her feet.

Thankfully, Mark and his ho were gone by the time they reached the parking lot.

"What's with that guy? Mark?" Brad asked on the drive home.

"What do you mean?" And here she thought they'd put the softball debacle behind them.

"The way he looks at you...I don't like it."

"Which you made perfectly clear tonight." She gave him a contemptuous sidelong glance at a stoplight.

"Is something going on between the two of you?"

"Brad! Absolutely not."

"Are you sure?"

"Positive." She ran her hand along his thigh, hoping to distract him from his current train of thought. The way his gaze dropped quickly to his lap then back up at the road showed her plan was working. Her hand settled between his legs and his chest rose heavily as he inhaled. "Are you jealous?" She smiled and leaned across the seat so she could kiss the side of his neck.

"No," he said a little too quickly. Then he sighed. "Okay, maybe."

"Don't be. I'm with you. I'm wearing *your* ring. Nothing's going on between me and my boss." But it wouldn't take much for there to be, which made it that much more important that she get her résumé updated this weekend and start sending it out. She kissed his neck again and felt the bulge beneath her hand grow. "I never knew you were the jealous type."

"Me, neither." He pulled up to her apartment building and shut off the engine. "I've been neglecting you lately, haven't I?"

It had been three weeks since they'd had sex.

"You've been busy."

He turned and kissed her. "Let me make it up to you."

"You wanna come up?" Her alter ego eagerly waved a whole stack of rain checks in her mind.

Without answering, he got out and joined her by the passenger door then followed her inside.

Once in her apartment, he eased his arms around her waist, and for the briefest of moments, Karma almost pushed him away and told him to leave. Suddenly, Brad's touch felt all wrong. Too stiff, not passionate or gentle enough.

Not Mark enough.

Instead, she let him kiss her...let him prod her toward the bedroom.

All the while, she was cringing inside. She couldn't win for losing. For weeks, all she'd wanted was for Brad to fuck her silly, and now that it looked like she was getting her wish, it was the last thing she wanted. Sure, Brad's definition of fucking her silly was tame compared to hers—and Mark's—but she still enjoyed it. Or, rather, she used to.

Was her reluctance because of how he'd acted at the game? Toward Mark? Or was her reluctance caused by weeks of resentment over him choosing work over her?

Or was there something more profound at work

here. Maybe her reticence had nothing to do with Brad's behavior at all. Perhaps she simply no longer wanted to be in denial and subconsciously recognized that Brad was just that. A mechanism of denial she'd clung to far too long. That possibility scared her, so she quickly abandoned it and forced herself back in the moment, where Brad's arms pulled her closer and his lips brushed over hers.

She had wanted this for weeks. She had wanted him to pay her some attention and take her to bed, only to be put off time and again. But now that she was getting exactly what she wanted—or *thought* she wanted—she no longer wanted it.

"I have an idea," she said, pulling away.

Brad pulled off his T-shirt. "What's that?"

"Let's play a game."

His face scrunched. "A game? What kind of game?"

She rushed into her exercise room, grabbed the Truth or Dare game from behind the books in her bookcase, and hurried back to her bedroom.

He took one look at the name on the box and frowned. "Truth or Dare?" He didn't sound too keen on the idea.

"Yes. You'll love it. I promise." She opened the box and explained the rules. "You pick a card, I tell you truth or dare, and then you read whichever one I choose. Then I do the same to you."

"I don't know, Karma..."

"Oh, come on."

He sighed. "Okay, fine." He sat down on the bed, and Karma swirled the cards go fish-style, facedown, on the comforter between them.

"I'll go first." She picked up a card. "Truth or dare?"

"Truth, I guess." He didn't sound as into the game as she had hoped.

She read the question. "What is the most you've ever masturbated in a single day?"

"What?" He blew out a frustrated breath. "Really? I'm supposed to answer that?"

"You have to. You chose truth."

He scratched his fingers through his hair. "I don't know, Karma. Maybe two or three times. I really can't remember."

Lame answer. But at least he answered. That was a good sign, right? "Okay, your turn." She set the card aside.

Brad tentatively pulled one from the pile. "Truth or dare?" He exhaled heavily, face drawn. Then his eyebrows furrowed as he read the two questions to himself.

"Truth."

Another sigh, then, "Describe my in-bed personality in three words." Something that looked a bit like insecurity flashed across his face.

He had reason to fear. The three words that immediately came to mind were tame, boring, and creatively lacking. She couldn't very well spill those to him, though, or he'd go into a sexual coma and she would be lucky if he ever made love to her again. Instead, she took this as an opportunity to show him how the game was supposed to be played.

Shifting to all fours, she crawled toward him and slid her mouth up to his ear. "Hot, sexy, and exciting," she whispered in her most seductive voice.

When she pulled away, his face was red, and he wore a self-conscious grin. "That was sweet."

"Just the truth." She picked up another card, feeling like a cad for lying. "My turn. Truth or dare?"

"Truth."

She really wanted him to say dare, but oh well. "Would you rather cuddle post-sex or jump in a hot shower together?"

Brad never did either, so his answer could give her a clue about how she could navigate their post-sexual activities in the future.

He shrugged and glanced away. "Shower, I guess. But I'd really rather just sleep."

"That's it?" The longer they played, the more she simply wanted to go to sleep herself. That wasn't how this game was intended to work. She was supposed to be getting hotter, not bored.

"Yeah."

"Okay. Well, your turn. Ask me again. Dare me this time." Maybe if she took a dare, he would, too.

He pressed his lips together then read, "Look around the room and find something to incorporate into our sex play."

Karma glanced at her dresser. She didn't have a lot to choose from. Her fishing hat, some jewelry, a couple of scarves. Wait a minute. She hopped up, grabbed a green scarf, and held it out to him. "Want me to blindfold you?"

"What? No."

Not willing to give up just yet, she waved the scarf in front of him as if tantalizing a thief with gold. "Do you want to blindfold me instead?" She mustered the most seductive voice she could under the less-than-sexy circumstances.

"Karma, come on. This is silly." He gestured toward the cards. "I don't want to play games to sleep with you. This stuff doesn't really turn you on, does it?"

Feeling a bit foolish, she lowered the scarf and glanced at the cards. When she had played the game with Mark, she'd been so turned on the only way to turn back off was for him to give her at least two orgasms. But playing with Brad was about as stimulating as cleaning her nails. "No, I guess not."

"Come on. Let's put these away." He began collecting the cards. "We've got a big day tomorrow, so let's just have normal sex and get to bed, okay?"

"Okay."

He put the cards back inside their box, took the scarf out of her hands, stood, finished undressing, and then helped her out of her clothes.

Feeling not the least bit desirable, she lay back on the bed, wrapped her arms around his shoulders, and stared up at the ceiling as he took her missionary style. Again.

The day Mark returned, she'd told Lisa that she didn't need passion to be happy.

She'd been wrong.

Right now, the only thing she wanted was passion.

Chapter 22

Saturday morning, Karma dragged herself out of bed and into the kitchen to prepare the truffles she wanted to give to Jade. Brad had left last night after they'd had sex, so she was on her own this morning. Thank God. After the lackluster events of the evening, she wasn't sure she could face Brad right now.

She pulled out the truffle recipe, gathered all the ingredients, and followed them to the letter. After combining the cream and chocolate, she set the bowl aside and got ready for her day at the zoo.

As the minutes passed, she grew more and more tense. It felt like her body was performing a preflight check to prepare for her day with Jade. Muscles? Tight. Jaw? Clenched. Headache? In the queue. But if she was marrying Brad, she had to find a way to coexist with his daughter.

She returned to the kitchen, formed the chocolate mixture into balls, prepped the chopped almonds, powdered sugar, and crushed peppermints while the truffles rested in the refrigerator, and then finished by rolling the chocolate balls in the crushed toppings.

They looked good, but when she bit into one, the ganache was grainy, as if the chocolate hadn't completely melted. This was the same problem she and Brad had encountered when they made truffles at Single Servings. What the heck was she doing wrong?

But at least they tasted good. Everything else was forgivable as long as they were delicious. No way could Jade not like these delectable things.

She carefully placed the truffles in a container and packed them in a cooler so they wouldn't melt. A few minutes later, Brad announced himself with a quiet knock.

Karma grabbed the cooler and joined him in the outer hall. Jade wasn't with him, which meant she'd stayed in the car.

"How's her mood?" she asked.

Brad's expression said it all. Jade was particularly sour today. "The usual."

"I made truffles for her. Hopefully that will help."

Wishful thinking. The moment she and Brad walked out the door, the battle was on.

"I asked you to please get in the back, Jade." Brad pointed for Jade to get out of the front seat and into the back.

Huffing dramatically as if he were asking her to do something as inane as cut grass with a pair of scissors, Jade threw the front passenger door open, glared at Karma, and got out. She was wearing black on black on black. Probably not the smartest wardrobe choice since it was unseasonably warm today. But Jade was in *that* phase. The one where she experimented with all manner of pseudo-Gothic dress in place of more practical jeans and a T-shirt.

"Hi, Jade." Karma gritted her teeth and forced a

smile.

"What happened to your eye?" Jade pointed. "Did someone beat you up?" Was that a smirk on her twelve-year-old mouth?

"I got hit with a softball." Karma dabbed her fingertips on her tender cheek, just under her eye.

"Cool." Jade sighed and rolled her jaw over what had to be a whole pack of gum as she gave her a two-finger wave that looked more like a hostile peace sign. "We doing a picnic?" She addressed Brad but gestured toward the cooler.

"No. Karma made something for you and she doesn't want it to melt."

Rebellious teenaged eyes narrowed on the cooler as if Jade instinctively knew she was trying to induce a truce. Karma could almost hear the plan backfiring already. Maybe the truffles had been a bad idea.

As soon as they were in the car, Jade opened the cooler, which Karma had set in the backseat.

"What the hell is that?"

Karma rubbed the tips of her fingers against her temple.

Brad's gaze shot to the rearview mirror. "What have I told you about the language, Jade?"

A derisive snort came from the backseat.

"They're chocolate truffles," Karma said, glancing over her shoulder as Jade pulled the container out of the cooler.

"Truffles? That sounds like something pigs eat."

"Jade." Brad's tone held an unspoken warning.

The beginning of a headache sprang to life behind Karma's eyes. "That's a different kind of truffle."

Jade tentatively picked out one of the treats coated in powdered sugar, spit her wad of gum into her other hand, and took a bite. A moment later, her face screwed up. "Ew, it feels like sand."

Karma faced front and pinched the bridge of her nose.

Brad reached across the seat and laid his hand on her arm. "That's enough, Jade. Karma worked very hard on those just for you. The least you could do is thank her."

"For what? They're, like, yucky. And they taste funny. Not like real chocolate."

That would be the coffee she'd added. Big mistake. Twelve-year-old girls didn't like coffee. Neither did Karma, but when she ate the truffles, she could barely taste it. Apparently, Jade's taste buds were more attuned than hers.

"Jade. Enough!" Brad squeezed Karma's hand as tears stung her eyes.

I will not cry. Sometimes Jade reminded her of her old childhood classmate and former coworker, Jolene. Jo had bullied her all through school, reducing her to tears more often than not. As an adult, Jo had channeled her bullying personality into walking all over Karma at work. At least until Mark came along. Mark had helped Karma find her voice and shut Jolene down once and for all. But how did you shut down a contemptuous, ungrateful twelve-year-old?

Thirty awkwardly silent minutes later, except for the wet chomping noises of Jade chewing her gum with an open mouth, they arrived at the zoo. Karma's headache had amplified, and the sun and heat didn't help as the three made their way from exhibit to exhibit.

If only Jade had brought a friend along, they could have gone off to do their thing to give Karma a break from all the mental hatred spewing her direction. As it was, Karma was stuck with the brooding preteen, and all the girl did was complain. One long, nonstop litany of complaints. It was too hot. She was too thirsty. The zoo was lame. It smelled like monkey poop. She wished she'd gone shopping with her friends. She had a bad taste in her mouth from the truffle. The exhibits stunk. The animals weren't active enough. She had to pee. Her stomach hurt from eating that nasty truffle.

By the time they wound their way back to the exit a few hours later, Karma felt like she'd been through war. Her body ached, her head pounded, and emotional *and* nervous breakdowns sat just at the edge of her sanity.

And she and Brad still hadn't told Jade they were engaged, which had been the whole point of today's trip.

When Karma had begun to think Brad was going to back down yet again and not tell her, he cleared his throat. "So, Jade, Karma and I have something we need to tell you." He squeezed her hand.

This was it. Get ready for the damn to break loose. If Karma had thought the past few hours had been hell, the next sixty seconds were going to be like a star exploding.

Jade's suddenly wary gaze shifted back and forth between them. "What?"

Brad hesitated, met Karma's gaze with a glint of worry mixed with a dash of hope, then looked back at his daughter. "I've asked Karma to marry me, and she's said yes."

Silence. The kind you hear in a vacuum or a soundproof room. But the stream of insults and accusations Jade threw from her glare was deafening.

"We're getting married," Brad said with finality.

"No." Jade turned and stormed through the parking lot.

Karma and Brad practically had to jog to keep up, which made Jade trot away even faster. She was practically running.

"Jade! Stop. Get back here." Brad let go of Karma's hand and ran after his daughter.

Jade finally stopped then spun and pointed blazing, tear-filled eyes her direction. "I hate you! You're not good enough for my dad! And I hope your eye hurts! I hope it hurts like hell and falls out!"

Karma gasped and covered her bruised eye with her hand.

A couple of rows away, a family of four stopped and stared. All Karma could do was shake her head and look away. This hadn't gone well. Worse than Karma thought it would.

Brad corralled Jade and knelt in front of her. He spoke in hushed but heated whispers, gripping Jade by the biceps. Whatever he said met with a lot of frowning, glares, and tears.

"She's young enough to be my sister!" Jade screamed. "I hate her! I hate her! She's nothing but a *SLUT*! A nasty, skanky *slut*!"

Karma's mouth fell open. Oh, hell no. She would not stand here and take this shit, even if Jade was only twelve. And if Brad didn't put a lid on that kind of talk, like instantly, let World War III begin.

"Stop it, Jade. Just stop it." Brad sounded like he was at the end of his rope.

"No! I hate her! You can't marry her! No!" Despite her tough exterior, Jade broke down in brutal sobs. "She's only using you!" She slapped her hands over her face and bawled.

Brad pulled Jade into a hug, leaving Karma standing like an abandoned dog beside the car. Really? He'd let his daughter call her a skanky slut and throw insult after insult at her, and now he rewards her with a hug?

"Ssshh, honey," Brad said, smoothing his hand down Jade's long black hair. "How about we go home and order a pizza, just the two of us? You and me, just like we used to."

And the rewards for bad behavior continued. It was like Karma wasn't even there. Brad was all about Jade. Poor Jade. His poor little spoiled brat of a daughter. She threw a temper tantrum and instead of making a statement by not giving in, Brad had just enabled her to throw even more tantrums in the future.

Jade sniffled and nodded as she wiped her palms over her cheeks. "Okay."

Awareness slammed into Karma so hard, she almost gasped. This was what she had to look forward to with Brad. A life of second place. Brad would always put his daughter first. Always. He would always bend when Jade cried…always give in and push Karma aside to tend to Jade, regardless of how badly Karma needed his emotional support.

What Jade needed was for Brad to show her that she couldn't twist him around her little finger and control him. That he had a life of his own and adult needs that were just as important as hers. Instead, he caved. He fucking gave in.

Karma turned away, feeling like a fifth wheel. This is what she had signed on for when she put Brad's engagement ring on her finger. This was the choice she had made. She'd thought Brad could provide the security and commitment she wanted, but now she felt brutalized, which was about as far from secure and safe as she could get. Was this the kind of commitment she wanted? One where she never took a priority in Brad's life? Where she would always stand in line behind his daughter? She deserved to be number one in her husband's life. Maybe not all the time, but at least part of the time. With Jade, it was clear Karma would never be number one.

Brad managed to get Jade into the car, and the three drove back to Karma's apartment in silence. Brad grabbed her cooler from the backseat and walked her up to the outer door.

"Here, maybe you should take these. I think they'll just upset her." He handed the cooler to Karma.

"Sure. Because we wouldn't want to upset Jade, now would we?" She gave him a hardened glare.

His eyebrows crinkled into a frown. "What's that supposed to mean?"

"Nothing." She looked away, too frustrated to look him in the eye.

"Karma? Why are you mad?"

"Because every time she gets just a little pissed off, you drop everything—especially *me*—to bend to her beck and call. I wanted to spend time with you tonight.

Me. Your *fiancée*." She slapped her palm on her chest. "But no, Jade's angry that we're getting married, so off you run, leaving me alone." She flapped her arm toward the car. "Again."

"You're being unreasonable. She's my daughter."

"Yes, and she needs to know that you have a life to live, too. She needs to learn how to respect that. And *me*. She needs to learn how to respect *me*. She called me a slut today, Brad. A skanky slut. She said some really hurtful, insulting things. And you did nothing to stand up for me. Instead, you walked away from me and coddled her. And when you walk away from me and give in to her tantrums, you're teaching her that it's okay to *disrespect* me. That *my* feelings don't matter."

"I don't see it that way."

"Really? You don't? She cries and throws a fit and you give in. Every damn time, Brad. You're empowering her to behave like a spoiled brat every time she doesn't like something or doesn't get her way, because every time she throws a fit, you give her what she wants. Maybe I need to throw a fit so I can get what I want once in a while."

Brad huffed and thrust his hands onto his hips. "Look, we need to talk about this later. You're obviously too upset to discuss this rationally right now."

Damn straight, she was upset. She'd held her tongue far too long as it was.

"Just go. Your *daughter* needs you, and I need to figure out an alternate plan for dinner since I thought I was eating with you tonight. But seeing that I'm not welcome around your daughter..." Karma threw him a pointed glare then yanked open the door and stormed inside.

Maybe she was being irrational and maybe she wasn't. Right now, she didn't care. She had a blinding headache, she was hungry, and she'd just spent the entire day with the human version of fingernails on a chalkboard. Even grownups had their limits, and Karma had reached hers.

She unlocked the door of her apartment, stepped inside, slammed the door, then just stood there, glaring out her window as she watched Brad back his Camry out of its parking space and drive away.

Damn him! And damn his entitled, spoiled daughter!

She spun around, marched back out, locked up behind her, and stormed down the stairs to the exit, not realizing she was still carrying her cooler until she got to her car. Climbing behind the wheel, she set the cooler in the passenger seat then pulled out. If she was going to eat alone tonight, she was going to do it at her favorite restaurant, Greek Tony's.

Chapter 23

The newspaper lay on the left side of the table, the half-eaten meatball sub Mark had ordered for dinner clutched in his right hand. After viewing houses this morning, he'd spent the afternoon at the office organizing his space, hanging pictures, and going through reports before calling it a day and stopping by Greek Tony's for dinner. There was a lot of catching up to do at work, but things were coming back quickly from when he'd worked at Solar a year ago.

Well, most things were. Karma was still holding him at arm's length.

He glanced up as the chimes on the door jangled.

Speak of the devil.

Mark set down his sandwich and watched Karma beeline for the counter. She didn't notice him sitting in the corner, but then she appeared distracted and frazzled—maybe even upset—her hair pulled into a haphazard ponytail, her face drawn and pale.

"Hey, Andrew," she said in a tired voice to the kid behind the counter.

"Hey, Karma. Whoa! What happened to your eye?"

She halfheartedly lifted her hand toward her face. "I got hit with a softball...and my fiancé's daughter hopes my eyeball falls out." The last she said with an edge of sarcasm.

Andrew's eyebrows shot into his forehead. "Ooookaaaay. That's not right."

"Tell me about it." Karma leaned on the counter as if she could barely hold herself up.

What the hell had happened to her today?

"So, the usual?" Andrew said.

"Yes, please."

"You look exhausted. Long day?"

Karma brushed a wayward strand of hair off her face. "The longest. Besides wishing me to lose an eye, my fiancé's daughter is a damn diva."

Mark tried not to listen, but couldn't help himself. The dining room was small and relatively empty. There were only two other occupied tables. He was actually surprised she hadn't seen him, but he *was* sitting at the corner table, tucked away from the main part of the room.

"Uh-oh. A diva, huh?" Andrew said.

"God, yes." Karma handed over her credit card. "We spent the day at the zoo, and all she did was complain, and when Brad and I told her we're engaged, she flipped out. Right in the middle of the parking lot. People stopped and stared."

Andrew chuckled. "Glad it's you and not me." He swiped her card.

"I wish it weren't." Karma plunked her elbow on the counter and rested her head in her hand. "The worst of it is that I made her homemade chocolate truffles as a peace offering, and she didn't even like them. I mean, chocolate, Andrew. *Chocolate.* What girl doesn't like chocolate? I give up." She straightened, but her shoulders still slumped.

The extent of what Karma had endured today had obviously taken its toll on her both mentally and physically.

Andrew handed back her card, turned, snagged a plastic-wrapped cookie off the back shelf, and set it on the counter in front of Karma.

"What's this?" She picked it up.

"Chocolate chip cookie. On the house. Maybe it'll help make things better." Andrew smiled. "It's got *chocolate* in it."

From his vantage point, Mark could see Karma's cheeks lift, so he knew she was smiling. "Thanks, Andrew. You're the best." She grabbed her ticket, cookie, and beverage cup, filled it at the soda fountain, then turned to look for a place to sit.

That's when she noticed him sitting in the corner watching her.

He sat back, lifted his hand, and offered a casual wave.

To his surprise, she came over and nearly collapsed into the chair beside him. "My day just gets better and better."

He folded his newspaper and tucked it away. "Good to see you, too."

She took a weary breath and set her drink and cookie on the table.

"Wanna talk about it?" He folded his hands on the table in front of him.

"Not really."

"Then why'd you come over and join me?"

She shrugged as if trying to appear aloof. "Glutton for punishment, I guess."

Something was way off about her. There was a distance in her eyes that made her seem as though she were wrestling with some serious mental shit. And she looked even more tired than he'd originally thought, with dark circles under eyes.

"Are you okay?" he said.

"Sure." She shifted in her chair but kept her head down.

He reached over and gently brushed his fingers against her bruised cheek. The air fell still around them as she pulled her gaze up to his.

"Are you sure?" He was concerned for her. "I've never seen you so...I don't know...you just look drained of life, Karma." If her relationship with Brad was doing this to her, then she needed to run and run fast. The Karma he remembered was so full of life and vitality. She smiled all the time and laughed. She was witty and smart. This new Karma was none of those things. In fact, he hadn't seen her smile once since returning to Indianapolis. She seemed stuck in perpetual oppression, a little sad all the time.

She pulled away from his hand. "I'm fine."

"No, you're not, you're—"

Her eyes met his, blazing with anger. "Just stop. You lost the right to weigh in on my life the moment you left, Mark."

Even though her words were directed at him, he got the impression that her ire was aimed elsewhere. Maybe her reaction was the result of bottled-up resentment over how their relationship ended last year.

Or maybe it was something else. Something having to do with Brad and his daughter.

Whatever the cause, he held up his hands in surrender. "I'm sorry." He dropped his hands and offered a disarming smile, not wanting to upset her any more than she already was. "But despite what you think, I never stopped caring." Far from it. She had been all he'd thought about. "I never stopped hoping you'd be happy. That's all I want. For you to be happy. Which makes seeing you like this that much harder."

"Then close your eyes."

That would make things a lot easier. It would also be easier if he didn't care so damn much about her.

"If only I could." He lifted his hand again and tucked a loose strand of hair behind her ear then brushed his fingers against her cheek once more.

She sucked in her breath as her eyes filled with cautious anticipation, as if she wanted to pull away but couldn't.

Unspoken words landed on the tip of his tongue but remained rooted there. *I love you. I've always loved you and want to be with you now and forever.* The power of his devotion surprised even him.

"You're not someone I can take my eyes off of that easily, Karma." He flattened his palm against her cheek. "You're special. You deserve to be happy."

For a long moment, she stared into his eyes, and the harsh bitterness of whatever had upset her seemed to dissolve. The lines around her eyes softened. The tension around her mouth evaporated, and she started to resemble the woman Mark remembered.

Then her nostrils flared, and she pushed his hand

away. "How was your date last night?" she said icily.

"My date?" The shift in direction had come so swiftly he had to regroup.

"The woman you left the Stacked Pickle with?"

He slowly leaned back in his chair, never taking his gaze off her as last night came back into focus. "That wasn't a date."

Indignation blasted him as she recoiled. "So, you just fucked her then."

How interesting that she was so angry about something that shouldn't have made one bit of difference to a happily engaged woman. Like when she'd brought him his coffee without him having to ask, her jealous reaction was proof she still had feelings for him.

"I didn't say that."

If Mark had been the one-night-stand type, he would have ended up balls deep inside the woman he'd left the Stacked Pickle with. She'd been eager and willing, and he hadn't had sex in a year, but after walking out with her as if he had every intention of taking her home and letting her ride him all night, he dismissed her in the parking lot without so much as a kiss and drove back to his apartment alone.

He would rather masturbate than defile his cock with another woman's body. The only reason he'd cozied up to her in the first place was to see how Karma would react. Looked like he had his answer. She wore jealousy well.

Andrew brought out Karma's food, which she had ordered to go, then quickly hurried away. Apparently he'd picked up the vibe that Mark and Karma were in the middle of an uncomfortable discussion.

"You expect me to believe you didn't sleep with her?" There was just enough doubt in Karma's voice for Mark to know she was considering he might have been telling the truth.

"I don't expect you to believe anything. Why does it even matter?"

"It doesn't." She jutted out her chin and lifted her shoulders. "You...I just...I thought—"

He held up his hand, cutting her off. "Truce. You're with Brad. You've moved on. I get that. I need to do the same."

Some of her bravado faded, and a flicker of the Karma he remembered resurfaced. She was still so beautiful. Even more than he remembered. But her light had dimmed. Was that his fault for leaving her, or was it Brad's? Did Brad suppress her energy, hold her back from being the woman Mark knew she wanted to be? Maybe it was both their faults. The thought that he might have contributed to Karma's loss of self by leaving her sat about as well on his stomach as rotten eggs.

"Look," he said, "I'm sorry for how I behaved toward Brad at the game last night. You're right. I was instigating him before the game." He might as well own up to his part in things. "My only defense is that I feel protective of you." A *lot* protective. "Last night, my protective side came out. I began asking myself if Brad's good enough for you. Is he the man you're meant to be with the rest of your life? Does he make you laugh? Does he treat you right? Does he respect you?" He paused and took her hand. "Does he love you?"

Karma's gaze bore into his, but she gave nothing away of her thoughts. Maybe that was because she didn't want to admit the hard truth, or perhaps she simply didn't know the answers.

"How did the two of you meet?" He still held her hand, and she didn't seem to mind.

She bit her lip and looked out the window. "Actually, I met him during Flirt Quest."

"Flirt Quest?" Had Mark missed something? What the hell was Flirt Quest?

Her cheeks colored. "Remember when you wanted me to start talking to men? When you assigned me to flirt with them and stuff?"

Cold dread dribbled into Mark's heart. He remembered the night he'd *assigned* her to talk to men all too well...and how much he'd regretted it afterward every time he imagined her talking to another man. "Yes."

"Brad's the guy I met at the book store. The one I told you about."

She had told him Brad hadn't been her type. Well, apparently he was. "I see."

"Yeah, well, fate has a funny way of working, doesn't it?"

It sure did. And right now fate was laughing at him...about to choke on its own spittle, it was laughing so hard.

Because *he* was the reason why Karma was now engaged to a man she didn't belong with.

Karma's dinner was getting cold, and her angry stomach growled at being teased but not fed. She should have been shoving meatballs and warm, soft bread down her throat, but she couldn't make herself stand up and go home.

After the day she'd had, the last person she'd thought she wanted to see was Mark, but then she'd come over and plopped her ass down at his table like there was no place else to sit, even though almost every table was empty.

"What are you doing here, anyway?" she asked.

He pulled his hand away from hers and sat back. "Having dinner." He smiled, and the gesture was sexier than he probably intended it to be.

Ask a silly question, get a silly answer, right?

Her face heated. Traitorous blush response. Mark could still make her blush without even trying. "No, I mean —"

"I worked all afternoon," he said, saving her. "I didn't feel like cooking anything, and someone once told me this was the best place to eat in Clover." One corner of his mouth curled upward.

She briefly glanced away at the reminder of their past then glanced back at him. "You worked?"

There was that sexy smirk again. "I have a new job. I need to impress my boss by getting up to speed."

She nodded at his familiar playfulness. It reminded her of old times. He was always such a playful man, but his easy manner often covered a web of ulterior motives. If she had learned one thing from their time together, it was that Mark never did anything without a reason. The most innocent statement usually hid a complex plan to dislodge the truth.

Her memory flashed to something he'd said a few minutes ago. *You've moved on. I get that. I need to do the same.*

Whoa. *I need to do the same.* Present tense. Perhaps the ever-tight-lipped and carefully spoken Mark Strong had just slipped. If he still needed to move on, then that meant he hadn't. And if he hadn't, then what was he doing here? And why was he pretending to be so understanding of her relationship with Brad?

Maybe that was what last night had been about. Was that why he'd spent the entire evening with that woman and left with her? To make her think he had moved on when he really hadn't? Or maybe he'd been trying to make her jealous or use reverse psychology in an effort to make her think he was no longer interested. Then again, perhaps she was reading too much into all this and he *had* moved on.

"Earth to Karma." Mark waved his hand in front of her face, bringing her back to the present.

"What? Sorry." She took a deep breath and blinked several times.

"I asked if I'm keeping you." He gestured toward her to-go box.

"Oh. Uh…" She closed her eyes and shook off the niggling feeling that there was something important she wasn't getting a solid grasp on. "No. You're not keeping me. I just…um…"

"Why don't you go ahead and eat?" He gently tapped the side of her sandwich box so that it scooted about a half inch closer to her.

The nightmare of spending a few hours with Jade,

only to be ditched by her beau when Queen Diva threw a temper tantrum, slammed back into her mind, and her headache, which had been waning, surged back to full strength. "Okay. Sure." She rubbed her fingers over her brow in an effort to massage away the ache. Maybe food would help.

"I heard you tell Andrew…" he gestured toward the counter, "that you spent the day at the zoo with Brad and his daughter."

She forced herself not to cringe. "Yes."

"And she's twelve, right. I think that's what you told me before."

She nodded. "Yes. Twelve going on bitchy."

Mark chuckled. "You know it's only going to get worse."

She frowned at him. "Gee, thanks for the optimism."

"Just keeping it real." He casually crossed his arms.

"Well, don't." She opened her sandwich box and pulled off a warm chunk of meatball sub.

"What happened? What's her problem?"

"Besides hating my guts and wanting me to lose an eye?" She shoved the fragrant mess of bread, meat, and sauce into her mouth. "Where do I start?"

"How about the beginning?"

Regarding him, she took another bite and washed it down with cherry Coke. Should she really divulge her private life to Mark? Doing so would just give him more ammo for needling his way back into her life. Then again, the man made for an awesome sounding board, and her willpower was about checked out for the evening.

"Jade is spoiled rotten," she said, swallowing

another bite of sandwich. "Brad and his ex-wife got divorced when she was nine. Overcompensating for their guilt, both Brad and his ex now give her everything she wants. She throws a fit, they give. She cries, they give. She rants and behaves like a brat..."

"They give." Mark bit back a smile.

"Bingo." Karma chowed down another hunk of sandwich, her hungry stomach pushing her to keep filling it.

"And she doesn't like chocolate truffles?"

"You did overhear my conversation with Andrew, didn't you?"

"Every word."

She sipped her Coke. "Yes, she hated my chocolate truffles."

"Why? Did she say?"

"*They're grainy.*" Karma gave her best Jade impression. "*And they taste weird.*"

Mark laughed. "Taste weird? How do truffles taste weird? That makes no sense."

"I think it was the coffee I added. Plus, I didn't use regular milk chocolate." She offered a dubious snort. "The child obviously has no taste for the finer things in life, such as Ghirardelli dark chocolate."

"Well, I'd love to try them."

Karma swallowed another bite of her sub. "Well, they're in the car." She gestured toward her Honda Civic.

He frowned and glanced out the window. "Aren't you worried they'll melt?"

"Would it matter if they did? I mean, they're *grainy* and *taste weird*." She shouldn't be so upset over the rantings of a twelve-year-old in the middle of an identity crisis, but screw that. It didn't matter if the perpetrator was twelve or twenty. Bullying and harassment, as well as disrespect, hurt.

He shot her a don't-take-it-personally glance.

"Don't worry, they're in a cooler." She waved him off. "I did my best to make sure they stayed perfectly intact, even though I knew there was a good chance I'd be rebuffed." She stuffed the last bite of meatball sub in her mouth.

"And yet you did the right thing, anyway."

When had this conversation taken such a pleasant turn?

"I tried." She lifted her drink and leaned back in her chair as she took a long swallow. "You know. I made a special point to get up early to make them. I really tried to make them perfect. Have you ever made truffles?"

"Once or twice." He said it like once or twice meant at least two dozen times.

"So you know how long they take to make."

"Yes."

"This was only my second batch, but I really tried, and I put in all that effort, and then she—"

"Karma." Mark sat forward with a stern expression on his face. "Repeat after me. You can't...please... everybody."

Seriously? He wanted her to do affirmations now? Rolling her eyes, she said, "You can't please everybody. I know."

"Then stop trying. The only person who matters is you. As long as you're happy, who really gives a damn? Are *you* happy? *Are* you?"

Was she? Right this minute, she was probably happier than she had been in a while, and that was only because Mark was making her smile. But all day, she'd been a disaster. As far away from happy as a person could get. And for the past month, she hadn't had much cause to smile, either. Brad was always brushing her off. His work always took precedent when Jade didn't. Karma seemed destined to receive the scraps and nothing more.

"I don't know," she said weakly. Could she really say she was happy when she felt so miserable?

He tucked his newspaper under his arm then reached down and picked up his briefcase. "Well, maybe you need to figure that out." He stood. "Now, are you going to let me try those grainy-assed, weird-tasting truffles or not?"

The way he said it and the comically exasperated look on his face made her smile. "Fine, but don't say I didn't warn you." She grabbed her cookie and her drink then joined him as he opened the door for her.

"See ya," Andrew called from behind the counter.

"Bye, Andrew."

She led Mark to her car, leaned inside the passenger door, and pulled the barely touched batch of truffles from the cooler. "Here you go." She turned around and pulled the lid off the container.

Mark selected one covered with chopped almonds and popped it in his mouth. A couple seconds later, he made a face and planted his palm around his throat like he was choking.

Great. Were they really that bad?

"Ack! Awful!" Then he winked and smiled as he dug

another one out of the bowl. "Just kidding."

"You asshole." She smacked his arm, making him laugh as he ate one of the peppermint truffles.

"They're not perfect, but they're delicious," he said, licking his lips. He selected one covered with powdered sugar. "The flavor's there, you just need to perfect the technique. You'll get it."

She put the cap back on the bowl. "You want them?" She held the container toward him.

"Don't you want to take them home and eat them yourself?"

"Not really."

He gently plucked the container from her hand. "Bring back bad memories, do they?"

"Something like that."

They stood in silence for several seconds. What had started out as a crappy evening had turned out all right. She was full, her headache was almost gone, and she had a smile on her face.

"Don't think I'm not on to you, Strong," she said, shutting the passenger door and pointing a warning finger at him as she started around to the driver's side.

"Me? Whatever do you mean?" Damn that sexy smile and the man that went with it.

"You know what I mean." He was working his way back into her life. Or at least trying to. And yet she couldn't quite bring herself to be mad at him for it. In fact, she kind of enjoyed the attention. "Enjoy the truffles. Oh, and I want my bowl back."

"Yes, ma'am." He lifted the container in acknowledgement.

With an exasperated shake of her head, she got in

her car and, with one last glance Mark's way, pulled out of her parking space and toward the exit. By the time she pulled into her apartment complex, she was tapping her fingers on the steering wheel and singing along with the song on the radio.

Chapter 24

The next few weeks proved unable to mend the broken fence between her and Brad. Karma wanted him to see the double standard he was setting and how he was enabling Jade to continue disrespecting her, and Brad couldn't see either.

To make matters worse, Brad had asked her to join him and Jade on a trip to Florida during Jade's fall break from school only to renege the offer. He and Jade planned on visiting his parents during the two-week trip, and Karma was supposed to spend the first week with them. Get to meet the future in-laws type stuff.

Nix that. After Jade's outburst at the zoo, Brad thought it would be better if he and Jade went alone. He claimed he could smooth things over better that way and thought the time together would help soften Jade to the idea of him marrying Karma.

So, instead of packing her bags and heading off to the airport for a week in sunny Florida, Karma had cancelled her vacation and now sat on her couch, eating a banana, watching reruns of *Miami Vice* on an overcast and chilly mid-October Saturday afternoon.

Not the view of Miami she'd hoped for, but it would have to do.

Around eight o'clock, she started sneezing.

By nine, her throat was sore.

By ten, she was running a one-hundred-degree fever and rising.

Great. Maybe she should have kept her vacation on Solar's books. Looked like she was coming down with one helluva cold.

By Sunday morning, she no longer thought it was a cold. This was full-on flu.

Her body felt like a train had run over it ten times, her chest was as congested as a Los Angeles freeway, and her fever spiked to one hundred three.

She wasn't much better Monday morning and called in sick.

Tuesday, she seriously considered drowning in the bathtub as she took yet another Epsom salt bath in an effort to coax the germs out of her body.

On Wednesday morning, she felt a little better, so she dragged herself to work.

Big mistake. By the time she reached the top of the stairs, she was out of breath and sweating profusely. Maybe that meant her fever had finally broken.

Or not.

At her desk, she blew her nose and tried focusing on her e-mail through a blurry cloud.

"Karma?"

She glanced up as a coughing fit seized her. Mark was standing at her counter, a look of concern on his face.

"Good mordink." She sounded like a bullfrog with a plugged-up nose.

"Oh, no, no, no." He flicked his hand toward her.

"You're going home."

Home sounded good. Real good. Especially her bed or the couch or even the floor, as long as she could lay down.

"I'm...ah...ah...*AH-CHOO!* Fine."

He shook his head. "You are not fine. You're sick." He walked around her desk and placed his hand on her forehead. "And you're burning up. How long have you had this fever?"

She had to think a second. Brain processes weren't high on her body's priorities under an apocalypse of germ warfare. "Since..." *sniffle,* "Saturday."

"Shut off your computer." He took a step back and waited. "Come on. Turn it off."

"Mark." His name came out sounding like *Bark.*

"I'm taking you to the doctor. Let's go." He picked up her bags and nodded toward the hallway.

Part of her didn't want to be treated like a baby, but the other part of her just wanted to suck her thumb like one. There was something calming about someone else taking control of her life for a change, because right now, trying to get from day to day was wearing her down. That was probably why she was so sick. She'd let herself get run down. She'd let the stress of what was going on with Brad and Jade mutilate her immune system.

Only half reluctantly, she shut down her computer, stood, and let Mark help her down the stairs. She was so damn weak.

"Nancy, I'm taking Karma to the urgent care facility," he said to the receptionist as he passed her desk. "Could you please cancel my meetings and take messages from anyone looking for me?"

"Absolutely."

"I'll call in later."

Nancy swooshed them out the door.

"You don't have to do this," Karma said as he loaded her into the passenger seat of his car and tossed her bags in back.

He didn't have to, but she was grateful he was.

He climbed behind the wheel. "I know, but I'm going to anyway. So, just relax and let me handle everything, okay?"

Fine. She would let him handle it. She closed her eyes and leaned her blazing forehead against the cool glass. Somehow, she dozed off, waking up as Mark pulled into a parking space at the local MedCheck and shut off the engine.

Once again, he helped her out and guided her inside.

Another coughing fit hit her, and she could barely stay upright as the spasms doubled her over.

The lady behind the desk took one look and knew Karma's ailment wasn't good. Luckily, the place wasn't busy, and within minutes, Mark practically carried her back to an exam room.

After a nurse took her vitals and made a few notes about Karma's symptoms, she left the room. Mark sat beside her and wrapped his arm around her shoulders. He felt good. Solid. A pillar of strength keeping her upright.

She rested her head on his shoulder and closed her eyes. If only she'd stayed home and not tried to go to work.

"I'll take care of you," he whispered against her hair,

rocking her as he caressed her face.

Her body relaxed, and she snuggled a little closer.

A few minutes later, the doctor came in.

Karma gently pushed away from Mark's body.

"I'm Dr. Kane," he said with a smile.

"Hi." Just one syllable was enough to send her into another coughing spasm.

"That doesn't sound good. How about you have a seat up here for me." He patted the white tissue paper covering the examination table.

She did as he asked, and he slipped his stethoscope up the back of her shirt and asked her to take several deep breaths.

After listening for a few seconds, he placed his stethoscope around his neck.

He continued to examine her then sat down. She took her seat back beside Mark.

"I don't hear anything that would indicate pneumonia, just a bad case of the flu," Dr. Kane said. "We've been seeing a lot this over the past few weeks. The violent coughing is caused by bronchospasms. I'm going to prescribe an inhaler that should help relax the bronchioles and put a stop to that."

"What about the fever?" Mark asked.

"Tylenol, lots of rest, lots of fluids, and cold compresses."

"That's it?" Mark's arm was back around her shoulders. "No antibiotics?"

The doctor smiled. "Antibiotics won't help this. It's a virus. But, of course, if your wife gets worse, that may indicate a secondary infection, which could require antibiotics, but right now, I think she's just dealing with a bad case of the standard flu."

"Okay, Thanks." Mark took the inhaler prescription and tucked it into his jacket pocket.

Wait. Rewind. What? Had the doctor just referred to her as Mark's wife?

A few minutes later, as she sat in the passenger seat of Mark's car, she glanced across the seat. "He called me your wife."

"I know. I caught that." He backed out of the parking space.

"You didn't correct him."

He kept his eyes forward, but Karma caught the way his jaw clenched ever so slightly. "I didn't think it was important enough to correct him."

Mark had smiled when the doctor called Karma his wife. She hadn't been looking at him at the time, so she missed his reaction, but something about someone else acknowledging how perfect they looked together was deeply gratifying.

On the way back to her apartment, he swung by the store, and while she waited in the car, he dropped off her prescription at the pharmacy, grabbed some Tylenol and cold medicine, then grabbed the ingredients for homemade chicken soup before heading back to the pharmacy for her inhaler.

"What's all this?" she said as he loaded the groceries into the car. Poor thing sounded like someone had run sandpaper down her vocal chords.

"I'm going to make you some soup."

"Mark—"

"Hush. I'm going to do this, and you're not going to stop me." He handed her the white pharmacy bag containing her inhaler.

She took it out and took two puffs, as Dr. Kane had instructed.

Back at her apartment, he helped her up the stairs and carried her bags inside.

"I'm going to go down and get the rest of the groceries. Why don't you go change into your pajamas and get in bed. I'll bring you some Tylenol and juice in a few minutes."

Without protest, she nodded and dragged herself toward the hall. Mark retrieved the groceries from the car, carried them into her kitchen, and dug out the bottle of Tylenol, along with one of the half-gallons of orange juice he'd bought. When he was sick, orange juice always made him feel better.

"Here you go." He pushed open her bedroom door and sat on the edge of the bed as she sat up. He placed the pills in her palm and watched her wash them down. Then he took the empty glass and set it on her desk as she lay back on her pillow.

The desk hadn't been here last summer. It had been in the spare bedroom.

They'd shared a lot of special moments in this room. He'd held her in his arms, kissed her hair, made love to her. They'd talked about so many things here, some important, some fanciful. In this bed, they'd laughed with one another, he'd kissed away her tears, and he'd experienced the most incredible physical connection he'd ever felt with a woman.

Memories he thought he'd forgotten surged to life.

How he'd lain with her in his arms and stared at the seascape on the opposite wall, wishing they were there…on vacation…years from now…celebrating their anniversary.

He brushed his fingers over her sweltering forehead. "Get some sleep. I'll check on you in a bit."

Her eyes were already closed.

He quietly shut her bedroom door behind him and peeked into the spare room where her desk used to be. There was a treadmill in there now, along with a professional-grade spin bike. She'd been busy while he'd been away.

On a bookcase beside one of the windows, he found all the books he'd had her read stacked on one of the shelves. He picked up the one she'd called the papaya book and flipped through the pages.

The memories continued to rush through him. Their first kiss. The first time he'd made love to her. Her incredible innocence and the way she had grown into a confident, sexual woman by the time their affair ended.

Being here again was both gratifying and heartbreaking. He didn't want to be alone, anymore, but he didn't want anyone but Karma to quell his loneliness. If only she would see how bad Brad was for her and how good they could be together.

Setting the book back on the shelf, he left the room and returned to the kitchen.

Everywhere he looked, he was reminded of their time together. She was sitting across from him at the breakfast bar, eating the brownie he'd bought her the night she'd opened up about her past. She was at the table, her face crimson as he opened the case of four dildos he'd bought for her to prepare herself for his girth. She stood in front him at the sink, filling a vase with water for the flowers he'd brought her.

Karma's breathtaking image was everywhere he looked, even though she lay in bed, feverish, sick, and — hopefully — asleep.

Which meant he needed to get busy making his flu-busting homemade chicken soup.

Now, where was the soup pan?

Karma awoke and checked the time. Seven o'clock. Was that seven in the morning or seven at night? She glanced out the window. It looked like night.

Dragging herself out of bed, she made a pit stop in her bathroom, splashed cool water on her face, blew her nose, and brushed her teeth. She didn't feel quite as bad as she had earlier, but not by much. Instead of being run over by a train, she felt like it had only been a large truck.

Every joint ached as she tucked her box of Kleenex under her arm, padded in her socked feet to the bedroom door, and stepped into the hall.

Mark looked up from his perch on the couch, his laptop sitting — appropriately enough — in his lap, his shoeless feet propped on the coffee table.

He sat up and set his laptop on the table. "How do you feel?" He stood and met her halfway across the living room.

"A little better." But her voice still sounded like death.

"You want some soup and crackers?"

She nodded. Soup sounded good. So did crackers.

"Have a seat. I'll fix you a bowl."

She collapsed onto the couch and turned on *Wheel of Fortune*.

Mark returned with a large bowl of steaming goodness and a plate of what looked like Chicken in a Biscuit crackers. She loved those things.

"Here you go." He handed her the soup and set the plate on the arm of the couch.

She hugged the bowl of hot soup to her chest and spooned up a bite. After blowing across the surface so it didn't scald her mouth, she slurped it up. Even though she couldn't taste anything, the broth and tender chunk of chicken felt delicious.

He sat down beside her.

"Aren't you going to eat any?" she said, nibbling the corner off a cracker.

"I already ate a little while ago. Besides, I made this for you."

"Oh." She sucked in another spoonful of broth.

"Finding a road map," he said.

"Huh?" She looked up to find him pointing at the TV.

"The puzzle."

She glanced at *Wheel of Fortune*, and sure enough, even though some letters were missing, *Finding a Road Map* was the solution.

"Good job."

He shrugged. "It's a gift."

"It is, is it?"

"Not really, but it sounded good, right?" His army green eyes flashed to hers.

"If you say so." She ate another bite of soup. "This is really good. You made it from scratch?"

"Yep. Secret family recipe guaranteed to throw the flu right out of you."

She smiled and took another bite.

Unlike Brad, Mark enjoyed cooking, and not from a box, a can, or a jar. And this stock was too rich to have been anything less than homemade.

Glancing back to the TV, she continued eating her soup in silence. Then Mark returned her empty dishes to the kitchen and spent the next ten minutes cleaning and putting away the leftovers.

When he came back into the living room, he handed her a cherry Popsicle and sat down beside her.

She stared at the Popsicle then smiled at him. "You really didn't have to do this today. You went way over and beyond here." He'd cancelled meetings and put off work just to take care of her.

He ruffled her already unruly hair. "Just taking care of my assistant. She's pretty darn important to me. I couldn't do my job without her."

His words felt like they held a double meaning, and she suddenly wished she hadn't sent out all those résumés a few weeks ago. She was beginning to think she might actually be able to pull off working for Mark. And there were other things she was beginning to think she could do with him, too.

She didn't really want to think about those other things right now, though. Because if she did, she would stress out over what exactly that meant, including figuring out what to do about the engagement ring on her finger, as well as what to do about Mark's phobic

Donya Lynne

aversion to commitment, which had left her hanging like rotting fruit on the branch last year.

"You gonna be okay if I head out?" He was still dressed in his slacks and dress shirt, even though his sleeves were rolled up.

She honestly didn't want him to leave, but it probably wasn't a good idea for him to stay.

"I think so."

"Well, I'm only a phone call or text away if you need anything. And I mean that. If you need anything, call me. I don't care what it is or if it's three o'clock in the morning. Okay?"

She sighed and offered a weak smile. "Okay, Dr. Strong."

He grinned. "And don't you forget it." He gathered his laptop and packed it into his bag then paused. "I know we've got a past, Karma, and I know you're with someone else now, but I'd still like to think we're friends." His gaze met hers. "You can count on me if you need anything."

She briefly looked away then met his gaze again. So much about Mark was ideal. He was handsome, healthy, intelligent, successful. He was the kind of man every woman wanted. If only he could get out of his own way and allow himself to be happy.

"Mark, you're a good man." She nodded tightly, remembering all the wonderful things she had learned about Mark last year, as well as the tragedy of his past. He had opened up to her, and she didn't think he opened up to many. Their time together had been so very special, and it was obvious to her that it had been special for him, too. They had shared something. A

246

common bond. An understanding. Somehow they just *got* one another, and even now, with her hand promised to another and her mind clouded by fever — or maybe *because* her mind was clouded by fever — their connection was almost palpable. "Right now, I think you're the only man I *can* count on." She quickly looked away as the truth of her own statement slammed into her.

Even though what they'd had last summer hadn't been enough to make him want to stay with her, Mark seemed more committed to her than Brad was. Her fiancé seemed more willing to push her needs aside than acknowledge them, whereas Mark pushed his own needs aside to put hers first. Right now, with fever draining her strength, she didn't want to think about what this revelation meant for her and Brad's future, but it didn't feel like a good thing.

Silence stretched between them, and then Mark knelt in front of her and put his hands on her knees. "I'll always be here for you, no matter what." He leaned forward and hugged her.

Damn, did that feel good. A full-on, unsolicited hug. She'd been starved for affection lately, and his solid warmth and tenderness hit the spot.

After holding her for several seconds, he pulled away, stood, and grabbed his bag. "Now, take two more Tylenol and rest. Don't even think about coming into work this week."

She crossed her finger over her heart. "I promise."

He grinned and headed for the door. "I'll check on you tomorrow."

With that, he was gone, leaving in his wake more

Donya Lynne

questions than answers.

Chapter 25

Karma's Blog
Sunday, October 28
"Football Could End My Engagement"

B doesn't like football. It's just one of the many differences between B and me. I love football. I love everything about it. The rush of a successful Hail Mary. The frenzy of the fans after the running back busts through the defensive line into open field, gunning for the end zone. The hurried field goal in the final seconds of the game that changes who wins and who loses in the blink of an eye.

For me, football is a religion. It's the seed of tradition and defines autumn. Without football, the departure of summer and changing of the leaves wouldn't be so special. It would be just another reason to dread the coming winter instead of cause to bundle up and brave the outdoors.

I once went to a football game at Notre Dame. A mighty feat, I must say. Not many can get tickets to a Notre Dame football game. The day was cold and dappled with drenching rain showers. The stadium seats were warped, uncomfortable wooden benches. By the end of double overtime, my feet were blocks of ice. But that day was one of the best times of my life.

B would have hated it.

These are the things I'm sacrificing by marrying him.

Do I want to sacrifice something I enjoy so much?

But football isn't the only way B and I are different. He's thirty-nine years old. I'll only be twenty-six in a couple of weeks. He likes classic rock. I prefer easy jazz. He's a workaholic. I want to spend more time living and enjoying life. And let's not forget his overly entitled, spoiled rotten daughter. B's and my ideas about parenting obviously lie at opposite ends of the spectrum.

Will he and I really be able to have children together if our styles are so vastly different?

About the only area where B and I agree is in our love of running, but marathons do not a marriage make.

Then there's M. Perfect, charming M.

He's the whole package. Everything about him aligns with everything about me. There's a give-and-take with him. He understands me without my even having to try, and he instinctively seems to know what I need before I do. It's always been that way between M and me.

This week, I've been sick, and M has checked on me every day. He took me to the doctor, made me chicken soup, brought me more meds and Kleenex yesterday. He's been terrific.

But I want to get married. I want to have a husband and a family. M isn't capable of that. The time I spent with him last year proved as much.

So, where does that leave me, other than between a rock and hard place? On one hand is B, who is ready and eager to commit, but who, the longer I'm with him, feels further and further apart from me. On the other is M, who fits me like a tailored suit, but who wants nothing of commitment.

How did I find myself here?

Karma logged out and set her laptop on the coffee table

then plunged her hand into the box of Chicken in a Biscuit crackers sitting beside her on the couch. Mark had brought her two more boxes yesterday, along with a half-dozen boxes of Kleenex, which should last her an entire year now that her flu was winding down. He'd also brought her cough drops, another container of orange juice, and more Popsicles. Oh, and then there was the giant Crock-Pot of chili. She couldn't forget the chili he'd made, which was a nice accompaniment to a day of college football.

And it would make a fine lunch and dinner for a day of professional football tomorrow, too. She turned on the TV and snuggled under her throw blanket.

Around four o'clock, her phone rang. She turned the sound down on the TV and picked up.

"Hey, Lisa." She still sounded awful, but at least she felt better.

"Hi, girl. How are you feeling?"

"Better."

"Good." Lisa's voice sounded tight, like she'd called for a reason but wasn't sure how to bring it up. "Glad to hear it."

"Is that why you called? To check on me?" Prodding Lisa when she got like this was the best way to make her spill.

"Partly. But...um..."

"Out with it, Leese."

"I just read your blog."

Karma's mind froze, and it took her a minute to process Lisa's announcement. "Wait, how do you know about my..." Then she remembered when Lisa and Daniel had helped her clear out her spare room last spring. "Ooohh. That's right. I told you about it when you and Daniel helped me move in my treadmill. Have you been reading it all this time?" She suddenly tried to remember all the posts she'd written and all the secrets she'd divulged.

"Off and on. I haven't read it in a while, but I looked at it today while watching the game, and…"

Oh no. Lisa had read her Brad and Mark musings. She dropped her face into her free hand.

"Karma, what's going on?"

"I don't know." She lowered her hand to her lap and glanced out the window. "I think I'm in trouble here, Lisa."

"Are you falling back in love with Mark?"

How did you fall back in love with someone you had never stopped loving? "Lisa, I don't think I've ever fallen *out* of love with him."

"You can't do that. You can't be in love with him if you're going to marry Brad."

"Tell that to my heart." She laid her head against the back of the couch.

"What about Brad?"

Just his name sent shudders down her back. "Brad and I just aren't working, Lisa. If you read my blog post, you know that."

"Yes, I got that impression. So, are you going to call off the engagement?"

"I don't know what I'm going to do." Brad wasn't a bad guy. He was a decent man. They just didn't see eye to eye about a lot of things, and there just wasn't any passion there. She didn't feel a connection to him like she did with Mark. "Do you think I'll ever find a man that's the best of both worlds?"

"What do you mean?"

"You know, a man who makes me feel like Mark does but wants to get married like Brad?"

Lisa laughed. "Gee, Karma, you're not asking for much, are you?"

She sighed. "I'm looking for the impossible, aren't I?"

"Naw, you're not." Lisa paused. "Like I said before, you *can* have both. I believe it's possible. And you know, you could do worse. A lot of married women would kill to have just a smidgeon of what you've got with Mark, and a lot of single women would give their left arm for what you have with Brad."

"What are you saying?"

"Just that no one's perfect, sweetie. But you have to decide who's closer to *your* definition of perfection. You're never going to get everything you want. That's why you have to weigh the pros and cons and compromise. What can you live with, and what's a deal breaker? If Mark wants to be with you — *really* wants to be with you — but just can't call it a commitment, then is that really so bad? It's just semantics, right?"

"True, but who says he wants to be with me?"

"Did you even read your own blog post? Of course he wants to be with you. Why would he be taking care of you like he is if he didn't?"

As always, what Lisa said made sense. "You've got a good point."

"Of course I make a good point. I'm awesome."

Karma started to laugh but ended up coughing instead. After catching her breath, she said, "Don't make me laugh or you'll kill me."

"I'm sorry. Couldn't help myself." Lisa snickered. "But hey, seriously, it doesn't take a genius to see Mark is still into you. And I mean *into* you. I'm not saying Brad's a bad guy or that you should ditch him, but, Karma, you deserve to be happy, and I just don't see you being happy with Brad. Sure, having Mark back threw you off in the beginning, and of course you were angry, but now things are settling down, and in the last few weeks you've been the happiest I've seen you in a long time. That can't just be coincidence."

"Okay, so the next obvious question is, what about my job? Let's say I decide to give Mark another chance. What then? I'm his assistant. You're in human resources. If he and I get involved, I can't be his assistant, anymore, can I?"

"We can figure it out. There's always a solution. First, you just need to decide what you want."

"Meaning Brad or Mark."

"Yes. You have to choose. If you want Mark and he wants you, then we'll deal with what to do about your job later."

Karma frowned and nibbled on her bottom lip. "What if I told you I'm already dealing with it?" She squeezed her eyes closed, unable to believe she was actually going to tell Lisa that she'd sent out résumés.

"What do you mean?"

"Lisa, don't kill me, but I started putting out feelers with other companies after Mark returned."

"You what?" Lisa's voice shrilled.

"I was upset." Karma slapped her hand on the couch. "I didn't think I'd be able to work with him, so I sent out a couple dozen résumés." And she'd actually received an e-mail from one of her former professors at Purdue with word about a possible position opening soon. But she hadn't heard back, yet.

"Have you been contacted by any of them?"

"No. Not yet." No sense telling her about the e-mail from her professor until she had more definitive news.

Lisa blew out a relieved sigh. "Good. Don't leave. You can't leave."

"But—"

"No. We'll figure it out, okay? Just...don't accept any offers if you get any."

"What if I receive an offer I can't refuse? You know, like more money and a chance to work in my preferred field?" She really wanted to use her writing degree someday sooner rather than later.

"You'd sell out like that?"

"I wouldn't be selling out."

"Oh, you know what I mean."

"Whatever." Karma glanced up at the score as it flashed on the screen before a commercial break.

"So, you're going to think about what I said?"

Karma dug another cracker from the box. "Yes, Mother."

Lisa laughed. "My vote is for Mark, but then I've never really warmed up to Brad. He's just too...I don't know...serious. Mark's like yummy, melted marshmallows on a bed of warm chocolate. Brad's cold graham crackers."

"Ah, but marshmallows and melted chocolate are just a gooey mess without graham crackers to hold them together."

"Oh, jeez. Listen to that philosophy."

"Just keepin' it real." Karma bit into her cracker. Pieces fell onto the blanket and she brushed them off.

"Well, I'll take the gooey mess and lick it off my plate. How's that?"

"Hey, that's *my* gooey mess you're talking about. If anyone's going to be doing any licking, it's me."

"You've got graham crackers, remember? You can't have the sweet, gooey mess until you throw out the crackers."

"Nice visual." Karma tossed the half-eaten Chicken in a Biscuit cracker back in the box.

"I'm here all night for your entertainment."

Karma forced herself not to laugh so she didn't erupt into another coughing frenzy. "How do our conversations always revolve around food?"

"I don't know, but now I'm hungry. I'm gonna go find some chocolate and marshmallows."

"Hey!"

"Hey yourself. You stop eating the crackers and you can have the chocolate."

"Fine. I'll think about it."

They said their good-byes and Karma glanced at the blue box with the chicken on the front sitting beside her. Then she smiled and shook her head. They weren't grahams, but wasn't it funny how she'd stopped eating those crackers just about the time Lisa told her to?

God, was she really considering doing this all over again?

And if she did, would Mark only break her heart?

Chapter 26

Friday, November 16

Mark smiled at the caller ID on his phone.

"Rob, hey." He stood and glanced out his office window.

"What are you still doing in Indianapolis?" Rob sounded uptight. Then again, this was his last weekend as a bachelor. Come Monday, he would be a kept man.

"Relax. There was an emergency with one of our clients, and I needed to oversee things. But don't worry. I'll be there."

"Just don't miss your fitting in the morning or Holly will kill me."

"Well, just make sure to keep the Valium coming and I won't kill you first." He'd promised Rob he'd be his best man, but just thinking about standing at the front of the church in his tuxedo gave him a queasy stomach.

"Yeah, yeah, you and your Valium. How's things with your little lady?"

"She's not my little lady," he said quietly, glancing over his shoulder to his open office door.

Things had softened between him and Karma since

the day he bumped into her at Greek Tony's, and even more since the day he took her to the doctor. But she still wore that godforsaken diamond on her finger, and until she broke things off with Brad—if she ever did— he wouldn't intrude. He refused to do to Brad what Antonio had done to him when he stole Carol out from under him seven years ago, going on eight. Becoming the very thing he loathed was not the solution and would just make things worse for all involved.

"Damn. I was hoping you'd show up with her and make it a double wedding."

"Fuck you." Mark tossed his gaze back out the window. "You're full of shit, you know that?"

"Yeah, but at least I'm happily full of shit."

Mark grinned. "I'm happy for you. And don't worry, I'll be there. I swear."

"You'd better be. I'm counting on you."

"Hey, you're the one who scheduled the wedding on a Monday. If you'd scheduled it on a weekend like a normal person I'd have been there days ago and we wouldn't be having this conversation. Who the hell gets married on a Monday?"

Rob chuckled. "It was Holly's idea. Relatives were flying in from out of town for Thanksgiving, and since everyone was taking the week off, anyway, she thought we'd save some money taking a weekday instead of a prime-time weekend slot."

"Smart woman you're marrying there, Rob."

"I know. But the weekend had been booked, anyway, so we didn't really have much choice."

"And now the truth comes out."

"And don't you breathe a word of it to anyone.

Holly likes people thinking I'm marrying a sensible, frugal woman."

"Aren't you?"

"Yes, but I guess making everyone think she purposely chose Monday to save money ices it."

Mark chuckled. "Okay, let me get off here. I just need to take care of a few more things and then I'm on the road. Car's already packed."

"Okay, see you later."

He hung up and reached for his coffee cup. He had a long drive ahead of him in a couple of hours, so one more mug of coffee wouldn't hurt, even though it was late in the afternoon.

As he approached his door, he heard Karma gasp from her desk.

"What? Oh no." She sounded upset.

He stepped out to find her on her phone. When he saw the look of dread on her face, he knew whatever news she'd just received wasn't good.

"Is she okay? What's wrong?" Tears sprang into her eyes and she covered her mouth.

Mark hurried to her desk and mouthed, "What's wrong?"

She shook her head and began to cry. "I'll be right there. Don't do anything, yet. Just let me get there." She hung up and immediately burst into tears.

"Karma? What's wrong?"

"It's my cat, Spookie," she said, grabbing her purse. "She collapsed and is struggling to breathe." She bolted out of her chair, dashing her fingers across her tear-streaked cheeks. "I have to go. I need to go."

Mark stepped aside. He knew what it was like to

lose a beloved pet. Growing up, they'd had dogs. He still remembered when they'd had to put down his favorite, a golden retriever named Rex. He'd cried for days.

"Do you need a ride?" He wasn't sure she should be driving if she was this upset.

She shook her head and darted past. "No. I'm fine. Thanks. I just want to get there."

"Be careful." He watched her rush down the hall and disappear around the corner.

If only there was something more he could do to comfort her, because his gut told him this wasn't going to end well. But comforting her was Brad's job, not his. Mark wasn't a philanderer, and he didn't take women from other men. Others could do what they pleased, but for him, a taken woman was off-limits. So, as much as he wanted to be the man to dry all Karma's tears and ease her heartache, he wouldn't break that one rule. He never had, and he never would.

But damn it, he wanted to fill that position if it ever became available again.

Karma raced to the vet's office, a million thoughts training through her head. What was wrong with Spookie? Would she live? Was she going to lose the best kitty in the world today? How old was Spookie, anyway? She was old. At least fifteen years. That's old for a cat. Why hadn't she seen this coming? She should have tried harder to find an apartment that allowed cats, because it looked like she'd run out of time.

Running up the sidewalk, she shoved open the

veterinarian's door. Her dad was waiting for her.

"Where is she?"

To some people, cats were just animals, but to Karma, Spookie was like her own child, or maybe a baby sister. Spookie was as much a member of the family as she and her brother were.

Her dad ushered her down the hall to one of the exam rooms. "They've got her in here." He pushed open the door.

Spookie lay on the exam table, panting. Karma's mom stood beside her, crying. Her tears splattered on the Formica countertop. This wasn't good.

"What's wrong with her?"

Her mom grabbed a tissue and blew her nose. "They say she has tumors in her lungs."

"T-tumors?"

Mom nodded, and the tears that had been balancing on her lower rims fell to her cheeks. "I'm sorry, honey, but—"

"No. Don't say it." Karma began to cry and knelt down.

Spookie turned her head toward her.

"She's purring," Karma heard the telltale ticking of Spookie's purr box. "That's a good sign, right?" She looked up at her dad.

He shook his head. "She's purring because she wants to be strong for us...to let us know it's okay to..."

Okay to let her die. That's what Dad had almost just said. That Spookie knew her time was up and that she wanted to let them know that she was ready to go. Well, Karma wasn't ready. She hadn't had enough time with her, yet.

Drowning in tears, Karma placed her forehead against Spookie's. "I'm not ready to see you go, yet, pumpkin."

The black furball gave her head a weak nudge.

"I love you, too, Spookers. Now hang on, okay. Just hang on for me." She didn't care, anymore. If Spookie made it through this, she would smuggle her into her apartment and keep her there in secret. Screw the apartment managers.

Then the veterinarian came in. Karma listened as he explained the prognosis, her heart falling with every word.

"The tumors have filled her lungs with fluid," he said. "We can drain the fluid, but there's nothing we can do about the tumors. In a few days, maybe a couple of weeks at the most, you'll be right back in here. Her quality of life will suffer."

Long story short. It was time to say good-bye. Karma's memory flashed back to when Spookie had been a kitten. A tiny bundle of playful black fur. From the moment she'd laid eyes on Spookie and vice versa, the two had been bonded. Spookie had been her constant companion growing up. Her one true friend when the kids in school teased her. Karma would come home from school and go to her room in tears. Then Spookie would snuggle into her lap, purring, and make everything okay.

And now she was dying.

"Can I stay?" If Karma had to say good-bye, she wanted to stay with her as long as she could and be with her right up to the very end...to give Spookie all that the little kitty had given her many times over.

"Of course. I'll give you a few minutes." The vet quietly left the room.

Her mom and dad kissed her on the cheek then took their leave to wait outside.

As soon as the door clicked shut, Karma broke down in uncontrollable sobs and picked Spookie up. Cradling her like a baby, she kissed her furry head and snuggled her close.

"I love you, pumpkin. I wish I could have spent more time with you, but, like a big dummy, I thought we had all the time in the world. That'll teach me to put off what's important, huh?" She kissed her head again then nuzzled her tiny black, triangular nose.

She would never give Spookie nose-kisses again. This was it. The big good-bye.

Their time together was all too short, and the vet returned a few minutes later. Karma set Spookie back on the table, keeping her palm resting against her furry abdomen as the vet injected the concoction that would send Spookie into Heaven.

As the life left her little body, Karma broke down again and could barely see the form authorizing the veterinarian's office to cremate her. Her tears filmed everything in blurriness. Somehow she scrawled her name on the signature line then turned over her precious baby to the caretaker who came and took her away.

Now came the long process of coping with her loss. More of the five stages of loss. Thanks to Jan, she knew what to expect. She was already well into the anger phase, because she was mad at herself for not taking more time and forcing herself to get off her ass sooner to find a new place to live. One that welcomed pets.

So, yeah. She was in anger. The time for denial and bargaining was over.

She met her parents in the lobby and waited for her dad to handle the paperwork with the desk clerk, and then the three of them trudged out the door.

"You want to come over?" her mom said, her eyes bloodshot. "We can have a nice dinner..." She dabbed a tissue under her nose.

"No." Karma just wanted to go home and cry. "But thanks anyway." She sniffled and wiped her eyes.

"If you need anything, just call. Okay, honey?" Her dad kissed the top of her head. "It'll get better."

She knew with time that the pain would pass and she would move on, but right now, her heart hurt. "Thanks, Dad." She hugged him then made her way to her car.

As she sank into the driver's seat, she pulled out her phone and texted Brad.

I need to see you. Maybe they'd had a rough few weeks, but tonight she needed him.

A moment later, her phone dinged. *Are you okay?*

No. I just put Spookie to sleep. Can you come over?

Long wait. *I'm really tied up tonight. We're way behind on this project. Can it wait?*

Really? Can it wait? As if she could roll back the clock and delay the lethal injection that had just sent her baby across the rainbow bridge.

Brad's lack of emotional support knew no bounds, and it was really starting to piss her off.

She sent a reply. *Never mind. I'll be fine.*

A few seconds later, he responded. *I'll make it up to you. Gotta go. Talk later.*

Just this once, couldn't she be his first priority? Oh but no. Once more, she was relegated to second place. Or maybe that was third. Jade was first. Job was second. And Karma got whatever was left over, if anything.

Was this what it would be like to be married to him?

She lifted her gaze and stared out the window as cold realization swept through her. Brad would never be what she needed him to be. He was nice. He was polite. He was handsome. But he just didn't align with Karma's personality or her soul. She chuffed and shook her head. A few minutes ago, she had needed Brad, but just that quickly—with one dismissive text—Brad had gone from being her fiancé, a man she *thought* she needed, to a nonentity. Her faith in him and their relationship had finally shattered. This was the proverbial straw that broke the camel's back, and now all she felt when she thought about him was...emptiness. Where she should have felt love, all she felt was a cold void. She would never get what she needed from Brad, and she was done trying.

She took off the engagement ring and dropped it in her wallet. If her head wasn't already such a mess over Spookie, she would return the ring to him now, but she needed time. Time to regroup and gather her thoughts. Time to grieve. She would deal with Brad later, when she had the mental fortitude and emotional strength to officially oust him from her life without breaking down in tears. She could only handle one loss at a time, and right now, dealing with Spookie's death was her priority.

Her phone dinged with a text. She almost didn't look at it, because she didn't want to see what else Brad had to say.

Are you okay?

It was from Mark.

A tiny starburst of warmth bloomed in the center of her chest. *Mark.* He would never dismiss her the way Brad had. He would always be there for her when it mattered.

She nibbled her thumbnail and glanced toward the vet's office. She'd just learned a valuable lesson. Never put off until tomorrow what you should do today. She'd wasted too much time not spending it with Spookie, and now she was gone. Karma would never hold her or hear her purr again.

She didn't want to make the same mistake with Mark.

With determination—and maybe an ounce or two of reckless abandon with a side of pissed-off-and-fed-up—guiding her, she typed out a text.

No, I'm not okay. Are you busy?

Within seconds, Mark replied.

I've always got time for you. How's Spookie?

Tears trickled down Karma's cheeks. *We had to put her to sleep.*

I'm so sorry. Can I do anything to help?

Unlike Brad, Mark seemed eager to help. To do whatever he needed to make her feel better. And not because he wanted to get with her, but because he was just that kind of man. Genuine. Caring. Compassionate.

Understanding.

Can you come over? She hesitated for only a second before hitting *send.*

I'm on my way.

He was supposed to leave for his friend's wedding, and yet he was willing to come over and give her his valuable time, which he had very little of right now. That spoke volumes about his character as opposed to Brad's.

As one life shattered inside her mind, another began piecing itself together.

Me, too. I'm just leaving the vet's office.

I'll wait for you if I beat you there.

Thank you. This means a lot to me. I know you have to leave for Chicago tonight. I won't keep you long.

Don't worry about that. Take all the time you need. Now, drive safely.

The minute she pulled in front of her apartment and saw Mark sitting in his car, she burst into tears again. She was an emotional wreck. All the way home, she'd vacillated between sadness over Spookie and anger at Brad, and now sorrow took over for good as Mark got out of his car and took a couple of hesitant steps toward her.

His generosity floored her. It was possible that he wasn't Mr. Right, but by God, he was at least Mr. Right Now.

As she climbed out of her car and walked up the sidewalk, tears streaming her cheeks, he strolled toward her, his face full of sympathy, his head tilted compassionately to one side.

"Ssshh." He collected her into his arms and rocked her as she huddled against his chest. "Come on. Let's go inside, okay?" He pulled back and lifted her face. His warm eyes beseeched hers.

She let him lead her inside and up to her apartment, where he helped her out of her coat and draped it over the arm of the couch with his.

"Want me to make you some tea?"

She nodded and trailed behind him as he went to the kitchen.

For all his faults—or rather for his *one and only* fault—Mark epitomized everything she wanted in a man. He was husband material, lover material, father material. He was all of it except for the commitment part. But as Lisa had said, did that really matter? As long as he wanted to be with her, did it really make a difference whether or not he tied their relationship up inside a legal document that bound them to love and obey one another till death do they part?

And Lisa was right about something else. He wouldn't be doing all this—taking her to the doctor, putting off his trip to Chicago, all of it—if he didn't still feel something for her.

She stared at his broad back as he filled her teapot with water then set it on the stove and dug through her cupboard for cups.

"You know," he said, turning. "We had this dog when I was a kid."

She sat down on one of the bar stools. He stood across from her.

"His name was Rex. Man, I loved that dog." His eyes glazed as if with fond memories. "He was my buddy. He slept with me, waited with me at the bus stop, met me there when I got home from school. Rex was my shadow, more like a brother than a pet."

She smiled at the wistful expression on his face.

"One day, Rex got really sick. He'd been losing weight for a while, but we didn't think anything of it at first. We took him to the vet, and they told us Rex had cancer."

Tears stung the backs of Karma's eyes, and Mark came around the counter. She turned to face him.

"We had to make the same decision you did today." He took her hand. "It was hard, but it was the humane thing to do. But man, I cried for days after that. Took me weeks to get over losing him."

"They're like our children or our best friends, aren't they?" She sniffled and cleared the emotion from her throat.

He nodded. "I don't think anyone who looks lightly on the death of an animal has much of a heart."

She tried to smile but ended up crying again instead. Mark pulled her into his arms and rocked her back and forth. "I'm sorry, sweetheart."

He didn't try to tell her it would be okay or that she'd be fine. He just held her and let her cry.

When the teakettle whistled a couple of minutes later, he slowly let go, returned to the stove, and turned off the burner. The loss of his warmth felt foreign. She wanted him back. Wanted to be in his arms again.

Scooting off the bar stool, she approached him from behind, hesitated for a slow heartbeat, and then eased her arms around his waist, pressing her cheek against his back.

His body stiffened then relaxed as he let out a quiet sigh and placed his hand over hers.

For several long moments, they remained like that in her kitchen, her hugging him from behind, her hold growing stronger with each passing second. Beneath his shirt, his hard abdomen felt like ribbed plywood, sturdy and muscular. She opened her fists and spread her fingers, pressing her palms against his torso.

His body rose heavily as he inhaled. "Karma..." he whispered, his voice gruff and filled with confusion.

This felt right. Her with him. Him with her. She lifted her cheek and kissed his back through his shirt. Just pressed her lips against him and fell still, absorbing his warmth.

The rise and fall of his body told her his breathing had accelerated, and the way he leaned forward and lowered his head confirmed his interest. He liked what she was doing. It was turning him on. She remembered the nuances of his body language enough to gauge how she affected him now, and his resistant shield was quickly evaporating.

And she wanted it to. She wanted the warmth he provided. The security. The closeness.

With her arms still around him, he slowly turned and took her face in his hands. His dark, turbulent eyes ranged her face then fixed on hers.

"Karma...?" He looked disoriented, his eyebrows furrowed, his mouth slightly open as if he were on the verge of speaking or trying to catch his breath.

Without saying a word, she lifted onto her toes, pulling herself up...until her lips met his. His breath caught and held, and his eyes drifted closed. So perfect. His lips still felt perfect against hers, even in such a simple, chaste kiss. His eyelids dragged open halfway, and she kissed him again, letting her lips linger as she let the tip of her tongue roll lazily against his bottom lip.

They were suspended in a bubble, hardly breathing, barely moving, locked eye-to-eye. The magic that had been them for four months stretched around them, blossoming like a rose, shimmering brighter as the seconds ticked by, coming back to life like a resuscitated butterfly, its wings fluttering, then beating stronger as it reanimated.

As she kissed him a third time and lightly nipped his lip, she felt his resolve snap.

The air rushed out of him as his arms wrapped around her waist and pulled her against his body. He nearly stole her soul as he claimed her mouth, his tongue diving to meet hers on a hungry exhale.

Her entire body flamed to life, having been starved for too long of physical affection. Stumbling backward, her back crashed into the wall, and his hands drove under her blouse. In the time it took to exhale, she was topless. Her fingers fumbled with the buttons on his shirt as he flung his tie to the floor then unfastened her slacks. In seconds, she was in her white lace bra and underwear, her fingers combing through the familiar trace of hair on his chest. He lifted her off the floor, and she wrapped her legs around his waist.

"You got a tattoo." She ran her fingertips around the dark circle and Asian hieroglyphs on his chest, just left of his sternum.

"Yes." Something about the look on his face revealed there was a special meaning to his ink. Had he lost a loved one in the year they'd been apart?

"What's it mean?"

"Not now." His breath came in urgent bursts. "Not like this."

He had lost someone close, hadn't he? The last thing she wanted to do was remind him of that loss now. Whatever his tattoo meant, it could wait. She would let him tell her later, in his own time.

"Make love to me," she whispered against his mouth.

He was already carrying her to the bedroom, where he lowered her onto the bed, coming down on top of her.

Yes. This was what she wanted. Him. Mark. She wanted Mark. They clicked. Everything about the two of them together felt right in a hundred different ways. For the first time in over a year, her body sang, and it was because of him. Her body had chosen.

Every nerve ending celebrated. Every cell rejoiced. She was home. With Mark, she was where she belonged.

Tears of realization sprang to her eyes as he pushed down his pants and kicked them off the foot of the bed. She had thought she'd moved on, that she was over him, when all along she'd only been in denial. She was nowhere near over him and never would be. She'd fought her feelings when he'd returned two months ago, but she'd only been fighting the inevitable. She couldn't fight fate, anymore. All she wanted was to feel him against her again. Inside her.

Before she knew it, he'd stripped her out of her bra and panties. There was nothing left between them but air.

Coming Back To You

"Condom?" he said between kisses. But he said it as if he were asking permission, as if he was giving her one final chance to stop him.

"Top drawer." She pointed to the nightstand. Permission granted.

He fumbled to open it then reached in, fishing a condom from the box.

"I've missed you," he whispered against her mouth. The sound of tearing cellophane made her heart skip impatiently. One step closer to finding her way back.

"I've missed you, too."

She'd barely spoken the words when he sank inside her. They both let out a ragged exhale, and she dug her fingers into the back of his shoulders.

So full. He filled her completely. Her inner muscles clenched, already eager to send her into the clouds.

"I won't be able to go slow." His jaw was taut, the skin around his eyes strained.

"I don't want it slow." She rolled her hips against him. What she wanted was hard and fast. She wanted to feel again. For months, she had felt nothing. Sexually, she'd been an apathetic vacuum, defunct and void of arousal. But right now, she was once again liberated. The shackles of resentment and sexual frustration fell away, and pleasure bloomed inside her.

"I don't want to hurt you."

"You won't hurt me." And even if he did, at least pain was feeling. But she was too aroused for that. "Now, fuck me."

Once more, his restraint snapped, and he was fucking her in a way she had never been fucked. Not even when he'd taken her against the wall in the

273

conference room—as savage as that had been—measured up to the vicious way his body took hers now.

It was as if he hadn't had sex in forever. As if he'd been starving for affection as much as she had. Just how long had it been since he'd slept with a woman? Surely, there had been others since he'd left. The woman from New Year's Eve, for instance.

But now wasn't the time to think of that.

Within minutes, they were both speeding toward climax, crying out with every stroke. Karma didn't care if her neighbors heard. Let them hear. Let them bear witness to the magical, wonderful moment when she and Mark had found their way back to one another.

"Oh God! Oh God!" She thrashed her head on the pillow, arching against him.

"Fuck!" His teeth grazed her shoulder as he gasped for air, pounding and thrusting into her body over and over.

She couldn't breathe. Her voice failed her. She was about to come. And not just come, but light up so severely she'd be able to energize a small town.

"I can feel you getting tighter." He grunted against her neck then raised himself to search her face. "You're going to come."

She nodded and met his gaze. "Yes." The word flew out of her mouth on a breath.

"Me, too."

And just the way they'd done so many times, they crested together, their bodies splintering into euphoria.

The muscles of his back and arms contracted and released repeatedly as he came harder than she could ever remember him coming. Wave after wave of spasms ranged up and down her body as she pulsed around his throbbing cock.

She held onto him as if letting go would kill them both, reveling in the way he tucked his face against her neck the way he used to. She loved that about him. Loved how he seemed to surrender to her as much as she did to him during their lovemaking.

Tears fell down her face as she closed her eyes. This was right. There was a chance she would regret her decision, but her heart wanted Mark. She'd given her brain a chance to get it right, but it had failed. Now it was her heart's turn. Hopefully, the damn thing knew what it was doing. If it didn't, and Mark left her again, it might be the last mistake her heart ever made.

Chapter 27

Mark stared up at the ceiling. He and Karma had made love almost non-stop for the last three hours. His lack of sexual contact for over a year had been too much to overcome when she touched him...pressed her mouth against his back...kissed him. He'd dreamed of this moment for so long, but now, lying in the darkness illuminated only by the street lamp outside, reality settled back in.

What had he done? Distress twisted inside his gut. This wasn't how he wanted to win Karma back. Not while she was still engaged. She belonged to another man, for Christ's sake. And yet he'd fucked her. He had fucked another man's woman. He had broken his cardinal rule.

Self-loathing roiled through his veins. He was no better than Antonio. He had become the one thing he had promised he would never be. A man who fucked over another man by sleeping with his woman.

Shit.

He rubbed his palms up and down his face then turned and looked at her. She was sound asleep. Still as a leaf on a windless day. If not for the heavy rise and fall of her chest, he could have mistaken her for dead.

Donya Lynne

But he'd never seen anything more beautiful than her that very moment. For a year, all he'd wanted was to have her back, but not like this. Not by coming between her and Brad so underhandedly.

This wasn't good.

As quietly as he could, he eased out of the bed. Damn. It was after nine. He should have been in Chicago by now. Not only had he broken a cardinal rule, he'd dropped the ball on getting back to Chicago in time for his fitting in the morning. If he left right now, he could be home by midnight and still not punk out on Rob. Then he could figure out how he was going to fix this with Karma.

After pulling on his pants and grabbing his shoes, he tiptoed back to the kitchen, where he retrieved his shirt from the floor and grabbed a piece of paper and a pen from the utility drawer.

Karma,
I didn't want to wake you.
Thank you for tonight.
Have to go. Will call you.
M

The note was short and sweet, but right now, he didn't know what else to say, and he didn't have time to figure it out. He was so unbelievably late already, and his head was a disaster area of emotional turmoil. He hated himself for what he'd done. How could he have been so careless?

Turning in a rushed flourish, he didn't see the note lift off the counter and slide down between the cabinet and the refrigerator.

Dressing quickly, he gave a final look around before grabbing his coat and slipping out the door.

In his car, he checked his messages. An hour-old text from Rob read *Where the hell are you? You're missing dinner.*

Damn. That's right. There'd been a dinner planned tonight for a few friends in the wedding party.

He typed out a quick reply. *Sorry. Delayed. On my way now.*

Karma woke with a smile on her face and her body aching in the most delightful way. She'd been dreaming about Mark.

She rolled over, ready to snuggle into him and persuade him into another round, only to be greeted by cold sheets and an empty bed.

"Mark?" She sat up, searching the shadows. The clock on her nightstand showed it was almost one in the morning.

Surely, he hadn't left. Not without saying good-bye. That wouldn't have been like him. At least not the Mark she remembered.

"Mark?" She got up and pulled on her robe.

The apartment was dead silent.

The light from the kitchen was on, and she smiled. Okay, he'd just gotten up for something to eat.

"Hey, what are you—" When she turned the corner, the kitchen was just as empty as the rest of her apartment.

She glanced into the living room and frowned. Had

he really left? Without saying good-bye?

That's when she noticed his clothes were gone.

Okay, so maybe he'd left a note. When she found none, she returned to the bedroom and turned on the light, coming up empty after searching the desk, the bed, the dresser, everywhere.

This wasn't funny, anymore. She could understand why Mark wouldn't want to wake her, but Old Mark wouldn't have left without at least leaving her a note. He wasn't that crass.

As dread began to filter into her heart, she dug her phone from her purse. Nothing. Not a single text or missed phone call.

She dropped her phone back in her purse and slowly sat on the edge of the bed, numb. It felt like all the air had been sucked out of the room, as if she were deflating like a hot air balloon with an empty propane tank.

Oh God, what had she done? She'd given herself to him...she'd taken a chance and opened her heart to him one more time. And now he was gone. Again. Without a word.

Of course he would leave. This very second, he was probably regretting everything they'd done to one another. Otherwise, why would he leave without saying good-bye or leaving at least a scribble of...what? Of gratitude? Of farewell? Her shoulders sagged. Could she blame him? She knew the score. Nothing had changed. He didn't want any long-term involvements any more now than he had before. Leaving covertly while she slept was his way of letting her know he still wanted what he'd wanted before. No commitments. No strings. Untethered solidarity. And even if he did want more, she was still technically engaged. That had to sit as well on Mark's stomach as poison ivy.

Speaking of which...she'd cheated on her fiancé. She'd cheated on Brad like a slut. A no-good, slutty, loose-between-the-legs ho.

Maybe Jade had been right.

It didn't matter that she'd taken off the ring or that, in her mind, she had already broken up with him. She hadn't actually said the words or returned the ring. She was no longer in love with Brad and needed to break off their engagement, but instead of doing that, she'd run behind his back and cheated. She'd thought she was a better girlfriend than that. That she would have at least had the gumption to break things off before sleeping with someone else.

Her only defense was that she'd been overcome by grief. Spookie's death had shattered her sense of reason and flipped her upside down. She had wanted the comfort. *Needed* it. But now she realized that even if Brad had come over, he only would have made her feel worse. Tonight had cleared her vision about Brad, but now her vision was totally mucked up where Mark was concerned.

She flopped back on the bed. Misery and disgust at her actions spilled through her brain.

Did she regret what she'd done with Mark? Honestly, no. Even though guilt riddled her over her behavior, she wouldn't have taken it back if given the chance. But waking up alone, with no note, no word from him, nothing...that shit hurt. Bad.

An echo of the heartache she'd suffered when he'd left last September resurfaced and bounced around inside her chest. A lump formed in her throat, and she rolled to her side, tears in her eyes.

Maybe it was time she counted her losses once and for all. She just couldn't see how any of this would end happily for anyone, least of all her.

Chapter 28

Karma's Blog
Sunday, November 18
"Time For a Change"

I've decided to leave my job. I can't work with M anymore knowing we have no future together. I love him. I admit that now. I never stopped loving him. All this time, I've tried to tell myself that I was over him, that I no longer loved him, that I could be happy without him. And then I slept with him Friday night.

I thought he felt the same way about me, but when I woke up, he was gone. No note. No good-bye. Nothing. If he loved me, he would have at least texted, right? His silence tells me he regrets what we did, and if he regrets what we did, then I can't work with him, anymore, because all I'll ever think about is how much I want to be with him, but how badly he regrets being with me.

So, I talked to an old college professor last night, and he has an opportunity for me. I might have to move to St. Louis, but it's a good job doing what I love. Writing. That's right. I'll be writing for a living. And moving to St. Louis will put distance between M and me. I'll need distance to move on.

I'm breaking up with B, too. He's not what I need. He was only a mechanism of denial, anyway. I see that now. I'm miserable with him, and the relationship was over months ago if I'm being honest with myself. Don't get me wrong. B is a nice guy. He's hardworking, and he'll make some woman a wonderful husband someday. But I'm not her. There's just too much that doesn't work between B and me.

So I'm going to start over. I'm going to leave all this heartache behind and begin a new life somewhere else. I think that's the only way I'm truly going to be able to move on with my life and let M go.

* * *

Mark had been caught up in a whirlwind of activity for the past forty-eight hours. There'd been little time to sleep, let alone think, and now was no different. Rob's wedding rehearsal and dinner was about to get underway.

At least the Valium took the edge off. Just acting out a wedding was enough to make his heart hammer uncontrollably.

He stood to Rob's right, his sweaty, trembling hands clasped in front of him. His heart rate was elevated, and he constantly shifted his weight from one foot to the other.

"Relax," Rob whispered. "You'd think you were the one getting married."

Mark ran his cottony tongue over his lips and nodded sharply. As soon as the Valium kicked in, he'd be fine. Maybe. Hopefully.

The reverend gave instructions to the group, and a few minutes later, as the bridesmaids giggled and sang a very out of tune rendition of "Here Comes the Bride,"

Holly floated down the aisle toward her groom-to-be.

Mark forced himself to take deep breaths, but by halfway through the fake ceremony, he started to relax as the Valium broke through his system.

An hour later and feeling much more relaxed, everyone piled into the rented limousines and headed to Boka, Holly's favorite restaurant.

He still hadn't talked to Karma about what had happened Friday night, but he couldn't make any sense of it himself. And until he did — and until he could find thirty uninterrupted minutes to devote to talking to her — he needed to hold his tongue.

"What's eating you?" Rob asked forty-five minutes later over appetizers.

"What do you mean?"

Rob tilted his head and narrowed his eyes. "You've been in a funk ever since you got here."

"I'm just tired."

"Bullshit."

Mark glanced at the table full of laughing faces. Friends and family. Everyone was so happy. He felt like the one gloomy cloud in a blue sky. "Not here. I don't want to talk about this here."

Rob leaned over and whispered something to Holly. She nodded and kissed him, then Rob stood. "Come on. Let's go."

"What?" Mark looked around the crowded room.

"You heard me. Let's go."

"Rob—"

"Are you really going to tell me no. You're here for *my* wedding. You don't get to tell me no." Rob practically dragged him out of his chair to the bar. Once there, Rob leaned his elbow on the polished wood and cocked his head to one side. "Okay, so what's up? You look like someone shot your dog."

After what had happened Friday with Karma's cat, Rob's analogy hit a little too close to home. "No, just my heart."

"Huh?" He waved the bartender over.

"Nothing, man." Mark tried to stand a little taller.

"Two Coronas," Rob told the bartender. Then he addressed Mark. "Is this about Karma?"

Lately, when wasn't anything about Karma? "Good guess."

"What happened?"

Mark glanced around then leaned closer. "I fucked her," he said under his breath. "Damn it, Rob, I fucked her."

No way could what he'd done be considered making love. You didn't *make love* to another man's fiancée.

The heavy expression on his face must have conveyed the severity of the problem, because Rob's eyebrows lifted as he gave a single, slow nod. "I see. I don't suppose she's broken things off with her fiancé, yet, has she?"

"Another good guess." Mark took the beer the bartender handed over and chugged a healthy swallow. "And therein lies the problem."

Rob raised his arm and rested his fingers on the top of Marks' wrist. "Hey, maybe you shouldn't be drinking. You did take a Valium."

"Then why'd you order me one?" He tipped the Corona toward Rob.

Rob dropped his hand. "Good point. Just limit it to

one. I don't need you comatose tomorrow morning."

"I'll be fine." He took another drink.

"So, you and Karma, huh?" Rob's face drew in tight, eyes pinched, mouth stretched into a thin line. "She wanted it?"

"It was her idea." Mark glanced toward the ceiling and ran his hand down his face, remembering how Karma had put her arms around him and how incredible she'd felt. Then she'd kissed him, and like an idiot, he'd let things get out of control. But it had been so long, and he'd wanted her so damn badly.

"It was *her* idea?" Rob's brow scrunched.

Mark explained what had happened Friday night, with Spookie, meeting Karma at her apartment, and then how she'd come on to him.

"What's wrong with that? That's a good sign," Rob said.

"How is that a good sign?" Mark shook his head and glanced across the room. "I slept with another man's fiancée, godammit."

"But *she wanted* to." Rob grabbed his arm. "Do you hear me. She *wanted* it."

"The way Carol wanted Antonio?" Mark glared at Rob, but his anger was directed at himself. "Isn't that what you mean?"

Rob's gaze went cold. The realization he'd just crossed a line without meaning to showed on his face. "This is different." Now he was trying to swim his way out of the whirlpool.

"No, it's not."

"Yes, it is. Give Karma a little credit. Do you really think she's going let this drag on with Bob or Brad or whatever his name is if she wants to be with you? Do you? She won't let things get to the point where he's standing in a church, waiting for her to come down the aisle. She'll break things off. So, this *is* different. She won't jilt him the way Carol jilted you. She won't make a fool out of anyone in front of hundreds of people the way Carol did. And she won't let that guy find her in bed screwing you on their wedding day. Karma's better than that."

"How do you know?"

"I can tell by the way you talk about her. And I met her, remember? She's a good person. A good *woman*. Good women don't hurt people like that."

"Carol was a good woman. She still is." Even though Carol had majorly screwed him over, it didn't make her a bad person. Not the most considerate, sure, but not bad.

Rob shook his head and looked away. "Hell, Mark. What do you want me to say?"

"Nothing. There's nothing you *can* say. This is my fault." Mark planted his open palm on his chest. "I'm the one who's fucked things up here. Whether Karma is a good person or not doesn't change things. It doesn't change that I did something I swore I would *never* do." He cursed himself, glowering at the shiny surface of the bar. "I slept with another man's fiancée, Rob. What kind of lowlife does that? What kind of asshole fucks another man's woman?"

Rob sighed and took a step back. "Do you love her?"

"What?" Mark's head snapped around. "Didn't you hear me? I messed up. I'm—"

Rob pushed toward him. "Do. You. Love. Her?"

"What kind of question is that?" He pulled back and took another drink, averting his gaze.

"One you need to answer. If not to me, at least to yourself. Now, do you love Karma or not?"

Mark clenched his teeth, glanced down into the round spout of his beer bottle, and shook his head. There was no way he could deny it. "Yes. All right? I love her. I love her more than anything. More than I've loved any woman."

"Then all this drama..." Rob circled his arm in the air. "Isn't doing you a damn bit of good."

"What drama?"

"All this sour shit about how you're just like that dick, Antonio, and how you've committed some unforgivable crime, yada yada yada." Rob flapped his hand like a puppet. "Drama!" Rob stabbed his index finger toward Mark. "When you love someone, you need to be with them, no matter what, especially if they love you back."

"She's engaged to another man. If she loves me, she has a funny way of showing it."

"Well, what has she said about what happened Friday night? What's her take?"

Mark took a deep breath and blew it out. "I haven't talked to her, yet."

"You haven't..." Rob trailed off and blew out an exasperated sigh, looked toward the floor, and pinched his nose. After a couple of seconds, he lifted his face and shook his head disparagingly. "Dude, you are seriously fucked up. You haven't talked to her?" He made a noise between a groan and a sigh. "And what was I just saying about drama?"

"Look, she was sleeping when I left, and I've been too caught up with you and the wedding and everything else since I got here. I haven't had two seconds to put two coherent thoughts together about what happened, let alone call and have a conversation with her."

"Then call her now." Rob waved toward the pocket that contained his phone.

"No."

"Why not?"

"Because I've decided this isn't something I want to discuss with her over the phone. When I get back to Indianapolis, I'll talk to her then."

Rob shook his head again. "God, Mark. What are we going to do with you?" He slung his arm around Mark's shoulders. "You're supposed to be the one who's got his shit together, not me."

"Well, things change." He swigged down another swallow of beer.

Ever since he'd met Karma, his life had been a roller coaster. Up, down, around, upside down. She had him in knots. Some good, some bad, but the bad ones were his own doing. Maybe when he got back to Indy, he could untie a few of them and get his life back on course. After a year of turbulence, he was ready for a little smooth sailing, even if it meant she would stay with Brad and tell him to get lost.

At least then, he might get a little closure.

Chapter 29

Karma sat across from Lisa in her office, the door closed.

"I thought you had decided to stay?" Lisa set aside Karma's resignation letter.

"Me, too." Karma had come in on her vacation to turn in her notice.

"What made you change your mind?"

She told Lisa about Friday night and how Mark still hadn't contacted her.

"I can't do it, Lisa." She shook her head. "I thought I could. I thought being with him would be enough, but then he did this. I feel like he's left me all over again, and I don't want to live like that, wondering when he'll leave for good. He obviously already regrets what happened. Even if we get past it, something else will just spook him later and he'll be gone."

"What about Brad?"

"It's over. I'm going to his house next. To give him back the ring." Honestly, she hadn't liked the ring all that much. She'd hoped the square diamond would grow on her. It hadn't. Just like Jade. Just like the monotonous sex and rain checks. None of it had grown on Karma, and it was time she set herself free. Not just from Brad, but from Mark, too.

"I don't want you to go." Lisa was genuinely sad.

"I don't want to, either, but it's time."

"Do you have another offer?"

"Yes."

"Where?"

"A publication in St. Louis. One of my college professors found me the gig. He lives there now. I'll also be helping him with research part-time."

"Have you already accepted?"

"Not officially."

"How about unofficially?"

Karma lowered her gaze. "I told him I was excited to get started, but that I wanted to discuss it with my family over the holiday before making it official."

When she met Lisa's gaze again, reluctant understanding mixed with sadness painted Lisa's expression.

"So, basically, you're already gone. The decision's been made."

Karma nodded, twisting her fingers together. "Yes. I can't stay here, Lisa. Not under these circumstances."

Lisa turned toward her computer. "You do realize the e-mail will go out today."

"What e-mail?"

"The personnel update. All the executives and upper management receive a personnel update when an employee terminates."

Now that she thought about it, Karma did remember hearing Don talk about the personnel report occasionally. She'd even seen the data in presentations he'd put together for team updates, but she'd never seen the actual e-mail.

Then her heart spasmed as realization dawned. "Wait a minute. Mark's going to receive it? Today?"

Lisa nodded. "While he's at his friend's wedding in Chicago. Are you sure you still want to do this?"

Good timing had never been Karma's friend, and now was no different. Sighing, she resigned herself that this was just how things needed to be. "Yes. Just do it. Get it over with."

"I'll hold it until the end of the day, but then I've gotta send it." Lisa stood and came around her desk, arms outstretched.

Karma stood and hugged her. "I'll miss you, Leese."

"Me, too. But that's what phones and e-mail are for, right? And weekend getaways." Lisa pulled away. "Daniel's going to be devastated, you know."

"I know. Let me tell him, okay?"

Lisa promised she would, then Karma left and drove to Brad's house.

"Hey, I wasn't expecting you," he said, opening the door. He was on vacation this week, too. Unfortunately — or fortunately, as the case may be — he hadn't planned to spend time with her. Jade was staying the week with him. Why would he possibly want to spend time with Karma when his daughter wouldn't approve?

"Yeah, this is kind of an impromptu thing." She followed him to the kitchen.

Jade was in the living room, sitting in a giant, purple beanbag chair, playing video games.

"Hi, Jade." A welcome wash of delight rushed through her just knowing she wouldn't have to deal with her, anymore.

Jade grumbled under her breath, rolling her eyes before turning her attention back toward the flat screen.

Brad gestured toward the fridge. "Can I get you a drink?" Even though they'd been dating for months, he still seemed so formal with her.

"Sure. I mean, no. No, thank you." She sat at the bar, still wearing her coat. "I just came by to return this." She pulled the ring out of her pocket.

Brad froze. Then frowned. Then cleared his throat and looked away. "Why?"

"Brad, it's just not working. We're too different."

"Is this about Friday? About your cat?"

"No, it's—"

"Jesus, it was just a cat, Karma. It's not like it was a person."

"Brad, no, that's not—"

"You're ending our relationship over a goddamn cat? It was *just* an animal."

Karma shot off the barstool. "Will you shut up and listen to me!"

Jade's head shot around at the commotion. "Don't you yell at my dad, you bitch!"

Karma spun on Jade and lashed her index finger at her. "I am so done with you disrespecting me. I'm through. I'm finished trying to make you like me. I really don't care anymore, because you're no longer my problem. So go ahead and hate my guts. No sweat off my back." She turned toward Brad and gave him a look. One that expressed she could no longer compete with his daughter when he wouldn't even catch her back.

All he could do was stand there, frowning as if he were stuck between warring factions.

She crossed her arms and took a step back, her glance flitting to the ring before meeting Brad's gaze again. With the peanut gallery silent once more, she returned to breaking off the engagement.

"First of all, Spookie was not just *some cat*...not some piece of furniture that broke and can be replaced. She was my baby. She was special to me. To me, she was just as human as you and I are. You have Jade. I had Spookie. She was *my* daughter. *My* best friend. So how dare you make light of my feelings for her, because I already know you would never allow anyone to say such things about *your* daughter." She waved toward the living room. "Second of all, that's not why I'm ending our relationship, but now that you've made your feelings known, it certainly confirms that I've made the right choice." She huffed and pushed the ring across the counter. "You're a good man, Brad, but you're not my good man. We just don't click. You don't get me. You don't understand what I need and what I want. You never stand up for me when your daughter starts in on me and calls me names. Don't you think I deserve at least that much?" She huffed when Brad didn't say anything. "And I don't get you, okay? If you think about it, you'll see I'm right. I'm not trying to lay blame here. We just don't work together. We don't. I'll always be third place to both Jade and your job, and I deserve to be first occasionally." She paused. "Okay, maybe more than occasionally. I *want* to be first once in a while, and right now, I'm *never* first."

"Yippee," Jade said, her voice uninspired. "Ba-bye." She gave a little finger wave. "Don't let the door hit your ass on the way out, be-yotch."

Karma offered Brad an exasperated grin as she gestured toward the living room. "Perfect example. She says things like that, and you don't say a word."

"Screw you, skank!"

"Be quiet, Jade!" Brad turned angry eyes on his daughter for the first time Karma had ever seen. "I've had enough! You don't talk to people that way."

Jade appeared stunned, eyes wide, mouth open. Then she threw down her controller, flung herself out of the beanbag chair, and stormed down the hall. "I hate you!"

A moment later, a door slammed.

"I'm sorry," he said. "I shouldn't have let her talk to you that way. From now on, I won't. I'll make sure she's nicer to you. I promise to be better."

Karma raised her hands, palms up. "It's too late, Brad. I'm tapped out. And Jade was only part of the problem. I just seem like an afterthought with you. That's not what I want."

"I can try harder." Brad moved toward her, his eyes filling with the realization she was really leaving him. That she was really walking away.

"No, Brad. You can't try harder. Because if you do, you'll resent me the way I've started resenting you. If it's not your daughter, it's your job. Or something else." She didn't want to hit him with how dull the sex was. She wasn't that cruel.

His face hardened. "It's your boss, isn't it?" The fury

flamed back to life in Brad's gaze. "You're attracted to him, aren't you?"

Karma took a step toward the door. "Leave Mark out of this. This has nothing to do with him." She would have ended their relationship regardless of whether Mark had returned or not. It probably just would have taken longer for her to realize she and Brad weren't a good fit.

"I don't want you to go," he said as she started for the door.

"I can't stay." She opened the door. "Good-bye, Brad."

For the first time in months, she was free. No entanglements. No burdens.

No Jade.

Breaking up with Brad had been the easy part, though. Now came the hard part. Now she had to start a new life in a new city, on her own.

Without Mark.

Talk about setting herself up for an uphill climb.

Chapter 30

His nerves calmed by Valium, Mark stood at the front of the church, a few feet away from Rob. Memories of his own wedding day threatened to consume him, but he cleared his throat, shook them off, and kept his focus on holding himself together.

The ceremony lasted all of fifteen minutes, but it felt like hours. Regardless, it did end, and finally he was able to escape. He practically dragged the maid of honor to the foot of the aisle and out the door to the waiting limousine, where he immediately downed a glass of champagne. Mixing Valium with alcohol be damned.

"Holly said you had an aversion to weddings," Tiffany, the maid of honor, said. She wore a crooked half smile and one eyebrow lifted knowingly.

Mark poured another glass of champagne, took a deep breath as he settled into his seat, and loosened his tie. "Here's to getting out of there." He nodded toward the church and lifted his glass toward Tiffany in a one-sided toasted.

She shook her head and laughed. "Men."

It was nearly four o'clock by the time they reached the reception, which happened to be at the same hotel where Mark had booked his room. Most of the out-of-town guests were staying there.

Feeling loose after two glasses of champagne and a Valium, he strolled in with the rest of the wedding party.

What he really wanted was to get back to Indianapolis. Last night, lying awake in his suite, he'd finally found time to mull over what had happened on Friday, as well as what Rob had said to him at the bar.

He did love Karma. Wasn't that what was important? She didn't belong with Brad. She belonged with him. And now that he'd had time to think about it, he realized Rob was right. This wasn't the same as what had happened between him and Carol. As far as he knew, Karma and Brad hadn't even set a wedding date. Mark and Carol had set the date, made the plans, shelled out the cash, and made it all the way to the big day before the truth came out about her involvement with Antonio.

Still, it didn't make him feel a whole lot better about sleeping with another man's woman. Mark was a lot of things, but he wasn't the kind who purposely sought women who were already taken.

And yet he'd pursued Karma and taken her to bed without so much as a hint of reservation.

So he was a bastard, but lying in bed last night, he'd decided he was going to fight for her. To hell with propriety and his noble sensibilities. If he was going to ride this out as the sign he'd asked the universe for last September, he needed to get in the game. And not just as an eager bystander. He needed to make his feelings known. He needed to confess his love. Not to himself, not to Rob, but to Karma. She needed to know. He needed to declare out loud...to the entire world...that he was in love with her and that he couldn't live without her.

"You doing okay?" Rob said as they waited outside the reception room for the wedding party's grand entrance.

"Yeah." He smiled at his best friend. "You were right last night. Thanks for knocking some sense into me."

"That's what friends are for, right?"

They hugged it out then clapped each other on the shoulders. "I'm happy for you, buddy."

Rob nodded. "Yeah well, just return the favor by getting your ass back to Indy and proposing to that sweet thing you're so crazy about. Then I can be the best man at *your* wedding. And this time we can do it right."

"You're getting a little ahead of yourself." Mark might be ready and willing to open his heart and let Karma in, but asking her to marry him was going to take more than a Valium, some alcohol, and a heart-to-heart conversation. "Let me cross one bridge at a time before you start marrying me off."

Rob grinned. "I hear you, but I think you already know she's the one." His grin turned into a crooked smirk.

Mark smiled back and narrowed his eyes. Was she? Was Karma the one? Yes. Yes, she was. The way he felt about her, she had to be.

The wedding coordinator shushed everyone. "Get ready, everybody. They're about to open the doors."

The party fell into two lines, one for the bridesmaids

and one for the groomsmen.

Tiffany wrapped her arm around his, and then the wedding party was ushered into the reception room. When Rob and Holly strolled in behind him, the guests stood and applauded.

He grinned, wondering what it would be like for him and Karma to be welcomed like that. As a married couple at their own wedding.

Dinner was served, and then it was time for him to make his toast.

Standing, he lifted his champagne glass. "Rob and I have known each other…well…it seems we've always known each other. We've been best friends forever." He glanced around the room then back down at Rob. "We've been through hell together. Through bad times and good. Mostly good. But when things were bad, Rob was always there. He always found the good in every bad situation and pulled me from the fire when I couldn't do it myself." Emotion clouded his words. Even Rob seemed to choke up a little. That's how deep their blood ran. Mark cleared his throat and looked into his drink. "Three weeks after he met Holly, he told me he was going to marry her."

Holly let out a tiny gasp, and Mark heard her whisper to Rob, "You never told me that."

Mark turned toward her. "It was the Fourth of July. The day I met you." Mark addressed the room again. "When he told me that, I thought he was crazy." A few chuckles broke through the gathered guests. "I thought he'd lost his mind. He'd only just met this woman, and he already saw himself walking down the aisle with her? The *avowed bachelor* who was my best friend had

suddenly found a woman he couldn't live without."
More chuckles, as well as a few *aaawwwees*. Mark
paused, smiled, and looked at Rob again. "But Rob
taught me a valuable lesson that day. Sometimes, you
just know. Sometimes something good comes along,
and you just have to grab on and not let go." He held
Rob's gaze for a long moment. Silent meaning passed
between them. Then he looked at Rob's bride. "Holly,
you are *that something good* that came along in my
friend's life. You're the woman who's made my friend
the happiest man in the world tonight, and I can only
hope that someday I'll know exactly how he feels.
Here's to both of you." He lifted his glass to a room full
of applause.

Rob and Holly kissed. It was sweet and chaste, but
Mark could feel the love and passion they had for one
another, and in that moment, his heart beat a little
harder for the woman he loved. His Karma.

Thirty minutes later, with hope in his soul, the band
playing, and the dance floor full, Mark absently took
out his phone. This was the first chance he'd had all
day to stop and check his messages and make sure
nothing had blown up while he was away.

He rifled through his e-mail. Mostly updates from
the team leaders. Nothing serious. Then he saw an odd
message from Lisa. *Regarding personnel report -You need
to see this* was the subject line. Huh? He opened the e-
mail. It was just a link. When he tapped it, a blog called
Chocolate Chunk Brownies came up.

Chocolate Chunk Brownies? Was this Karma's blog?

The brownie analogy was something he'd used with her and was too coincidental for it not to be.

His heart began to beat a little harder, almost panicked. Something didn't feel right. *Regarding personnel report*. That's what Lisa's subject line had said. He flipped back to his e-mail, found the report, and opened it.

Resignations: Karma Mason.

No. NO! He burst out of his chair and dialed Lisa's number as he rushed away from the noise and laughter of the reception, searching for someplace quiet. But he was wasting his time by calling the office. It was past eight o'clock in Indianapolis. The office was closed. He disconnected even before Lisa's voice mail picked up and rifled through his list of company contacts as he paced in the outer hall. He was pretty sure Lisa had a company cell phone. He nearly jumped out of his skin when her name came up in the company listing and he stamped his thumb on her link to dial her.

One ring.

"Come on, come on. Answer."

Two rings.

Shit, Lisa needed to pick up.

Three rings.

"Hello?"

"Lisa! What's going on? What's wrong?" His urgent thoughts tumbled out of his mouth in no particular order.

"I guess you got the personnel report."

"Yes. What happened? Why is Karma leaving?"

"Did you get my other e-mail? The link?"

"Yes. Is that Karma's blog?"

"Yes." She sighed. "She'd kill me if she knew I sent it to you...or that I'm even talking to right you now, but—"

"Lisa, why is she leaving? Where is she going?" Despite having enough alcohol and Valium in his system to put down the Incredible Hulk, his heart raced and his hands shook.

"She told me about Friday night. Why did you bail on her like that, Mark?"

"Bail? I didn't bail. I had to leave."

"You didn't leave a note. You didn't—"

"Yes I did. I left a note on her kitchen counter."

"Well, she couldn't find it, and now she thinks you regret what happened."

Wait, what? Karma hadn't seen his note? What had happened to it? And now she thought he regretted what they'd done? Well, in a way he did, but not for the reasons Karma probably imagined.

"Do you?" Lisa said. "Do you regret it, Mark?"

"No. I mean, yes." He rifled his hand through his hair, almost frantic with confusion. "I mean...in a way, I did, but not because of her. She's *engaged*, Lisa. What I did was wrong. I never—"

"Not anymore."

Mark's breath caught, and he froze in the hallway. Had Lisa just told him Karma had broken off her engagement?

"What do you mean?" He began pacing again, his fingers combing through his hair over and over.

"She broke up with Brad today. Gave back the ring and everything."

That was good news, right? Great news. It meant she

was free and clear. But that still didn't answer the question about why she was leaving Solar? "I don't understand. Why did she turn in her notice?"

Lisa huffed. "Because she's in love with you, Mark. She can't work with you when she doesn't think you'll ever want to be with her."

Mark stopped, dumbfounded. "I..." Words suddenly failed him.

"Mark, after you left last year, she went into a major emotional meltdown. I swear, there were times I wasn't sure she'd recover. Thankfully, she did, and then you came back, and she started falling in love with you all over again, even though she didn't want to. She knows how you feel about commitment, so she tried to keep her distance, but she just couldn't. From what she told me today, as well as what she's written on her blog, she had decided that maybe she could accept that you didn't want to get married as long as you still wanted to be with her. That's partly my fault, by the way, but the point is, Karma was willing to look past your inability to commit, and then you took off without a word Friday night. Now she's worried she'll always be wondering when you'll leave for good...that you regret what the two of you did and that you'll always be a flight risk. She doesn't want to live that way. She doesn't want to always be wondering what will spook you and scare you away for good."

Oh God, oh God. This wasn't good. "I can't lose her. Not again." The words whispered from his mouth before he could catch him.

"Then you'd better do something to stop her, and I mean fast, because she's not just leaving Solar. She's leaving the state. This new job she's been offered is in St. Louis."

He combed his hand through his hair again. This was a major cluster fuck. How had he let this happen? If only he hadn't felt so filthy for enabling her to cheat on her fiancé.

"Did she break up with Brad because of me?" *Please don't let the answer be yes.* He didn't want to be the reason for something so devastating.

"No." Lisa's voice held a touch of understanding. Somehow she knew this was important to him. "She broke up with him because they were too different. She wasn't happy with him. You just helped her see that."

"How?"

Lisa sighed. "Because she's happy with you."

"Then why is she leaving?" None of this made sense.

"Didn't you hear me a second ago? She's leaving because she's afraid you'll leave her again. And she can't take that kind of pain a second time, Mark."

Mark knew better than anyone what that kind of pain felt like, so he couldn't blame her for not wanting to go through that.

He planted his fist on his hip and spun on his heel, lifted his gaze toward the ceiling, then exhaled heavily. "She never told me." Then again, he hadn't told her, either, so could he blame her?

"She didn't know how. And honestly, I don't think she even put all the pieces together about how she felt until recently."

He was surprised Lisa was giving him this information at all. She was Karma's best friend. As such, shouldn't she be siding with her right now?

Divulging Karma's secrets could be construed as breaking the bonds of friendship.

"Why are you tell me all this, Lisa? Aren't the two of you friends?"

"That's why I *am* telling you. Because we *are* friends."

"I don't get it." He collapsed onto a nearby settee.

"Karma can get in her own way sometimes. That's something I think the two of you have in common, by the way."

"Touché." How was it that Lisa and Rob could see right through him when he could barely make sense of what he was feeling? This must be what was meant by being unable to see the forest for the trees. He was so deep in the thick that he couldn't even tell what direction he was going, but Lisa and Rob, from the outside, could see all.

"You make her happy, Mark. She loves you. And if I'm not mistaken, you're pretty crazy about her, too, aren't you?"

"You're good at this."

"I try." Lisa huffed. "So how are you going to fix this? You can't let her leave."

"I'm not sure I can make her stay. If she's already decided—"

"Mark, you're the only one who *can* make her stay. But you don't have a lot of time to do it. She's already *unofficially* accepted the other job."

No, no, no. "She can't."

"Then get your ass back here and tell her how you feel."

Good idea. He had to leave tonight. Right now. He

didn't want to waste another minute of what little time he had being three hundred miles away from her.

"Lisa, I've gotta go."

"That's what I want to hear."

He hung up, raced back into the reception hall, and corralled Rob. "I'm sorry, but I have to leave."

"What's wrong?"

"It's Karma. I have to get back."

"Did something happen?"

Mark turned for the exit with Rob hot on his heels. "She's leaving. I've made a mess of things and need to set things right."

"Whoa. Wait a minute. You're not driving back tonight, are you?"

He pushed through the doors and turned toward the elevators. "I have to. I can't let this happen, Rob. I can't let her leave."

"You can't drive." Rob emphasized each word. "You're on a cocktail of Valium and champagne. Are you crazy?"

"Then I'll take a cab to the airport and catch a flight."

"There's a winter storm coming in. Flights are already being cancelled. Holly and I just got word that ours was."

The elevator doors slid open and Mark stepped inside. "I'll find a way. One way or another I'm going back to her tonight."

The doors closed but not before Rob shook his head and mumbled something that ended with *crazy bastard*.

In his room, he wasted no time and frantically tossed his things into his suitcase before shutting off the light and hurrying back downstairs.

Holly and Rob met him at the checkout desk as he was negotiating with the clerk to help him find transportation.

"Tell him I'll give him a thousand dollar tip if he takes me," he said to the clerk, who was on the phone with the second limo service they'd tried.

The clerk shook his head. "I'm sorry, Mr. Strong, but he still says no. They can't risk it with the storm."

Mark hung his head.

"Our limo driver said he'll take you," Rob said. "He's got family in Indianapolis he says he can stay with."

Mark turned toward them. "I can't do that."

"We want you to." Holly nodded and pulled Rob's hand into both of hers.

Rob placed his hand on Mark's shoulder. "Like I said, our flight's been cancelled. We're not going anywhere. We have no use for a limousine."

"We're going to stay here and ride it out." Holly smiled. "That'll probably be better, anyway." She snuggled against Rob. "It will sure make our honeymoon memorable being snowed in."

These two had been made for one another. They were both glass-half-full people.

"I owe you guys."

"Just get down there and make things right with your girl," Rob said. "That'll be enough."

Mark removed the key to his car from his key ring and retrieved his valet ticket from his wallet. "Take my car. I'll come back and get it next weekend."

Rob tucked the key and ticket into his pocket. "Will do. Now go. The limo's waiting for you."

Mark hugged them both then hurried out into the spitting snow. The stretch limousine sat at the curb.

"There's a thousand dollar tip in this for you if you can get me there in one piece," he said to the driver.

"Yes, sir." The chauffer grinned and held open the door for him. He didn't waste time loading his bags in the trunk and just tossed them into the back.

Less than a minute later, they pulled into traffic and headed for the interstate.

For the next two hours, Mark read Karma's blog on his tablet.

He started at the beginning, reading about how he'd been her first true love. She'd used his initial instead of his name, but that didn't diminish the impact of learning how she felt, and his heart broke and mended with each post he read.

As he continued to read post after post about him and their time together, he felt like a voyeur, peeking through the window of her soul. No detail was spared. No memory left out. She'd written about how she suspected he felt as strongly for her as she did for him, her thoughts about how he'd told her Carol was in the past but how she felt Carol was still affecting him even now, and about how she didn't think she'd ever find another man who made her feel the way he did.

Why hadn't she told him all this when they'd been together?

But that was like a maple leaf accusing a blade of grass of being green. Hadn't he withheld his own feelings? He'd loved her two months into their affair, and yet he'd never told her. Except for one night when he whispered the words to her as she slept, he had never admitted his love aloud.

He continued to read, but when he got to the part about when she met Brad, he had to take a break. Reading about their relationship proved difficult, even though they were no longer together. Or maybe that was why it was difficult, because he had the gift of foresight. He knew how their story ended. So, despite her blogged professions of how she loved him and had finally moved on from "M," he knew better. She'd only been denying her true self.

The other thing that bothered him was that she'd had to see a professional to battle the depression she'd fallen into after he left. He hadn't realized. For months, he'd wanted to call her, text her, confess that he loved her, but he'd worried she had moved on and would rebuke him. Now he knew the truth. She'd wanted to hear his voice as much as he'd wanted to hear hers. If only he could go back and do things differently, but he'd been so caught up in trying to wrestle control from the universe by demanding a sign, he'd failed to miss the most obvious sign of all. That his heart beat only for her and that they belonged together regardless of the cost.

All of the cloak and dagger and missed opportunities were his fault. Instead of taking a more active role in his destiny, he had sat back and done nothing, letting invisible forces control his life.

Well, no more. That ended tonight.

Tonight, he took back control. He was the master of his own destiny from now on.

Another thirty minutes passed, and Mark saw the green exit sign for Indianapolis as he stared out the window at the lightening landscape as snow layered over the night-darkened fields on either side of the interstate. It was almost midnight, and even though they'd had to drive slowly, they'd beaten the worst of the storm.

Around twelve thirty, the limo crawled along the empty street in front of Karma's apartment complex then turned in. He guided the driver around to her building then handed over his credit card to pay for the ride. When the driver handed him the slip to sign, he scribbled in the promised thousand dollar tip.

"Thank you, sir."

"Thank *you*." Mark grabbed his things and began to scoot toward the door.

"Shall I wait? Just in case no one answers?"

Mark glanced around the parking lot and spotted Karma's car. She was home. "No, thank you. I'm good." Even if it took until morning for her to answer her door, he wasn't leaving until he saw her.

"Good luck, sir."

"Thank you, Elijah." He'd had the opportunity to chat with the driver a few times during the trip. "Drive safely. Enjoy the holiday with your family." He pulled his luggage out of the car and into the snowy drizzle that would turn to all snow by daybreak, carried his bags up the sidewalk as the limousine pulled away, and then climbed the stairs to her apartment.

This was it. No more hiding. No more secrets. No more going back.

It was time for him to take his rightful place by Karma's side.

Chapter 31

Karma groaned from sleep as the ringer on her phone cut off. Who the hell would be calling her at...she checked the clock...almost one in the morning. Most likely a wrong number. She got wrong-number-drunk-dialed in the wee hours of night once in a while.

She rolled back over and closed her eyes.

Knock-knock-knock!

Her eyes fluttered open. Was someone knocking on her door?

Knock-knock!

She sat up, suddenly on high alert, and clicked on her bedside lamp. She'd heard horror stories about women who answered their doors at night only to be raped or mugged...or murdered.

Climbing out of bed, wearing nothing but a pair of flannel pajamas, she tiptoed into the kitchen, grabbed a knife, and then darted quietly to the door just as another insistent knock startled her.

Then her phone began ringing again from the bedroom.

What the hell was going on?

She stuck her eye up to the peephole and caught her breath. It was Mark. He had his phone to his ear, and his hair was sticking out in all directions like he'd spent the last twelve hours running his fingers through it.

"Come on. Pick up."

She could just make out what he said from behind the door.

Taking a step back, she set the knife on the window ledge and unlatched the deadbolt.

When she opened the door, he lowered his phone.

He looked a mess. His hair was trying to imitate Einstein's up-do on a bad day, his eyes were bloodshot, and his tuxedo was a wrinkled nightmare. His tie hung limply around an open collar. What the hell had Mark gone through to get there? A stampede of elephants?

She crossed her arms, not about to give in. "What are you doing here?"

"Can I come in?" His voice sounded worse for wear, hoarse and gravelly.

Barely holding her emotions in check, she stepped aside and warily waved him inside.

He set his suitcase next to the couch as she closed the door. Then he turned and disappeared into her kitchen. Okay, that was odd. What the heck was he doing? The light flicked on as she remained in the living room. She heard a quiet rustle.

"There it is," he said softly.

A moment later, the light turned off. He reappeared and crossed the room toward her. He held a small slip of paper in his extended hand.

"What's this?" She took it and read.

Karma,
I didn't want to wake you.

Thank you for tonight.
Have to go. Will call you.
M

When she looked back up at him, he glanced down at the note and gestured. "I didn't want you to think I left Friday night without saying good-bye."

"Oh." She nibbled the inside of her bottom lip.

How had he known she had thought he'd walked out on her? She felt like she was watching a TV show that was part of a series and she hadn't seen one of the earlier episodes.

Despite her wariness, an expectant excitement hummed down her spine, but she didn't dare hope his arrival at such an insane hour meant anything important, but she couldn't deny the bubble of hope that it did. Had he gotten the personnel report and, in a panic, returned to Indianapolis? If that was the case, what exactly did that mean? That he loved her? That she'd been wrong about him?

Clearing her throat and squaring her shoulders, she set the note aside and crossed her arms again. She couldn't let him affect her like this. She needed to show him she no longer needed him.

"It's late, Mark. Why are you here?"

He frowned and dropped his gaze to the floor before closing his eyes. He seemed to be wrestling with something she couldn't see. His inner demons, maybe. Then he lifted his head and opened his eyes again. When he did, raw anguish burned into her.

"Don't leave me." The heartbreak in his whispered words nearly crushed her. "Please don't leave me."

She took a step backward as if his words had nudged her. In a way, they had, because he had it backward. She hadn't left him. He'd left her. He'd done it twice. Once over a year ago then again Friday night.

"Mark, *you* left *me*." Quiet agony laced her whispered words.

He took a step toward her, and she backed away another fraction of a step. His gaze beseeched hers, pleading an unspoken yearning. "Please don't go. I can't lose you again."

Her retreat came to a sudden halt as her brow screwed into a knot. What was he saying? He wasn't making sense. "Mark...I—"

"I love you." His Adam's apple bobbed up and down. "I've always loved you. I just never knew how to say it." His gaze devoured her face as he took another small step toward her and pressed his palm to her cheek. "I can't live without you. I *can't*, Karma. You're all I've ever wanted. You're everything." Turmoil and primal honesty shone from his dark eyes. "That's why I came to Indianapolis. That's why I took the job at Solar. It was the sign I'd been asking for. For almost ten months, all I'd wanted was a sign that we were meant to be together, and when Don offered me that job, I knew that was it. That's why you can't go to St. Louis. Because I came here to be with you. *You*. Don't you understand?"

Karma couldn't think. She couldn't speak. She could hardly breathe. Mark's staggering declarations flooded her senses, making it impossible for her to digest any of it. Was he saying that all this time he'd been in love with her and hadn't told her? That he'd let her suffer for months when all along he'd wanted nothing more than to be with her again? Why would he make her endure that? Why would he leave her to bear the weight of his absence alone? He hadn't even called. Just hearing his voice would have helped, but he hadn't even given her that.

Tears stung her eyes, but she wasn't sure if they were tears of joy or anger. Maybe both.

"Did you hear me?" Mark's hand pressed more firmly against her cheek, his fingers pushing into her hair. "I love you. I want you." His eyebrows dug inward toward the bridge of his nose as he gazed heavily into her eyes. "I *need* you."

A year of heartache, frustration, sadness, confusion, anger, and so much more pushed its way up Karma's spine like rising lava. "All this time...?" Tears dropped from her eyes. "All this time you've loved me and didn't tell me?" She pushed against his chest. "You left me here all alone thinking I meant nothing to you?" Her voice rose, and she pushed him again, harder this time. Like a brick wall, he didn't budge, and that just made her angrier. "How do you think I felt after you left, Mark?" Tears gushed down her face, but she didn't care. "How do you think I feel now?" She wasn't sure if the ache in her chest was because her heart was breaking all over again or mending together with such ferocity that it created physical pain.

"I love you."

"Stop saying that." She swatted his chest again, but he wrapped his arms around her and refused to let go.

"I...love...you." His tear-filled gaze drilled into hers.

"Damn you!" She beat his chest with weak fists.

"Damn you, Mark!" She thrashed, trying to worm out of his embrace, sobbing.

He pulled her more securely against him. "I love you," he whispered against her ear.

The fight drained out of her, and she wilted and hung her head, her hair spilling over the sides of her face. Surrendering, she leaned into him, pressed her face against his solid, warm chest, and bawled heavy, ugly sobs. The tears came hard and fast, and she clung desperately to his tuxedo jacket, gripping the fabric inside her fists.

A year's worth of emotional cleansing flooded her system for several gut-wrenching minutes as she tried to process what had just happened. Mark stood solid, holding her, caressing her back, kissing her hair, letting her expend herself. When the tears stopped coming, and only the aftershocks of her tumultuous emotions remained, he loosened his embrace and brushed his hand over her hair.

"I love you," he said again, speaking against the top of her head. His breath warmed her scalp.

Feeling lighter than she had in over a year, Karma lifted her head, sniffled, and stared into his eyes. The last vestiges of resistance swept away like mist on the wind. "I love you, too."

For a heartbeat, their gazes locked, and pure love flowed unabashedly between them. Then his lips crashed down on hers, and she sobbed against his mouth as naked honesty ripped her open and stripped her bare.

"Don't leave me." She sounded like she was begging. "Please don't leave me again."

"I won't." He lifted her off the floor and cradled her against his body as he carried her down the hall to the bedroom.

All she could do was press her face against his chest and wrap her arms around his neck. Everything was different now. This was a side of Mark she'd never seen. He was a changed man. No longer the master of control, he seemed to have given in to something larger than himself. He seemed like a man fighting for what he wanted, ready to expose his heart and soul.

He placed her on the bed and shrugged out of his jacket, determination making him regal, his shoulders squared, his chin high. No longer did he look like a mad scientist, but a man lost to passion, driven to claim what he knew rightfully belonged to him.

And she did belong to him. For months she'd tried to deny it, but truth had found her, and it was good to be found.

Without tearing his gaze from hers, he tugged the tie from around his neck and tossed it aside, removed his shimmering Jacquard vest, then began unfastening the buttons of his shirt.

His intent was clear. Tonight, he would make love to her. Truly *make love* to her. Heart open, soul bared, nothing but honesty and devotion between them. There were no more lies. She wasn't hiding from him or the truth, and neither was he. That much was clear.

Sitting on the edge of the bed, she gazed up at the powerful, masculine body that now belonged to her. The enormity of that realization made tears spring to her eyes again.

"Is this really happening?" she whispered.

He knelt in front of her, lifted her hands from her lap, and placed them on his chest. Her right palm lay against his circular tattoo, the meaning of which she still didn't know.

With a subtle nod, he grinned. "Yes, it's really happening. Feel me. Feel my heart beat."

She pressed her hand more firmly against his warm, solid chest. The strong pounding of his heart thumped against her palm.

"That's for you," he said. "Every beat of my heart from this day forward is for you."

She stroked her fingers through the soft waves of hair that arced toward his sternum. "When did you get so romantic?"

His fingers pushed up the sides of her thighs. "Since the moment I realized what an idiot I was to return to Chicago without you." He pushed her knees apart and situated himself between them.

"You *were* an idiot." She ran the backs of her fingers down the stubble on his chin.

The corners of his mouth lifted. "You've no idea." He pushed forward and locked his lips to hers at the same time he pushed his hands under her pajama top.

Idiot didn't begin to cover his blundering behavior over the last fourteen months. But he wouldn't make the same mistake twice.

Lifting her top over her head, Mark's gaze dropped to her fair-skinned breasts. At one time, she'd been self-conscious about letting him see her naked, but, to him, she was perfect and beautiful. She moaned as he took one pale-pink nipple into his mouth and rolled it against his tongue. It instantly hardened into a tiny pebble, and she leaned back on one arm, her other hand driving into the hair on the back of his head as if she wanted to hold him in place. She needn't worry. He wasn't going anywhere. He was where he wanted to be.

He trailed his tongue across her flesh to her other breast, swirled it around her nipple, and then closed his lips to feast once more. She sighed, and he looked up through his lashes as her head fell back, opening her neck to him.

Not one to refuse such an offering, he rose on his knees and left a trail of kisses from her ear, down the side of her neck, and between her breasts to her stomach as he eased her down to the mattress. Her legs encircled his back.

There were so many things he wanted to tell her. So many admissions about what he'd gone through since he'd left, all the unsent text messages he'd written and deleted. But right now, all he wanted was to love her. Really love her.

Admiring the vision of her naked torso and pert breasts, he tugged on the waist of her pajama bottoms, dragging them down her legs, leaving her in nothing more than an innocent-looking pair of white cotton panties. He loved seeing her in white. So pure. Angelic. Just like her.

But even purity had to go, and he hooked his thumbs around the elastic waistband and peeled them from her body.

Still kneeling on the floor, her legs on either side of

his shoulders, he leaned forward and brushed his lips up the inside of her thigh, all the way to the apex of her body. Her reaction was instantaneous. She rolled her hips, shifted on the bed, and let out an airy breath from between her heart-shaped lips.

The first time he saw her — in Chicago at the charity benefit a year-and-a-half ago — she'd reminded him of a princess at her debut. Statuesque yet timid. She was a woman worthy of worship, and as he knelt before her, spread her with his thumbs, and slowly ran the length of his tongue over her clitoris, that's exactly what he was doing. Paying fealty to the woman who'd quietly — almost stealthily — burrowed her way into his heart.

Her hips rotated against his face. She moaned and dug her blunt nails into his scalp, begged him with her body not to stop until she cried out, back arched, and clamped her thighs against the sides of his head, his tongue pressed hard against her pulsating core.

His. All his.

After several long, delicious moments, her legs relaxed, and he leaned back and rose to his feet, unfastening his belt as he did.

She reached into the nightstand, pulled out a condom, and sat up as she ripped open the packet.

When he was fully naked, she rolled the condom on as he watched, then slid back on the bed to make room for him.

And then he was inside her, her bent leg supported by his arm.

She was tight, her core still contracted from her previous orgasm, and the snugness felt good as he thrust into her.

Her gaze locked to his, and he couldn't look away even if he wanted to. He fed off the awe and devotion shining back at him. Tonight clearly held as much meaning for her as it did for him, if not more.

She licked her lips, and the sight of her glistening tongue sent a shock into his libido, making the base of his spine tingle. He remembered what she could do with her tongue, and the knowledge that from this point forward no one but him would benefit from her oral talents licked his erection and bolstered his ego in a way nothing ever had.

Her breath hitched, and her body shuddered. She was going to come again.

And this time, he was going to come with her.

"Don't stop." She moaned and gripped his back.

Eye to eye and mouth to mouth, he wouldn't have stopped even if there'd been an earthquake. This was their moment. Finally, they were one. Truly, honestly, one.

His orgasm rushed up like an attacking lion, and he grunted as pleasure gripped him by the balls.

"I love you." As the words left his lips and he buried himself inside her, the intensity of his orgasm doubled. "God, I love you."

Beneath him, she fell into vicious, rapturous contractions, her arms locking hard around his back, holding him against her. "I love you, too."

Peace. He was finally at peace.

And he didn't need a sign to tell him he was exactly where he belonged.

Chapter 32

Karma stirred awake, lying on her stomach, her arm hanging off the side of the bed. God, the things Mark had done to her. He'd made her feel things she'd never felt, but then, she'd never been this in love.

She lifted herself and turned toward the other side of the bed. Mark wasn't there.

Oh no. Not again.

"Mark?" She sprang upright. "Mark?"

"In here," he called from the living room.

She relaxed and pulled herself out of bed. It was five o'clock, still dark, except...not as dark as it should be. She peered out the window as she pulled her robe around her. The ground was covered with snow. The first real snow of the season.

Barefoot and salaciously tousled, she pattered into the hallway to find Mark sitting on the couch, shirtless, wearing a pair of grey sweats. In the middle of the living room floor, his suitcase was open. His laptop sat in his lap and his bare feet rested on the coffee table.

She crossed the living room to the couch. That's when she heard the music playing through the speakers. It was a slow acoustical number, full of lyrical guitar, and sounding like a warm spring day after a rain shower. Soft sounds of ocean surf filled in the background. "That's nice. What is it?"

He clicked and pulled up his player as she sat down. "A song called 'Sweet Inspirations' by Eric Bernard." He turned up the volume then leaned over and kissed her. "It's kind of a perfect song for right now, isn't it?"

Everything about the song spoke of the peaceful tranquility between them. And the love. "Yes." She tucked her feet under her and rested her head on his shoulder. "Did you sleep?"

"A little."

"What woke you?"

He shrugged. "I don't know. Excitement maybe. I just felt like I didn't want to miss anything." He pressed his lips to the top of her head.

"Why'd you come out here?"

"I didn't want to wake you."

She sat up. "So what are you doing? Besides listening to music."

He clicked again and brought up her blog. "Reading your blog."

Warmth filled her face, and she bit her lip, fighting an embarrassed smile. "How did you...?"

"Lisa sent me the link." He scrolled down.

She was going to have kill Lisa later.

He was reading one of the entries she'd written about him. The one Jan had asked her to write detailing what she liked and didn't like about Mark.

"It says here you only didn't like one thing about me." He rubbed his palm over his stubbly chin.

"That's right." As hard as she'd thought, only one thing had come to mind for Mark's list of cons. In her mind, he'd possessed a lot more pros.

He pointed and read aloud. "*That he left me.*" He turned and looked at her. "That I left you? That's the only thing you didn't like about me? Really?"

She giggled and ducked her head. "Really. That's it."

"I don't snore?"

Her eyes met his again. "Maybe a little."

"And that's okay?"

She nodded and snuggled a little more against him. "Yes, as long as you're snoring next to me."

He closed his laptop and set it on the coffee table before pulling her into his lap. "I think I can manage that from now on." He rubbed his palms up and down her legs. "And now that I'm back? What about now? Is there anything you don't like about me now?"

She laid her cheek against the top of his chest. "That you waited so long to return."

"Well, there's nothing I can do about that, but I can try to make up for it."

"I'd like that." She traced the lines of his tattoo. "You never told me what this means."

He glanced down. "What? My tattoo?"

"Yes. Does it have a special meaning?"

"It does." He placed his hand over hers so that her palm flattened against the ink.

Once again, she worried at its significance. "Did you lose someone close to you?"

When her gaze met his, he blinked slowly and a tender smile touched his face. "I did."

"I'm sorry." She let her gaze fall. "I didn't mean—"

"Ssshh." He placed his fingers over her mouth. "It's okay. I found her again." He dropped his hand to hers.

"My tattoo is your name. The glyphs stand for karma."

She looked at them again, more closely. He'd tattooed her name on his body? "When? When did you do this?"

"About a month-and-a-half after I returned to Chicago last year."

"Mark..." Words failed her. Yet again, he had done something she hadn't expected.

Karma's reaction was exactly what he'd expected. Her mouth fell open, her wondrous eyes searching his.

"It was my way of reminding myself of you every day. Of remembering the promise I made on my way back to Chicago."

"What promise?"

He let go of her hand and brushed back her tangled hair. "Karma, leaving you was the hardest thing I've ever done. I almost turned around a dozen times before I even reached Lafayette. I couldn't help thinking I was leaving the best part of myself behind. You. But I was so messed up. You know I was." He gestured toward his laptop. "You wrote about it on your blog. I couldn't get out of my own way long enough to see what was right in front me." He paused and caressed her face. "So I made a deal with the universe. I agreed to return to Chicago and let the universe decide. If I was meant to be with you, the universe would bring you back to me."

Her eyes glistened, and she tilted her head to one side. "You could have just called me."

He blew out a puff of air. "Do you know how many

times I typed you a text only to delete it. I almost called you so many times."

"Why didn't you?"

"Because that's not how it was supposed to work. I'd given up control. I had to be patient and become the man I needed to be to deserve you. Besides, I thought you'd already moved on."

She exhaled and shook her head. "And now you know I didn't."

"Now I know you didn't. And neither did I."

She sighed and bowed her head. "Since we're being so honest, I might as well admit that I watched you leave."

"When? My last day?"

"Yes."

"How? You weren't there that day. You'd called in sick."

She lifted her face, her cheeks pink. She bit her lip. "I was in the parking lot across the street. I saw you get in your car. I was sitting there crying when you texted me."

"Oh, Karma." He pulled her against him and kissed her temple. "If you hadn't replied, I would have come here looking for you. If I'd done that, I don't think I could have left."

"And I almost didn't reply. I almost raced home to meet you here."

He grinned and slowly shook his head. "What a mess we made of things. We both went to such extremes to chase the other away." He caressed her cheek. "And it almost worked. We almost lost one another. But here we are."

Donya Lynne

"Together again."

"Yes. And being more honest with one another than we've ever been."

"Finally." She snuggled closer and looped her arms around his waist.

He chuckled and kissed her hair. "Just shows that when something's meant to be, nothing can get in the way."

She raised her head, and her gaze searched his. "And we're meant to be?"

For a heartbeat, he lost himself in her eyes. "I hope so, because that's the only way I'll have it. I'm not leaving you again, Karma. From now on, where you go, I go."

Chapter 33

Thanksgiving

Except for a few hours when Mark borrowed her car and made a trip to his apartment for a duffel of clean clothes and made a grocery run, she and Mark spent the next two days tucked away in Karma's apartment, making love, making plans, ignoring phone calls, and getting reacquainted with one another.

Thursday morning, Karma woke early and hopped in the shower as Mark continued sleeping. She had a batch of truffles and homemade stuffing to make today for Thanksgiving dinner at her parents'. Hopefully, these truffles would turn out better than her previous two attempts.

She prepped all the ingredients for both dishes before starting in on the truffles, then crossed her fingers as she put the cream on to boil.

A couple of minutes later, Mark strolled into the kitchen wearing boxers and a T-shirt, his hair damp. He smelled like Irish Spring and aftershave.

"Good morning." He cozied up behind her, wrapped his arms around her waist, and planted a full-lipped kiss on her cheek. "Mmm, truffles for breakfast, but I'd rather have you."

She giggled as he nibbled her neck. "These are for Thanksgiving dinner. I promised I'd make truffles. I just hope they turn out this time."

He stepped out from behind her and checked the cream. "They will. I can feel it."

"Is it ready?" She deferred to Mark's expertise. The man was a veritable genius in the kitchen. She'd sampled the proof more than once in the four months they'd been together.

"Almost. A few more seconds."

She scooted the bowl of chopped chocolate toward the stove and grabbed the sieve.

"Okay, that's good." Mark shut off the cream then took it off the burner and let it rest several seconds then gestured for her to pick up the pan.

"You want me to pour it?" She'd hoped he would. That was the only way she would learn.

"Sure. This way you get a feel for it."

She picked up the pan and held it suspended over the chocolate as Mark eased behind her again, one hand around her waist, the other resting on her arm.

"Slowly," he said. "Pour the cream in slowly." His hand skimmed up to her shoulder and brushed aside her hair. His lips closed on the side of her neck.

How the hell did he expect her to concentrate on pouring cream when he was doing that?

Once the cream was in the bowl, she set aside the sieve and picked up the whisk.

Mark's hands found her breasts. "Take your time. Don't rush it. Let the cream seduce the chocolate into submission." His deep, seductive voice stroked her like a feather as she slowly stirred the cream and chocolate together to the same rhythm with which his hands squeezed and released her breasts in sultry circles, over and over. "Let the cream gently make love to the chocolate so they become one...until they're inseparable." He pressed his erection against her backside and released her breasts, only to wrap his arms around her torso.

Little by little, as he ground himself against her in time with her stirring, the nibs of chocolate melted into the cream until she had a smooth, creamy bowl of ganache.

She wasn't sure how much longer she could maintain control. When Mark got this way, she was practically candle wax under a hot flame.

"Is that what we are?" she whispered, picking up the coffee and pouring it into the ganache.

"What? Inseparable?" He kissed her shoulder.

She added the vanilla and whisked it in. "Yes."

He took the whisk, tapped it on the side of the bowl, and set it on the counter before turning her around. "Yes. That's what we are. Like ganache, you and I are better together than we are apart." He inched closer, his gaze burning her from the inside out. "Now, what do you say we explore all that togetherness while we're waiting for the ganache to set?"

She'd barely had a chance to nod when his lips seared hers as he lifted her, spun her around, and slammed her back against the refrigerator as she wrapped her legs around his waist.

The jars in the door rattled as he swallowed her breath.

For two days, Mark had been gentle but passionate, loving her body, kissing her mind, cherishing her. Now it was as if he'd only been a dam with a tiny leak, and the leak had finally burst to let the water gush through. He was all over her. In her, on her, surrounding her. God, the overwhelming assault was like nothing she'd ever experienced. He was practically consuming her.

His hands gripped the bottoms of her thighs, and he hiked her against him, banging her against the refrigerator again. A box of crackers she'd set on top tumbled off the edge and bounced across the floor.

Jesus! Karma gasped as he broke the kiss and latched onto her neck with a guttural growl.

The refrigerator shook again as he thrust against her, his erection grinding between her legs as if two layers of flannel didn't separate them.

Every breath was a moan. Every movement a stroke of pleasure.

And then he lifted her away from the refrigerator, carried her to the bedroom, and tossed her onto the bed before crashing down over her.

They wrestled and rolled, peeling away their clothes in a frantic, possessive battle.

His hand wrapped around the back of her neck. A split second later, he fisted her hair and yanked back her head before frisking her neck with his teeth.

Yes! He'd never pulled her hair. Not like this. The memory of their first true night together — when they'd played Truth or Dare and he'd told her he loved when a woman pulled his hair — flashed into her mind. This was what he'd meant. This unabashed feeling of wanton lust. No wonder he liked it so much.

He rolled with her and sat up, still tugging viciously, directing her head where he wanted it, until his mouth devoured hers again in a rush of fire.

Theirs was a battle of passion. Two bodies entwined in a war of mutual dominance, seeking only pleasure. His hunger stoked her own. Unable to stop herself, she clasped her arms around his shoulders, dug her fingers into his hair, and grasped two healthy handfuls. As she held on for all she was worth, he growled, and his hold intensified.

"You're mine now." He tossed her to the side, reached into the drawer for a condom, hastily rolled it on, then flipped her to her stomach.

She slapped one hand against the headboard, breathless, moaning, needing him inside her. A year away from him seemed to be culminating in this one electrifying moment, even though they'd already spent two days enjoying each other.

The front of his body crashed down over the back of hers, and he split her open with his knees. This was feral sex. Raw and basic. Karma's entire body shuddered in anticipation.

His hot breath washed over the back of her neck as he shoved her hair aside and laved her nape. Then she felt his cock nudge between her legs, and then...

She gasped as he penetrated her in one swift stroke. Hard.

This was fucking. This was the against-the-conference-room-wall office sex they'd had two summers ago times fifty.

The bed rocked and banged the wall, providing an erotic beat to his rhythmic thrusts. His fists planted on either side of her torso as he lifted and pounded harder.

Within seconds, Karma shrieked as she came, the relentless impact with her G-spot too much to hold back.

He raised to his knees and gripped her hips, lifting her rump higher as she pressed her cheek against the mattress.

Oh God, she was going to come again. So fast. So soon after the first.

Gasping for air, unable to comprehend the profound attack on her senses, her body seized again, breaking into violent tremors as he continued to drive into her. It was as if he was determined to remind her who she belonged to, how much pleasure he could give her, and how strong their chemistry was.

If there had been any doubt before, there was none now.

His hand smacked her right cheek, and she sucked in her breath. He'd never spanked her.

"Again!" She could barely speak through her urgent panting.

His hand whacked her ass a second time, and the pleasure that rippled through her core sparked a third orgasm to life.

"AGAIN!" She needed more. Her third orgasm needed to be set free.

His hand landed a third time, harder than the previous two, and the sound of flesh slapping flesh was as erotic as the act itself.

"Fuck, Karma!" Mark grunted. Obviously, he could feel how close she was to another orgasm so close on the heels of the first two.

She gripped the headboard, arching her back to intensify the contact with her pleasure zone. Shit, but this was dirty sex. The kind that porn stars had on camera, hot and sweaty and all lust. And she fucking loved it. For too long she'd had saltine sex with Brad. This was gourmet-crackers-with-caviar-and-foie gras sex, just without the refinement. There was nothing refined about the way Mark drilled her like a relentless battering ram. His gritty urgency and slaps to her ass blew her mind in such a welcome way.

The pleasure built, deepened, and doubled on itself. When the orgasm struck, she almost blacked out.

In an instant, Mark pulled out, fell to his back, and pulled her on top of him.

"I want to see your face when I come," he hissed urgently.

Still in the throes of her third orgasm, she raised herself then sank down on his shaft. His eyes rolled back and he reached around to grip her tender ass, pushing and pulling her against him as he pounded into her from below.

In this position, she could grind her clit against him, and that sent a completely different sensation through her core.

Lifting up, she dug her blunt nails into his chest, briefly grinning at his tattoo. He was branded. She *owned* him.

Leaning down as she rotated her hips around and around, she pierced his gaze with hers. "You're mine now." It was what he'd said to her earlier, and in the moment, she knew the promise went both ways.

Realization and acceptance flashed through his gaze

as a tight moan fluttered from his chest. And as swiftly as a bird takes flight, the control shifted from him to her. She felt his body give. Felt him relinquish control and acknowledge his place as hers to do with as she pleased.

"Then take me," he whispered, his voice shaking.

She grabbed his arms and flung them out to the sides against the mattress before locking her hands with his. Holding him down, she ground herself against him, driving her body against his, urgently seeking her fourth climax but more determined to drag his first out of him.

He moaned and gripped her fingers, his whole body tight as a drum. "Hold me down. Claim me."

Shoving his arms up the bed and over his head, she lowered herself against him, pressed her breasts against his chest, and licked his lips.

"Who owns you?" She snagged his bottom lip between her teeth and tugged. "Hmm?" She let his lip go. "Who owns you, Mark?"

He groaned, and his eyes glazed over, his pupils fully dilated. "God, you! You own me." The skin around his eyes tightened. "Oh God!"

She knew the signs. Knew them so well. He was close.

Fucking him harder, she nipped his bottom lip, making him groan. His face tensed, and he sucked in a desperate breath. "Fuck, don't stop." He drew in another tight breath and held it, never looking away from her eyes. He took several shallow, pinched breaths as his faced strained. Then he blew apart.

She released his hands, and he drove his arms

around her, clutching her body to his. His biceps pulsed in time with the contractions of his lower abdomen as his cock emptied in a series of spasms inside her.

Mark coming was a glorious experience. His entire body got in on the act. He seemed to feel it everywhere, right down to the tips of his fingers. Every muscle jerked. Every cell seemed to climax. And to think she'd given him that.

When they'd finished ravishing each other, and they were lying in a breathless heap with their arms around one another, she closed her eyes and thanked whatever power had brought him back to her.

His fingers tenderly stroked up and down her arm.

"You know," he said quietly, "there was no one else while we were apart."

She drowsily lifted her head and looked at him. "What do you mean?"

He blinked and his gaze met hers. "I haven't slept with anyone else."

Narrowing her eyes, she raised up on one elbow. She almost couldn't believe she'd heard him right. "What are you saying?"

He licked his lips and smiled. "What do you think I'm saying?"

"It sounds like you just said you haven't had sex since the last time we—"

"I haven't." His eyebrows popped as his gaze quickly danced around her bedroom. "Well, except for here the last few days, of course."

Her mouth opened, but she couldn't speak. Had he seriously withheld himself from other women for the last year?

"Is that so hard to believe?" he said, curling toward her, his hand on her hip. "That I didn't find anyone else worthy enough to share a bed with?"

She shrugged. "I don't know. I guess. I just…" But she couldn't find the words. "What about New Year's Eve?"

He frowned. "New Year's Eve? What do you mean?"

"I saw a picture of you. It was New Year's Eve. You were with a woman. I thought…didn't you…? Are you saying you never slept with her?"

Mark's face was the picture of confusion as he tried to follow along, and then realization dawned. He chuckled. "That was just a blind date." He rubbed his palm over his face. "And not a good one, I might add."

"But…" All this time, she thought he'd been dating that woman. That she'd been his girlfriend, at least for a little while. She'd been wrong on all counts.

He pulled himself up on one elbow and ran his hand down her cheek. "Karma, no one else measures up to you. How could I sleep with someone else when I was in love with you? It's only you I wanted. It's always been you."

In that moment, she knew without a doubt. There would never be another man in her life. Ever.

Mark was *it*.

Later, after another quick shower to wash away the sex and sweat, they returned to the kitchen, finished preparing the truffles, made the stuffing, and then loaded everything into her car.

"Thanksgiving dinner is more like a late lunch with my family," she said as they fastened their seatbelts. "Then everyone eats leftovers for dinner…if they're still hungry."

Mark settled into the passenger seat. "My family does a huge, formal dinner. Since I was a baby, they've invited members from their studio and do up a massive table."

This was nice hearing about the more personal details of Mark's life. For all he'd told her, he hadn't revealed much about his family.

"Were you supposed to spend the holiday with them?"

"Yes, but I'd rather be here." He squeezed her hand. "This is where I need to be."

The man could render her speechless with just a look, and she leaned across the seat and kissed him before putting her Civic in gear and pulling out of her parking space.

"You sure you're up to this? My dad's probably going to flip when he sees you instead of Brad."

"Then I'll just have to prove his worries are unfounded."

Her dad wasn't one to easily forgive and forget. He wouldn't care that Karma was happy and in love. All he would see was a man who had hurt his daughter and would hurt her again. It would take a lot more than a handshake and a promise of Mark's faith to win her dad over.

But this was what Karma wanted. In nine months with Brad, she hadn't been nearly as happy as she was after only two days with Mark. But then, she had history with Mark. A wondrous, incredible, life-changing history.

Mark was the reason she was the woman she was today. He was the reason she'd overcome her insecurities. The reason her confidence was at an all-time high and her closet was filled with a wardrobe of fashionably sexy clothes and high heels. Mark had helped her find her voice when she'd thought it would be lost forever. Today, she would need that voice to silence her father's misgivings. Because, without a doubt, Dad was going to blow a fuse when she walked in on Mark's arm.

Her brother Johnny's Audi was in her parents' driveway when she turned onto their street.

"Shit."

"What?"

"I forgot that Johnny was going to be here today." She had told Mark all about Johnny last year. How he'd made her childhood a living hell and was the cause for much of the insecurity Mark had helped her clear.

"Your brother?"

She nodded. "When he sees you with me, he's going to know that Jolene was telling the truth last summer." Jolene. Johnny's friend. Ex-Solar employee who'd gotten the boot at Mark's hands.

"I can handle him." Mark patted her thigh.

She shrugged and pulled into the driveway behind Johnny's car. "I guess everyone's going to learn about you sooner or later. Might as well be sooner." She shut off the engine and started to get out.

"Hey, wait a minute." Mark grabbed her wrist.

She turned. "What is it?"

He cupped her face in his palm. "I love you. No matter what happens in there, we'll get through this."

Just hearing him say the words emboldened her. "I love you, too. And, yes, we will." They were ganache, inseparable, better together than apart. Her family would just have to deal.

He held her gaze a moment longer then kissed her. "I'll be right by your side the entire time."

They gathered the truffles and stuffing and approached the front door. The partially melted snow crunched under Karma's boots, and a cold wind bit her face.

"Here goes nothing." She opened the door and led him inside.

Warmth embraced her, and the smell of roasted turkey and homemade rolls made her mouth water. Her mom refused to have store-bought rolls on Thanksgiving. She made what she called three-leaf clover rolls. Karma had helped her make them as a child. They were always the highlight of the Thanksgiving dinner table.

The sound of today's pregame show and a baby crying came from the family room. Johnny and Estelle's one-year-old daughter, Whitney.

"Shall we go say hello?" Karma gestured in the direction of the voices.

"Sure." He raised his eyebrows and nodded toward the family room as if to say it was now or never. "Might as well."

Mark seemed to be taking the potential for pending chaos better than she was, but that was probably only because she knew what they were in for. He didn't.

Still holding the containers of truffles and stuffing, she led him into the family room and promptly stopped.

"What's she doing here?" Not only were Johnny and Estelle there with Whitney, but so was Jolene. Her nemesis. The devil herself.

Jo's eyes formed into slits the second she saw Mark. "I knew it!"

As if today wasn't going to be hard enough, seeing Jolene there was the icing made of shit on a rock cake.

Karma spun around and stormed into the kitchen. "What's Jo doing here?"

Her mom turned away from the stove. Her dad was pulling a perfect, golden brown turkey out of the oven.

"Honey, hi. We didn't hear you come in. We were beginning to think you wouldn't make it in time." Her mom stepped forward to hug her.

Her dad set the turkey on the counter. "Where's Brad? Have you two lovebirds set a date, yet?"

"Not exactly." She clunked the bowl of truffles on the counter. "Now, will one of you please tell me what Jolene is doing here?"

In the living room, she heard Jolene bitching to Johnny and Estelle about her and Mark.

Her mom and dad exchanged exasperated glances. They didn't like Jolene, either, so it made no sense why they'd invited her for Thanksgiving dinner.

"She didn't have anyone to spend the holiday with. Her parents moved to Florida last winter, and she couldn't afford to fly down and be with them." Her mom sighed. "So I told Johnny she could join us. It *is* Thanksgiving, after all. No one should spend

Thanksgiving alone. Surely we can all get along for a few hours, right?" She nodded, looking from Karma to her dad.

Her mom had no idea. Tensions were already going to spike once Dad saw Mark, but with Jolene there they would be catastrophic.

From the living room, Jo's voice grew more shrill, as did Whitney's wailing.

"Come on, honey," her dad said. "I'm willing to suck it up for the day if you are." He patted her shoulder. "Having you and Brad here will make things a lot ea...sier." His voice dropped, which was Karma's cue that Mark had just entered the kitchen behind her.

She turned as he set down the stuffing beside the truffles.

"Mr. and Mrs. Mason." He held out his hand.

Her dad glared at Mark's polite gesture and pointedly stuffed his hand in his jeans pocket. Her mom looked like she'd just seen Adolf Hitler's ghost as she glanced back and forth between them. Karma could almost hear the questions racing through her mind. *Who's this and what happened to Brad?*

Mark lowered his hand and she slipped hers around it. "Mom, Dad, I want you to meet Mark. He's my..." What exactly was he? Friend with benefits? Fiancé? Lover?

"Boyfriend. I'm Karma's boyfriend."

She turned and smiled at him. "Okay, yes. He's my boyfriend."

Her dad cursed and threw the oven mitt he'd been holding onto the counter. "Damn it, Karma."

"But...what about...?" Her mom looked completely

lost. "What happened to Brad?" Her gaze dropped to Karma's hand as if searching for the engagement ring she'd been wearing only a few days ago.

"I broke up with him." Karma jutted out her chin, forcing her shoulders back.

"You what?" Her dad slapped his palm against the counter. "No, I won't let you do this, Karma. Absolutely not."

"It's done, Dad! You can't stop it."

Jolene rushed into the fray, Johnny right behind her. Estelle must have stayed back with the baby.

"You bitch!" Jo said, glaring between her and Mark. "I knew it! You made me out to be a liar. I lost my job because of you." She surged forward as if preparing to take a swing.

Mark's arm shot out, and his hand latched on to Jo's shoulder, forcing her to stay at arm's length. "Let's get one thing straight. You lost your job because you were completely inept, pawned off your work on everyone else—mostly Karma, weren't accountable to your job, and stirred up trouble everywhere you turned. *That's* why you lost your job. And the extramarital affair with your boss didn't help."

Jolene gasped and jerked backward as if slapped. "Fuck you!"

Mark smirked. "No thanks. I'm perfectly happy with what I've got right here." His hand tightened around Karma's.

"I bet you are." Jo lunged forward again, getting past Mark this time. Her hand shot out and slapped Karma across the cheek.

Oh hell no!

Karma let go of Mark's hand, cocked her arm, and punched Jo in the chin before Jolene even knew what hit her.

Jolene cried out and shielded her face from further assault as Johnny stepped between them to help break things up.

Tense silence unfolded over the next several seconds as the aggression calmed.

Her dad still wasn't finished, though. "Karma, I won't have this man in my home." He jabbed his finger toward Mark.

Her mom turned concerned eyes toward him and covered her mouth. "John, don't—"

"No, Cathy." Her dad waved off her mom. "This man is the reason our daughter has been in therapy since *last* Thanksgiving." He slashed his arm through the air as if that indicated going back in time. "He took advantage of our baby, used her, then left when he was finished. And he'll do it again, mark my words."

Karma's hand latched onto Mark's with such ferocity it was a wonder she didn't snap the thing clean off.

"That's not true!" She refused to let her father belittle what she and Mark had.

"I never meant to hurt her." Mark pulled her against him as if protecting her. "I love her. I've always loved her. I want to marry her."

What! Karma's gaze flashed to his. Had he just said he wanted to marry her?

"Over my dead body!" Her dad took a menacing step forward, fists clenched.

Her mom grabbed onto his arm. "John, calm down. Don't."

"Get out of my house!" Her dad swung his finger toward the door.

"Dad!" She couldn't believe her father was kicking her out on Thanksgiving.

Her dad's gaze met hers. His pain and disappointment sliced into her. "I love you, honey, but you're making a mistake. A big mistake. He'll only hurt you again, and I won't stand by and watch this time while he does."

Karma glanced around at the accusing faces. Jolene seethed with self-satisfaction, even though her face was swelling. Johnny frowned as he looked from her to Dad and back again. Her mom's shocked and dazed expression made Karma feel sorry for her. But her dad's stern, resolute scowl spoke the loudest of them all.

"Fine." She let go of Mark's hand and grabbed the truffles off the counter. Mark picked up the stuffing. "If you're going to make me choose..." She scanned the room one last time then glared at her dad. "Then I choose Mark."

This hadn't gone at all as she'd wanted, but that wasn't her fault. Shoving Johnny and Jolene out of the way, she marched to the front door and back out into the cold.

The door slammed behind Mark as he joined her at the car.

"Would you like me to drive?" he said quietly.

As tears formed on the rims of her eyelids, she nodded. "Yes, please." With trembling fingers, she pulled her keys from her purse and handed them over.

He helped her into the passenger seat, took his place

behind the wheel, and didn't say a word as he drove them away from her parents' house.

After a few minutes, he reached for her hand. "You okay?"

She wrapped both her hands around his, leaned across the seat, and placed her forehead on his shoulder. "Yes." Shit had gone south with her dad, but as long as she was with Mark, everything would be fine.

"I'm sorry. I didn't mean to cause so much trouble."

"It's not your fault." Hopefully, it would just take her dad a little time to come around and realize Mark was good for her. That he was here to stay this time.

They drove around for a while until they found an open convenience store. Inside, there was one cooler devoted to frozen foods, and they pulled out two turkey and gravy TV dinners.

At home, they turned on the football game, heated the dinners, then took the stuffing, the truffles, and the white sectioned trays of heated food into the living room and parked behind the coffee table.

"Not exactly what you'd anticipated for Thanksgiving, is it?" Mark swirled his fork in his instant mashed potatoes.

She smiled. "No, but at least you're here."

A puff of air burst from his nose. "Are you sure that's such a good thing? I'm the reason you're not stuffed with a real Thanksgiving dinner right now."

She set down her fork and took his hand. "This *is* a real Thanksgiving dinner. What would have been fake is if I'd shown up at my parents' house today with Brad. I didn't love him. Not like I love you."

She kissed him, letting the perfection of her feelings pour from her soul into his. She didn't care what they ate, as long as they were together.

"I'll make it up to you," he said. "This weekend, I'll make you a real Thanksgiving dinner."

"With pumpkin pie?"

"Absolutely." He caressed her face. "And we can stay in, just the two of us. We'll watch football and make love."

She smiled. "And get to know one another again."

His lips brushed hers. "Definitely. I have so much to tell you. So many things I wanted to say and never did."

"Me, too."

After dinner, Mark helped clear the dishes then disappeared in the bedroom for a couple of minutes before meeting her back in the living room. He held a shallow white box and set it in her lap as he sat down beside her on the couch.

"What's this?" She picked up the box. It weighed hardly anything.

"I bought it for you last Christmas. I grabbed it yesterday when I went to my apartment, so I could finally give it to you."

"You bought me a Christmas present last year? Even though we weren't together?"

He nodded. "I was trying to be optimistic."

"I see." She ran her fingers over the white box, touched at how much he'd thought about her in their time apart.

He gestured toward the box. "Go ahead. Open it."

She lifted the lid to find the most beautiful pleated

Hermès scarf in vibrant shades of green and blue. She didn't know much about scarves, but she knew Hermès was expensive.

"Mark..."

He lifted it from her hand and wrapped it around her neck, securing it with a loose knot. "It looks perfect on you."

Her fingertips caressed the rich silk. "You didn't need to buy me a gift."

He leaned forward and rested his forehead against hers. "Yes I did," he whispered. "It allowed me to feel closer to you and gave me hope I'd be with you again."

Since he put it that way, she could understand. She'd done the same with the pillowcase and sheets she'd tucked away in her keepsake box for similar reasons.

After a long, intimate moment, he pulled back, grabbed one of the truffles from the bowl, and lifted it toward her. "Would you like to do the honors?"

"What? See whether I got it right this time?"

A serious expression fell over his face as he slipped the truffle into her mouth. "No. To see whether *we* did."

She bit into the truffle and succulent, smooth, perfect ganache spilled over her tongue. "Mmmm." She nodded. They'd most definitely gotten it right. "It's perfect."

"Because *we're* perfect," he said. "Perfect for each other." His lips closed over hers, once more sending her heart into orbit.

Mark gazed drowsily at the ceiling, his body still loose

and relaxed from the orgasm he'd just had. Karma lay curled on her side against him, his arm around her.

Today had been a disaster, but at least they were public now. There were still a lot of questions that needed to be answered, especially about her job, but that could wait another day or two. He wasn't finished soaking up just being with her again.

"Mark?"

"Mmm?" He blinked and turned his head toward her.

"What you said today. At my parents'."

"Which part?" Except he already knew.

"You said you wanted to marry me."

He grinned and kissed her hair. "That's right."

She lifted onto her elbows. "Did you mean that?"

"Every word." He had a ways to go to overcome the trauma of his past before walking down the aisle again, but somehow, some way, he would. Because he wanted Karma to have his name in a way that was almost primal.

She smiled and lowered herself into the crook of his arm again. "This is so surreal."

"What do you mean?"

"Us. You. Me. Together again." Her fingers brushed lazily over his chest, and she did that thing he liked so much, where she plucked at the tufts of hair.

"Crazy, isn't it? I loved you from the moment I saw you, but then I let you go." He grinned to himself as he remembered the old saying. "If you love someone, set them free," he said.

"If they come back to you, they're yours forever." She squeezed him.

"If they don't, they never were."

Karma lifted her head. Her face was so close to his their noses almost touched. "Are you mine forever now, Mr. Strong?"

He lifted her left hand and kissed her ring finger, right where he planned to put a ring someday. "I dare you to try and get rid of me, Miss Mason."

She grinned and shook her head. "That's one dare I refuse to accept."

"Smart woman, because I'm here to stay now." He stroked the backs of his fingers down her cheek, letting his gaze drink in her face. "Thank you for coming back to me, little bird."

She leaned into his touch and shook her head. "You've got it wrong. *You* came back to *me*."

He thought about it a moment. "So I did. And I'm never flying away again."

Epilogue

Karma's Blog
November 23
"This is Just the Beginning"

They say you never forget your first true love.

That's how this blog started, and that's how it's going to end. Because now I'm starting a new chapter in my life. One I get to share with my first true love.

M has returned, and I'm unbelievably head over heels in love.

Turns out M fell in love with me, too, just as I suspected, and all this time he's been searching for a sign that we belonged together. Being offered my boss's job at the company where I work was that sign.

And now here we are again.

Obviously, the fact we're back together poses a few problems. I can't very well remain his assistant now that he's my boyfriend. And I can't just accept the job offer from my old college professor since that would require I move to St. Louis. But the issues extend beyond just professionally. My dad is furious that I broke my engagement to B and that I'm now "shacked up" with a man who will "only hurt me." Dad actually kicked us out of his house yesterday — Thanksgiving. So, yes, my decision will have far-reaching repercussions, some which could be a struggle to get over.

But I love M.

The struggles will be worth it, and I can't wait to see what the future holds.

This is only the beginning of our story. Where we go from here and how our story ends has yet to be seen. But I can't wait to take the journey with him.

Another journey. Another adventure. But then, with M, everything's an adventure. Stay tuned. Things are about to get interesting.

About the Author

Donya Lynne is the author of the award winning All the King's Men Series. Making her home in a wooded suburb north of Indianapolis with her husband, Donya has lived in Indiana most of her life and knew at a young age that she was destined to be a writer. She started writing poetry in grade school and won her first short story contest in fourth grade. In junior high, she began writing romantic stories for her friends, and by her sophomore year, they had dubbed her *Most Likely to Become a Romance Novelist*. In 2012, she made that dream come true by publishing her first two novels and two novellas. Donya has many more novels and novellas planned for years to come.

For more information on Donya's books or just to say hello, visit her on Facebook or swing by her website.

https://www.facebook.com/DonyaLynne

www.donyalynne.com

www.ingramcontent.com/pod-product-compliance
Lightning Source LLC
Chambersburg PA
CBHW032135190626
46814CB00005BA/1709